Comments on L. C. Hayden's Writing

I can't put her books down after I start them. **Kate Mutch, Andover Public Library**

If you relish suspense, her books are definitely for you. **Lizzie Hayes, Mystery Women**

With her unique and thrilling stories, Hayden offers readers a look at characters so real we might know them. **Karen Williams, The Bookshelf**

The strongest point in Hayden's novels is her ability to create a truly readable story. By interweaving false leads with fascinating side plots, the author keeps her readers guessing until the very last page. **Myrna Zanetell , El Paso Scene**

Hayden does an excellent job of creating atmosphere. Her characters are well developed and there are enough back stories to keep readers wondering exactly where the true danger lies. **PJ Nunn, Raven Feathers**

Interesting and absorbing novels. **Nancy Mehi   The Charlotte Austin Review**

WHO'S SUSAN? Here's one hot mystery story with a child in jeopardy, amnesia, a chase in the Southwestern desert. It's a novel with real people in real trouble. Highly recommended. **New Mystery Magazine**

WHEN COLETTE DIED This is fine example of a women-in-jeopardy novel. The heroine is appealing and vulnerable, the hero handsome and brooding and the situation fraught with menace. This is a fun book to kick with and enjoy. **Toby Bromberg   Romantic Times**

Get the latest reviews at L. C.'s Internet Website at
http://lchayden.freeservers.com

C0-AZD-285

WHERE SECRETS LIE

Lc Hayden

WHERE SECRETS LIE

BY
L.C. HAYDEN

Top Publications, Ltd. Co.
Dallas, Texas

This is for

Sebastian Everett Hayden

My first grandchild

My own little angel

Acknowledgments

I would like to thank the Adoption Awareness Center for their kind help. Even though they were busy, they always took the time to answer my many questions.

A bunch of kudos also goes to all who proofread the manuscript. Their suggestions were invaluable and they helped to make the story a ton-and-a-half better. My hat goes off to Ray Whiteman, Kathy Porter, Ken and Martha Bland, Charlene Tess, Phyllis Caves, and Margie—and also to Mary Barton and Pamela Walford from Ponder Publishing Co. for their great suggestions on Chapter 1.

I'm indebted to JoAnne Lucas who suggested using the Who, What, When, Where, Why, and How in all of my non-series titles. Great idea, JoAnne. This book would have been called SEARCHING had you not come up with a much better idea.

Also, thanks to my publisher, editor, and friend, Bill Manchee and all the people at Top Publications. You're a bunch of neat folks.

Lots of hugs and kisses to my family, Richard, Donald, and Robert for their unending support—and to you too readers whom without you, this would not be possible. Please feel free to contact me at *lchayden@lycos.com* and please visit my website at *http://lchayden.freeservers.com.*

Finally, both Lisa Littau and Bobbye Johnson honored me by allowing me to use their names as my main characters. However, even though I used their names, any similarities between the characters and the real persons are strictly coincidental.

Where Secrets Lie

A Top Publications Paperback

First Edition

Top Publications, Ltd. Co.
12221 Merit Drive, Suite 750
Dallas, Texas 75251

ALL RIGHTS RESERVED
Copyright 2001
L.C. Hayden
ISBN#: 1-929976-06-2
Library of Congress #2001 131573

The characters and events in this novel are fictional and created out of the imagination of the author. Certain real locations and institutions are mentioned, but the characters and events depicted are entirely fictional.

Printed in the United States of America

Chapter 1

June 1975

The worst part of a murder is the digging.

Surely, there had to be a better way.

James Johnson wiped the sweat off his forehead and folded his arms on the top of the upright shovel's handlebar. He figured what? Maybe six, eight more inches?

No use postponing it. Better hurry up and finish. The sun had already started to set and soon it would grow dark. A course shiver racked his body, and he wondered if the culprit was the cool evening breeze or the task he was undertaking. He turned back toward the ground and continued disturbing its peace.

Once James finished digging the hole, he dragged the body and dumped it in. He stared at it and contempt made his stomach boil. "Goodbye, Bobbye," he said.

He knelt down and grabbed a handful of golden hair. With his other hand, he reached for the scissors and began to cut away. "You'll be all right once all of this ugly mop is gone. You'll see."

He grabbed another handful of hair and continued to hack away. Its silky texture against the palm of his hand horrified him. As though he had been burned, he jerked his hand back. The young woman's body crashed back into her newly dug grave.

"You're not Bobbye," he told the dead woman. Vacant eyes stared back at him. "You don't even know Bobbye, do you? You'd like her. When she gets to be your age, she'll probably look a lot like you. Same damn blond hair." James reached down, grabbed some more hair, and continued to chop.

"I'll get you, Bobbye. I swear you'll be next."

He picked up the shovel and continued with his hideous task. It took him less than thirty minutes to bury the body. Tomorrow the truck would come to pour the cement. Construction on the swimming pool would continue. He wondered if the first time he dove into the sparkling pool, he'd think about the blond-headed, nameless woman who was buried there.

He walked into the study, picked up the phone, dialed, and waited for an answer. "Maria, put my wife on," he told the maid.

"Sorry, *senor*, but Ms. Kathy–she no want to talk to you. She still mad."

"Put her on."

James heard the phone being set down. Seconds later, a rustling sound indicated the phone was picked up. "James." The familiar softness in Kathy's voice had vanished. "I'm leaving you and I'm taking Bobbye with me."

The hum of a disconnected line buzzed in James' ear. He stared at his wife's portrait enclosed in a heavy oak frame on the opposite side of his desk. Her thick, jet-black hair contrasted with the mahogany framework. Slowly, he stretched out his hand, curved his fingers into a claw-like position, and scratched the image of his wife.

* * *

Kathy's heart pounded so hard she was afraid it was going to explode. She took in deep breaths and exhaled slowly. She had done it. She had actually told him she was leaving. She was proud of herself. She had to do it. For Bobbye's sake. For her sake.

She had been with him now for five years, and in all fairness to James, they had not all been bad years. In fact, the first year had been, if not ideal, at least bearable.

Then she became pregnant.

James had stared at her and between clenched teeth hissed, "Get an abortion." He stormed out of the room.

Kathy had refused and in the end, he agreed to let her keep the baby provided she promised it would be a boy. She knew, of course, that she couldn't promise him anything like that, so she said, "For your sake, I hope it's a boy." She couldn't look at him in the eye, so she looked away. "But I can't promise you that."

"His name will be Robert, and he will have black hair like yours." He pointed a finger at her to emphasize his words.

Nine months later, blond-headed Bobbye Johnson was born and nothing was ever the same again.

The ringing of the phone brought an end to Kathy's brooding. It also sent adrenaline pumping through her body. She let the phone ring a long time before she picked it up. "Yes?"

"Kathy, I've got a surprise for you." James' voice sounded as if nothing was wrong between them. "I'm here at our cabin. I'm having a pool put in because I know how much you love to swim. What do you think about that?"

Kathy let out a long-drawn sigh. "I already told you. By the time you get back home, Bobbye and I will be gone." He didn't answer and Kathy messaged her temple.

At long last he said, "You've talked before about going to a counselor."

"Yes, we have. We've talked about it many times, but you've never done it."

"If it means that you'll stay, I'll go with you."

"The counselor is for you."

James laughed. "Darling, why would you think I need a counselor?"

"Ever since Bobbye was born, you've changed." She sounded like a broken record. How many times had she told him this before?

An awkward pause passed and Kathy knew she should slam the phone down, grab Bobbye and whatever items she could, and get out.

Then she heard James say, "Kathy, in spite of what you think, I love Bobbye. She is my daughter. But if you feel that a counselor will help, then we'll go."

"It's too late now." This was the first time she had verbalized her doubts. She loved James and she had wanted her marriage to work, but now it was too late and the thought left her feeling cold and empty.

"If you leave me, Kathy, you won't get a single penny." James' tone carved Kathy's heart with an ice knife. "Think of all that money you'll never be able to spend. Then think of Bobbye. How is she going to feel when she finds out she could have been a rich little girl? If you leave me, Kathy, you can kiss all of that money goodbye."

I know. I know. I'm so confused. Aloud, she said, "I need to think. I'm going to go out for a drive. Call me in an hour." She slammed the phone down, grabbed the car keys, and ran out of the house.

All she had ever wanted was a happy family life. When her parents got divorced, she had promised herself that she would always love her husband. Sure, at times he was distant, but he wasn't a bad man. Not really.

Failing to buckle up, she threw the car in reverse and sped away. If she stayed with James, she would live like a queen. Already he was becoming a very influential figure in the world of finances.

Kathy glanced down at the speedometer. She was doing fifty in a thirty-mile zone. What was she thinking?

She was thinking about James and Bobbye. Why didn't James love Bobbye? She was an adorable three-year old. But the way James looked at Bobbye when he thought Kathy wasn't looking frightened her. There was an evil glint in his eyes.

But that was ridiculous. James was not a murderer. He wouldn't harm Bobbye. She had only imagined the look. Everything was in her mind. James was okay. She was the one who was all messed up. After all, didn't the world worship him? He was a hero in everyone's eyes.

Tears blurred her vision, and she angrily wiped them away. In so doing, the car swerved sharply to the right.

Immediately Kathy turned the steering wheel to the left.

My God, was she really doing seventy? She needed to slow down. Who would protect Bobbye?

Protect Bobbye? From whom? Not James. Oh God, not James. This man was her husband. Why would Bobbye need protection from him?

The sobs, which raked her body, stole her breath away. She gasped and pounded the steering wheel. "Bobbye is safe. James is okay. It's all in my mind."

The constant blast of a horn brought her back to reality. Bright lights heading directly toward her blinded her. She swerved to avoid the head-on collision, but even as she did, she knew she was too late.

"I love you, Bobbye!" she screamed.

The crushing of metal, followed by a bolt of pain turned Kathy's world first into a soft gray then, pitch black.

* * *

Kathy knew she should open her eyes, but part of her wanted to stay in this never land where there was no pain, no sorrow. But if she stayed, who would take care of Bobbye?

That sudden thought forced her to open her eyes and wish she hadn't.

The first thing she saw was James' face.

"What. . ." Why was it so painful to talk? "Wh. . .where?"

"Hush," James said. "You're in the hospital. You've been in a horrible car accident. Do you remember the accident?"

Did she? She remembered. . .fighting! Fighting for Bobbye. Why? Her mind was so confused.

"Bob. . .bye."

"She's home with Maria."

"Who'll. . .watch. . .Bob. . .bye?"

A shadow moved past James' eyes. Had she imagined it? No. She was dying and suddenly she knew. With a strength that surprised her and James alike, she reached for James' arm and squeezed it. "If I ever meant anything to you, if your dream to succeed is so important to you, then promise me, Bobbye will be safe with you."

James tried to yank his arm away, but Kathy's grasp was strong.

"Promise me!"

James hesitated for a second—an eternity to Kathy. Then he looked her straight in the eyes and said, "I promise."

Kathy released her grip on him and sank back onto the bed. *Who will take care of my Bobbye?* She wanted to ask him this but instead she said, "James, why do you hate your daughter so much?"

She gasped for air and slowly closed her eyes.

* * *

At the eulogy, James sat in the front row. He could not comprehend the meaning of the words the clergyman said. His thoughts were elsewhere.

He had been lucky, he knew. He'd killed several times, but none of those deaths had touched him. In a way, he'd been responsible for Kathy's death, and now that she was gone there was a vast emptiness deep inside of him. Had he actually loved Kathy? He never thought he'd be able to love a woman, but here he was feeling empty, sad. There would be a void within him that would never be filled.

He had promised Kathy that Bobbye would be safe. That was a promise he intended to keep. He knew that the only way she'd be safe was if he sent her away.

He also realized that the killings had to stop and the only way to accomplish this was to shut down all of his emotions. From here on, he would never feel a thing. Not love, not hate, not joy, not sadness. Not even anger—especially anger. From here on, he would be a man with no emotions.

He could do this.

He had to do this.

Chapter 2

June 2000

Lisa Littau slammed the palm of her hand against the steering wheel. She had thought that by taking Loop 410, she would reach the hospital faster, but she should have known better. After all, regardless of the time, San Antonio's freeways buzzed with the heavy traffic.

Lisa bit her lower lip as the memory of the phone call came rushing back to her. "Lisa?" The voice over the phone sounded nervous. "This is Marie, your mother's next-door neighbor. I've got some bad news for you. It's your mom—she, uh, had a. . .heart attack. . .about half an hour ago. We're at Southeast Baptist Hospital. You better get down here. It doesn't look good. Lisa, I'm sorry. I'm awfully sorry."

Someone honked and Lisa's thoughts returned to the present. She could feel the tears welling in her eyes. In an effort to keep them under control, she once again bit her lower lip and tasted the coppery saltiness of blood.

It hadn't even been two years since her dad's death. Then her divorce, and now this. Lisa inhaled deeply. *Hold on, Mom. Please hang on. Don't die.*

Please don't die.

Lisa pressed down on the accelerator.

* * *

"You may go in now," the nurse at the cardiac unit said, "but only for five minutes."

Lisa opened her purse, retrieved her compact and stole a quick glance in the mirror. She knew Mama would comment on her appearance. Her blond hair was disheveled and she seemed rather shook up, but she thought she could pass

Mama's test. She straightened herself up, returned the compact to the purse, took a deep breath, and slowly opened the door.

Lisa's hand flew to cover the scream of anguish she felt building in the pit of her stomach. Five leads were taped to her mother's chest. Lisa noticed that with each strained breath her mother took, her chest expanded in exaggerated heights. Behind her, an electrocardiograph monitor recorded the irregular beatings of her heart. "Ma?"

Mrs. Foster's eyes flickered open. Even near death, her face brightened at the sight of her daughter. "Lisa." Her voice was barely above a whisper.

"Shh, Ma." Lisa reached for her mother's hand and gently patted it. "Save your energy."

"Can't. . .you must. . .know." Mrs. Foster stuttered, gasping for breath.

"Later," Lisa said. "You can tell me later."

"No, now. There's. . .no. . .later." Her weak, yet firm voice conveyed her urgency.

Fear grasped Lisa as her mother tried feebly to raise herself off the bed. "No, Ma, lie back. Save your strength." Lisa gently, but firmly, placed her hands on her mother's shoulders and pushed her back onto the bed.

"Lisa, your father. . .and I. . .we have always. . .wanted the best–" Mrs. Foster took several short, rasping breaths before continuing. "But what. . .we did–" She strained so much that her face took the shade of an over-ripe apple. "–was wrong."

A warning bell rang inside Lisa's head. Whatever her mother had to say, she didn't want to hear it. "Ma, please don't talk. I'm leaving now. I'll be outside."

Mrs. Foster grabbed Lisa's arm with a sudden savage ferocity derived from exasperation. "Stay. Listen. Your dad and I–we love you."

"I love you, too, Mom."

Mrs. Foster closed her eyes and shook her head angrily. "I wanted to tell you sooner, but I didn't know how." Her urgent tone told Lisa that what her mother had to say was important.

"There's no need to say anything. When you get better, we can talk."

"No, Lisa. . .now. Your father. . .is dead and–"

"I know, Ma."

"–and now I'm...dying. I know all we have are lots of bills." She turned her face and a tear rolled down her cheek.

Images flooded Lisa's mind. As a child, Lisa had to have the latest, most expensive toys. They were later replaced by exclusive brand-name clothes. Then later, she realized that most of her high school peers had cars. Why couldn't she? College was, of course, out-of-town. Elite. Expensive. Mom and Dad paid for the toys, the clothes, the car, the college, and they did so without complaining. They gave, then gave some more.

Lisa now knew how selfish she'd been, but in spite of this, she now expected—no demanded—the best for her daughter. Mom and Dad always helped her out even though it must have drained their retirement fund. That is, if they ever had one at all.

Money, the finer things in life—these had always been so important to her. But now they didn't matter. Somehow she had to make Mama realize that. "That's not important. What matters–"

"But there is lots of money. Lisa, listen."

Lisa felt her mother's hand wrap tightly around her wrist. Someone with so much strength couldn't possibly be dying. *Mama, please don't leave me. I don't know what I'll do without you.*

"Lisa, promise me. . .that you will find. . .your father."

Lisa closed her eyes. "Ma, he's dead."

"Your. . .*real* father, Lisa."

"Wh-what?"

"Check my medical r-re-records. I've always. . .been sterile. Michael and I. . . we–" She gasped for breath.

"I'm. . .adopted?" The concept hit her like a jolt of electricity. She felt as though the air had been taken out of her.

Mrs. Foster nodded. "But it was. . .illegally done." She paused as she struggled to breathe. "We paid ten-thousand dollars...for you. I realize it was wrong. I know...we shouldn't...have done that...but we have always loved you...like our own. Promise me, you'll find him and...and claim what rightly...belongs...to you." Having said this, she exhaled deeply and visibly relaxed. A look of peacefulness overshadowed her face.

During the quiet that followed, confusion gnawed at Lisa's innermost thoughts.

"Promise me!"

Startled, Lisa quickly said, "I promise, Ma."

A triumphant smile spread across Mrs. Foster's lips. "Check the bottom. . .of my jewelry box."

Lisa held her breath and frowned. "Your jewelry box?"

Mrs. Foster feebly nodded.

"I will, Ma, but I need to know who my–uh, real parents are."

Mrs. Foster's lips moved but no sound came. Lisa bent over so close that her ear almost rested on her mother's lips. "Bo. . .Bo. . .B. . ."

"I don't understand," Lisa said.

"Bo. . .Bo–" Mrs. Foster gasped for breath, and her eyes went blank. Behind her, the electrocardiograph beeped one last time. The sound was replaced with a steady hum.

"Ma!" Lisa screamed. "Oh, my God, somebody please help her!" An overwhelming feeling of helplessness ripped at her heart. If only she could wrap her arms around her mother and make her well.

Several precious seconds passed before a nurse brushed past her, followed by a doctor. Soon Lisa felt herself being led into the hallway.

Her confused thoughts quickly gave way to mindless shock.

Chapter 3

June 1975

A blond-headed, four-year-old girl wandered throughout the mansion. Close to her chest, she clutched a raggedy doll known as Ms. Molly. As she searched one vast empty room after the other, she looked like a drenched kitten with a wide-eyed nobody-loves-me look.

"Mommy?" Her whisper vibrated in the empty house, disturbing the silence. "Mommy?" Tears swam in her eyes.

"Hey, *bonita*, your Mama, she not home." Maria stopped her dusting chores and bit her lip. She smiled kindly and quickly glanced away. "She be back real soon. You see." Maria picked up her dusting rag and continued to polish the coffee table.

Bobbye squinted several times and raised her eyes toward Maria. "I want my Mommy," she mumbled.

"I know, *bonita*. She be here real soon. Okay?"

The little girl nodded hesitantly. "Where is she?"

Maria let out a nervous laugh. "I go sweep outside. You need me, I be outside. Okay?" She ran out before Bobbye could answer.

Once again Bobbye nodded, even though she knew Maria couldn't see her. She stood quietly, staring at the empty space Maria had just occupied. Bobbye sniffed and wiped her nose with the back of her hand, clutched Ms. Molly tighter, and shuffled down the hall. Behind her, the grandfather clock ticked the days away and still no Mommy. Where was she?

Abruptly she stopped. Daddy stood at the top of the

stairs, his hands resting on his hips. His eyes, like always, filled her with terror. Bobbye took a step backwards and mumbled, "Mommy?"

The scary man glared at his daughter. "It's the blond hair, isn't it? It makes you stupid, doesn't it?"

Bobbye ran her fingers through her hair. Had she forgotten to comb her hair this morning? Mommy would know. She fought hard to control the quiver in her voice. "I want Mommy."

"You can't have her, ever again. She's gone and she's not coming back. She's gone and left you behind."

Sobs shook Bobbye's body. "She'll come back!" she screamed. "She'll come back!"

"No, she won't." Daddy's eyes were pinpoints of anger. "Do you know why?"

Bobbye clutched Ms. Molly tighter to her chest. She tried to answer, but the words caught in her throat. She shook her head.

"She's dead," he said and walked away.

Bobbye dropped Ms. Molly. She didn't understand *dead*, but from the tone of his voice, she figured that it had to be something bad.

She screamed.

Chapter 4

June 2000

Lisa jerked upright in her bed, perspiration beading from every pore in her body. It had been a dream—only a dream. But she had dreamt this nightmare before.

When she was little, the dream came almost every night. She'd cry out for Mommy, but another woman would come rushing in, assuring her that she was confused, that she was Mommy. She'd stay with her, hugging her and holding her, until she returned to sleep. Eventually the dream went away.

But now it was back. Lisa tightened her eyes and an image formed in her mind. A gigantic white house with a pool loomed before her. It wasn't a happy place, but rather a mansion filled with sorrow. She had thought of these images as nightmares, but could they be memories instead? She was tired of these vivid visions which haunted her not only during the nights, but also during the days.

She reached for her purse, retrieved her wallet, and found her parents' picture. "All right, Mom, you win. I'll try to find my birth parents." She sighed. She knew she had no choice. Not if she wanted the nightmares to stop. "I can't do this alone," she told the picture. "I need your help. Where do I begin?"

From the recess of her mind, a voice that could only belong to her mother whispered, "Check the bottom of my jewelry box."

"Yes, of course, that's what you told me at the hospital," Lisa said aloud.

"Who are you talking to, Mommy?"

Startled, Lisa turned. Her five-year old daughter Tracy stood by the bedroom door, looking very sleepy. Her soft, blond hair cascaded down to her shoulders.

"No one, sweetheart. Actually, just myself." She squatted down and spread her arms. "How would you like to play at Sharee's house today?"

Tracy eagerly nodded as she cuddled safely in her mother's arms.

"After breakfast, I'll call Donna and see if I can drop you off there. Then you and Sharee can play."

Tracy frowned. "You're not coming, Mommy?"

She gave her daughter a tight hug. "No, sweetheart, I'm going to Grandma's house."

"Can me and Sharee come? We can help clean Grandma's house."

Lisa planted a kiss on her daughter's cheek. "No, sweetie, you'll be better off at Donna's."

* * *

In her mother's right-hand dresser drawer, Lisa found the jewelry box. It had been an anniversary gift from her father; a gift bought in Chinatown during one of their frequent trips to California.

Lisa carefully carried it to the bed and sat down. The top of the cherrywood case contained an etching of some Oriental trees and two Chinese lovers. Lisa's mother had often joked that the lovers were she and Pa. Lisa gently stroked the box. "Oh, Ma," she said and wiped away her tears.

She opened the jewelry box and "Laura's Theme" began to play. She scooped out the mixture of costume necklaces, bracelets, earrings, and rings and set them on the bed. She stared at the empty box. "That can't be," she muttered.

She turned it upside down and pounded it. Nothing. She searched among the jewelry and once again came out empty-handed. She checked inside the jewelry case again. Had that lining always been there? She felt all around it. There was something there. A picture, a piece of paper, something.

She found a sharp knife, felt where the item was, and began to cut around it. Lisa had thought that this would be a relatively easy task. She was wrong. Mom must have glued it down with the idea that it was going to stay glued forever.

When Lisa finally finished, she realized that the item she had felt was a newspaper clipping that had been folded in half. Unfortunately, some of the glue used to hold down the lining had accidentally gotten inside the folded newspaper article. Lisa tried to separate it, but in so doing, parts of it stuck together, making it impossible to make out any of the words.

The only thing Lisa read was the word "Dallas." Even the date had been obliterated.

Lisa placed the article in her purse and walked out of the house. In less than five hours, she would bury her mother. "Oh, Ma," she whispered.

* * *

Lisa had just finished packing when the doorbell rang. Slamming her suitcase shut, she dragged it into the living room and hurried to answer the door. She sucked in her breath when she saw her ex-husband carrying a bouquet of roses.

David's light brown, wavy hair fell over his forehead much the same way it had when they first met, and his boyish good looks contrasted sharply to his large frame. When he saw Lisa staring at him, he flashed that same Mona-Lisa smile she had fallen in love with. He handed her the flowers.

"Thank you, Dave." She let him in.

Even before he stepped all the way in, he began, "Lisa, I'm so sorry. I just heard. I wish I'd known earlier about your mom. I would have gone to the funeral. I always liked your mother. How are you and Tracy doing?"

"We're fine," she mumbled. She wished she could stop loving him. She led him into the living room, reached for a vase, and carefully arranged the roses. When she finished, she noticed David staring at the suitcases.

"Going some place?" he asked.

Lisa nodded. "Uh huh. To Dallas, just for a short time."

She knew David wouldn't approve, so she quickly added, "Would you care for a drink? I'm not sure if I have any beer, but I do have some Pepsi or—"

"No, no thank you."

"Coffee, perhaps?" She sat on the couch.

David shook his head and sat next to Lisa, their legs barely touching. "So where's Tracy?"

Of course, she should have known he had come to visit Tracy. If she'd known he was coming, she would have put on some make-up or worn something else. Her hands automatically traveled to her hair in an attempt to fix it. "She's next door playing with Sharee. If you want me to, I'll go get her."

"I can walk over—later," David said. He leaned back and in so doing their legs rubbed against each other. A tingling sensation traveled through Lisa's body, and she felt the blood rush to her cheeks. She stole a glimpse at David.

He was smiling at her with a smile that, had they been in a bar, would have either gotten him slapped or shown him a very good time. Lisa cast her eyes downward then stood up. She strolled toward the stereo unit and stroked her mother's picture.

"Lisa, are you sure you're all right?"

Do you really care? If you did, you wouldn't have walked out on me. Aloud she said, "Yeah, sure. Well, maybe not. I just buried my mother, and at the same time I found out that after all this time, she was a stranger."

"A stranger? What do you mean?"

"Before she died, Mama told me that I had been adopted."

David's mouth slowly dropped open. Then he shook his head in stunned disbelief. "What? Do you think that's really possible?"

Did she? She hadn't wanted it to be true, but now, the more she thought about it, the more her dreams made sense. Slowly, she nodded. "I guess I do. Do you remember how I told you about my dreams or nightmares—whatever you want to call them?"

David didn't answer. Instead, he studied Lisa with a look that penetrated deep into her soul.

She continued, "These dreams are not dreams at all. They're bits and pieces of my past. I can't explain it, but somehow I've got to get hold of those pieces. It's like a part of me is missing. I won't feel complete until I know who I am."

"You're Lisa Littau, the mother of my daughter. What difference does it make who gave you birth? The only ones who really matter are the parents you know and love."

Lisa flopped down on the couch. "I know that should be enough, but somehow it isn't. Besides, David, before she died, I promised Ma I'd search for my natural parents."

"I can't pretend I understand, but you've got to do what you've got to do." He pointed to the suitcases. "Is that why you're leaving?"

Without looking at him, Lisa nodded. "I'm going to Dallas."

"Why Dallas?"

Lisa reached for her purse and retrieved the newspaper clipping. She handed it to David who looked at her with a questioning frown. She related the story behind finding the article.

After he had listened to her narrative, David said, "Lisa, I don't think it's wise to pack and leave for Dallas. How can you be so sure that Dallas is the place to begin?"

"Because Ma and Pa were originally from Dallas. Whenever I mentioned that city's name, my parents would exchange a knowing look, then quickly focused their attention on something else. I didn't understand then, but now I do. My parents must have bought me in Dallas, and then, for safety's sake, moved over here."

"Wait, back up. *Bought* you? What do you mean?"

"Mama told me it was an illegal adoption." She plastered her hands to her face and tried not to cry.

David sat down beside her, hesitated for a moment, then wrapped his arms around her. "I'm sorry, Lisa."

In the comfort of his arms, Lisa released the pent up anguish she felt. "I feel. . .so betrayed," she sobbed. "It's as if my entire life has been a lie. Why didn't my parents tell me I was adopted? And why didn't they go through normal channels instead of buying me like you buy an animal or a piece of furniture?"

"I don't know." He held her tighter. "I wish I had the answers."

"I do too and I guess that's why I'm leaving—to find those answers." She sat up right and David removed his arms from around her.

"Are you sure that's what you want to do? Do you have any idea who your real parents are? Do you know their names?"

Lisa stood up, walked over to the stereo unit, and focused her attention on her parents' picture. She shook her head.

"Any details?"

Again, Lisa shook her head.

"Then how are you going to find them?"

Lisa shrugged. "I don't know. I just know I have to. My so called dreams tell me that I used to live in a big, white mansion with a fountain out front and a peanut-shaped pool in the backyard."

"That's not much to go on."

"I know, but at least it's a beginning."

David raked his fingers through his hair, stood up, and walked toward his ex-wife. He held her gently by the shoulders. "Lisa, if you want my truthful opinion, I think you're just wasting your time. You don't know a soul in Dallas–"

"I know Harry Bronson."

David smiled and nodded at the same time. "Oh, yes, good ol' Harry Bronson, the ma'am guy."

"Huh?"

"Don't tell me you haven't noticed? He calls everyone *ma'am*. Last year when he came to visit Donna–he even called her *ma'am*."

Lisa giggled. "I remember. I did think it was strange for a father to call his own daughter *ma'am*."

David moved his hands down to Lisa's upper arms and stroked them. "So what can Bronson do for you?"

"He's a detective in the Missing Persons Division, and according to Donna, a damn good one."

"True, but you don't know this Bronson guy all that well. Are you sure you can count on his help?"

Lisa shrugged, releasing David's hold on her. "All I know is that I've got to try." She walked away from David and sat down in the recliner.

"This could get to be quite expensive." He remained standing by the fireplace.

"I know, but I don't have a choice. I plan to live off my savings account."

"You only have a couple of thousand dollars in your savings account, don't you?" He sat back down on the couch.

"Including the money we saved for Tracy's college, I've got close to ten-thousand dollars. If I'm lucky, that will keep me for several months."

David frowned. "You'd use Tracy's college money?"

"I'll pay her back. She hasn't even started school yet. I'll have plenty of time to raise the money."

"And in the end, if you find that you weren't adopted, then you will have wasted all of Tracy's money."

"What do you care? It's my money as well." As soon as Lisa blurted it out, she was sorry.

For a second David looked stunned, but he quickly recovered. "That's not really true. Half of that money came from me."

"What are you saying? You want your half back?"

"No, I don't want it back. That's supposed to be Tracy's money. It's not meant for you to waste it away."

"Waste? Since when have I wasted money? All I've ever done was save our money so we could open up our own business." She bolted out of the recliner, pointing an accusing finger at him.

"*Our*?" David's face contorted spasmodically. "Since when did it become *our* business? You're the one who wanted it. Not me."

"I wanted it for you–for us."

"No, you didn't. You wanted it for you. I'm a car salesman–and a damn good one–and I don't need or want my own business to boost up my ego."

"It wasn't your ego I was thinking of. I wanted you to be something better. That's why I was always saving our money. But no, you had to go out and waste it all on worthless junk!"

"Worthless junk? Is that what you think of that diamond necklace I got you?" David was on his feet now, his hands closed into tight fists, his eyes glaring at his ex-wife.

"I didn't ask for the necklace. I–"

"Ungrateful. You've always been so damn ungrateful."

"You missed the point. It wasn't that I didn't appreciate it. It's just that we needed to open up our own business. You know so much about cars. We could have our own store where we sell all sorts of things for cars."

"I didn't–and still don't–want my own business. You never could get that through that thick skull of yours."

All feelings of tenderness had evaporated. Lisa found it easy to remember why she had divorced this man. "I won't have you come into my house and insult me!"

David closed his eyes, took a deep breath, and with a slow shake of his head, said, "I didn't come to fight." His voice sounded calm and gentle again. "Believe me, Lisa, that was the last thing I wanted to happen. I want that part of our lives to be over. We could never see eye-to-eye about my lack of ambition and your over-ambitious attitude. That's why we divorced. So there's no use rehashing old problems. Please, let's be friends." He reached over and caressed her cheek, then walked toward the door. "I'd be willing to keep Tracy so you can go to Dallas."

Lisa watched as David walked away from her. She wanted to run to him and have him hold her as he did before. She realized that all he had to do was smile and she would take him back. She was his puppet, and she hated her weakness. "Thanks, I appreciate that, but right now I need her." She crossed her arms in front of her as she talked.

"She's only five. How can she help you?"

"I need the companionship. David, I've lost everything. I couldn't bear to be away from her too."

"I understand. I was just offering." He smiled–warmly, seductively–and winked. "I'm going next door to say good-bye to Tracy, and from there I'm taking off. Call me when you get to Dallas." He gently closed the door behind him.

For a long time, Lisa stared at the closed door. She stormed into Tracy's bedroom and began to pack her clothes. As she did, a sense of impending danger engulfed her. So strong was her feeling, that she almost began to unpack, then stopped. "I promised Ma," she told herself. But the premonition caused a chill to run from her neck down to her back.

Lisa shook the feeling off. After all, what could possibly be so dangerous about searching for your parents?

Chapter 5

"Is this our new home, Mommy?" Tracy had just stepped inside, and her face was still flushed from running.

"Yes, sweetheart. What do you think of it?" Lisa asked.

"It looks bigger from the outside."

"That's because this is a duplex."

"What's a puplex?"

Lisa smiled. "Duplex, with a *d*. That means we have neighbors living right next door to us."

"Like Sharee, back in our other house?"

"No, sweetheart. They have their own house. This is like two houses put together."

"Oh." She shrugged and Lisa realized that her daughter probably still didn't understand what a "puplex" was.

"How long are we going to be here?" Tracy asked. "We've been here a long time."

"This is only our third day and guess what? We are going out today."

"Yea! Where are we going?"

"To the place where they make newspapers."

"Will that be fun?"

"Probably not, sweetie, but I tell you what: after we leave the newspaper office, we'll go do something fun. Would you like that?"

"Yeah," Tracy answered, throwing her arms around her mother.

* * *

Mando Perez slammed the papers down on his desk.

He flopped in his seat and folded his arms. He glared at the ad layout he had just designed for the next issue of the *Dallas Morning News*.

Anthony Bowler glanced up from his desk. "You got a problem, man?"

Mando pointed with his head. "It's the Queen Bitch. She's on my ass again. She says my ad production is down. Can you believe she threatened to fire me? Doesn't she realize I have nothing to do with the number of calls or walk-ins we get each day? Of course, to her that doesn't matter. She says I'm not *closing* enough of those prospects. Hell, if I lose a sale it's because of all the damn rules I have to follow. I wonder what she'd do if I let a cocaine dealer advertise?"

"I don't know, man," Anthony said.

"She'd love it 'cause she'd have all that cash coming in."

Anthony nodded sympathetically.

"Do you know what she called me?" Mando continued. "She called me a lazy Mexican. I have half-a-mind to sue her."

Their conversation came to an abrupt halt when an attractive blond in her mid-twenties entered their office. Both Anthony and Mando would have been tripping over each other to help her if it wasn't for the blond-headed little girl with her.

Still, Mando flashed her a smile. "May I help you?"

"I hope so," the woman replied. "My name is Lisa Littau, and I'm looking for the advertising department."

"You're looking at it," Mando said.

"In that case, I have an ad that I'd like to put in the paper."

Mando turned toward Anthony and wiggled his eyebrows several times, then turning to Lisa, he said, "I'll be happy to help you. What are you selling?"

"Selling? Oh, nothing. I'm adopted, and I'm searching for my biological parents."

Mando turned to Anthony and flashed him a frown. Then he turned back to Lisa and shook his head. "Oh, . . . I'm sorry. Our attorneys won't let us publish that kind of ad. Too risky, they say."

"Oh no, but I've got to place this ad. . . Please. I'll pay anything and sign a release so that the newspaper won't in any way be responsible. This is really very important to me, so please give me a chance." Her voice broke with emotion.

Mando frowned and ran his fingers over his lips several times. He looked over at Anthony for help.

"Have you tried the Internet? You can find just about anybody there. It would be a lot cheaper too," Anthony said.

No, she hadn't tried the Internet, but she knew that would be a dead end. She had, after all, been illegally adopted. "I'll do that," she said, "but I also want to run this ad."

"You'll probably end up with a lot of calls from some real strange people," Mando said.

"I realize that, but I'm willing to take that chance. I've even thought of getting a post office box, but I'm afraid if I do, my birth parents might think it's a trap or that I'm not on the level. Please, let me put in that ad."

She seemed on the verge of tears, and Mando had a definite weakness for weeping ladies, especially if they were pretty, like this one. Besides, didn't the Queen Bitch demand he close more sales? "You're that determined, huh?"

"That desperate."

Anthony and Mando exchanged looks.   Mando shrugged, turned to Lisa and said, "Okay, let's lay out the ad and maybe I can slip it by my supervisor."

Relieved, Lisa nodded and they got to work. Halfway through the layout, a middle-aged woman approached, then stood back and listened to them. Lisa looked up at her and smiled. The woman continued to stare at her. Lisa shrugged and turned her attention to the ad.

When they finished, Mando stuck the ad in front of a busy supervisor who approved it without taking the time to read it. Mando smiled at Lisa, gave her a copy of the ad and directed her to the billing department. "Show them this ad and give them your name, address, and phone number. In about two to three days, they'll bill you."

Lisa thanked him, slipped him a twenty dollar bill for his

trouble and then left.

Anthony walked up to the counter, looked at the woman who had just walked in, and said, "May I help you?"

She ignored him.

"Can I help you?" Anthony repeated.

She continued to stare at the door Lisa had just used. When she turned to face Anthony, her eyes were narrow slits in her face.

Chapter 6

James Johnson always read the newspaper while peddling his Schwinn Airdyne Bicycle for half-an-hour. As always, he read the first three-to-four paragraphs of each front-page article before going on to the next section. Then he read a few editorials, most of the headlines, and a few features. Finally, he would find the financial section and spend the rest of his time carefully analyzing and digesting the current trends of the market.

But today as he prepared to reach for the financial section, a picture caught his eye and for one horrendous second, he moved back through time. It was twenty-five years ago, and he was staring at his wife's picture. But no, that couldn't be his Kathy. She was dead, wasn't she? Besides, the woman in the picture had blond hair and his Kathy had luxurious black hair.

But even assuming she were alive, she would be somewhere in her mid-fifty's. The woman in this picture couldn't be much over twenty-five. Who was this woman who so strongly resembled his Kathy? Eagerly, he read the quarter-page ad:

ARE YOU MY FATHER OR MOTHER?
I was adopted probably in Dallas when I was about four years old. My adoptive parents were Michael Edward Foster and Marie Williams Foster. I was born on April 11, 1975. My full name is Lisa Foster Littau. If you are my biological parents, please contact me. I need to

talk to you.

The bottom of the ad listed a local phone number.

Like the tremors of an earthquake, James' old desires resurfaced: the suffocating warmth in his chest, an urgent stirring in his groin, the sense of something unfinished, and the need to punish. "No!" he said as he dropped the paper. "Stay away. I don't need you. I don't want you. Stay away before it's too late."

The shock caused James to gasp for breath. Without realizing it, he had been peddling faster than usual. He felt like an overheated engine—and it was her fault.

Always her fault.

Her—and her beautiful blond hair.

James' thoughts were interrupted by his son's voice. "Father, are you all right? You look so pale, and you're shaking like a leaf."

James noticed the creases on Thomas' forehead. He was a handsome young man who maintained a tight reign over his own life. He stood well over six feet with a slim and agile built. His dark, wavy hair framed a perfectly shaped oval face. His strongest asset by far was his eyes, green like his father's, and what ladies often referred to as bedroom eyes.

James deliberately waited to answer. He had to control his thoughts, his emotions. "I'm fine, Thomas. I think I just overdid this damn bicycle." As James attempted to get down, he staggered and Thomas hurried to his side.

"Father, do you want me to call a doctor?"

James shook his head. "No. I said I was fine." He stood, tall and straight. "Now let's get ready for work. Johnson Enterprises can't run without us. What's on the agenda?"

"At ten, Senator Herman is coming to discuss his special project. At eleven-fifteen there's a board meeting with representatives from the Paris, Mexico, London, and Rome branches. Then at—"

"But nothing before ten?"

"No, but we were going to discuss the Alison Project."

"That can wait."

Thomas gasped. "What? That's a three hundred million-dollar project. We simply can't postpone it. Father, are you sure you're all right? You have never–"

"I have some business to tend to. That's all. Later on in the day, we'll reach a decision on the Alison Project."

Thomas frowned.

"Look, Thomas, you know that in an hour's time our company makes, gains, and spends millions of dollars. The Alison Project is just simply not that vital."

"But it's my project," Thomas said between clenched teeth.

"Then you make the decisions." James stormed out of the room and slammed the door behind him.

Thomas' eyes shifted back toward the discarded newspaper. His eyes narrowed as they focused on the crumpled pages.

* * *

Joe leaned against the hood of the Rolls Royce, a gleaming, black Phantom IV limousine. As soon as he saw James walking out of the mansion, he straightened up and opened the door for him. "Good morning, sir."

James nodded once as a response and got inside. He waited until his chauffeur was in the driver's seat before he spoke. "We're not going to the office today. We're going to Dunkin' Donuts."

Joe gasped. "Which one, sir?" He couldn't keep the surprise out of his voice.

"The one on Mills Avenue," James said and pressed the button that raised the partition between him and his chauffeur. Even though he stared at the changing scenery, his mind focused on the newspaper ad.

Once they reached the doughnut shop, James lowered the partition and said, "You may go. I'm meeting a friend here. He'll take me to the office."

Joe could see inside the shop through its glass windows. Other than the employees, no one was there. He got out and opened the door for James. "Would you like for me to wait here until your friend arrives?"

"No, you may go. I'll call you if I need you." He stepped out.

"Yes, sir," Joe said. He closed the door, hopped back in the limousine, and drove off.

James waited until he could no longer see the car before he crossed the street and entered the car rental office.

Chapter 7

The ringing of the doorbell startled Lisa out of a peaceful night's rest. She stared at the alarm clock: it was only six fifty-six. Who would be ringing her doorbell so early in the morning? She sprang out of bed and grabbed her robe.

By the time she reached the hallway, the gooey embrace of sleep had left her. The hope she had felt before now, turned to disappointment. In the ad, she had put down a phone number only. There was no way her natural parents could know her address.

The doorbell rang again. "I'm coming," she yelled. But instead, she went into Tracy's bedroom. The noise had not disrupted her sleep. Lisa threw her a kiss and closed the door behind her.

She parted the living room curtain just wide enough for her to see a man giving her his back. He turned slightly and Lisa recognized him as Detective Harry Bronson, her best friend's father. She straightened her hair with her fingers and swung the door open.

Bronson, a solidly built man with high cheekbones, coarse black hair, and a very pleasant smile, seemed happy to see her. "Lisa, ma'am," he said as he offered her a sloppy salute.

"Mr. Bronson!" she said, stepping aside, allowing him to enter.

"I'm sorry to be intruding at such an ungodly hour, but I was on my way to work, and I wanted to stop by here first." He sat down on the worn-out beige sofa.

"That's fine," Lisa said closing the door. "You're always

welcome here." Suddenly a thought occurred to her. "Is Donna okay?"

"What? Oh, yeah. Sure." He rubbed his forehead as though confused. Then his face lit up. "Oh, you mean because I'm here, you thought something was wrong with Donna." He glanced toward the kitchen.

"Something like that."

"Well, to be truthful, I've been awfully busy, and I haven't gotten around to calling her. She called up the other day and she talked to her mom, but I haven't talked to her. But as they say, 'No news is good news.' Right?" Once again, he glanced toward the kitchen.

Trying to figure out what he wanted, Lisa followed his eyes. "Right," she said.

"Do you by any chance have some coffee? I just can't seem to function without my morning cup."

Lisa smiled. "I know what you mean. I was just getting ready to make some." She stood up. Once in the kitchen, she took out a pot. "Sorry," she said, "all I have is instant. I've just moved in."

"Yes, ma'am, I know. That's what Donna told the Mrs."

Lisa smiled when she heard the word *ma'am* and remembered how David had called him the ma'am guy. "So Donna put you up to this." Lisa took out two green plastic cups.

"Uh, well no, not really. She did call to give me your phone number and address. Said she passed on the information to David, just like you asked her to."

Lisa nodded. As soon as she had her phone installed, she had immediately called Donna to give her the new address and phone number. She wanted to call David too, but every time she talked to him, the emptiness in her heart plunged to new depths. It was better if Donna called him. Maybe by being away from him, she'd stop loving him.

"Anyway," Bronson continued, "the reason I'm here is because of this." He pointed to the newspaper.

Lisa stopped stirring the coffee and stared at Bronson.

"My ad? Why?"

"I know you live in a small, friendly community on the outskirts of San Antonio, and I know everybody over there trusts everybody else. But here in Dallas, it's a bit different. Things are not so simple over here."

The doorbell rang again, and Lisa stole a quick glance at the door. "Excuse me." She peeped out the window and saw a woman she didn't recognize. She made sure the bolt remained secure, then opened the door as far as the chain allowed. "Yes?" she said.

A woman in her forties stared at Lisa. Her hands played with the creases of her blouse.

Lisa searched her memory. Now that she had a chance to see her up close, she realized she had seen this woman before but couldn't quite place her. "Can I help you?" she asked.

"You don't remember me, do you, Lisa?"

"I've seen you before–" Where? Where? Then it dawned on her. "I know! I saw you at the newspaper office when I went to put in the ad. Is there something I can do for you?"

"Oh, Lisa, you really don't know, do you?" Her voice was soft, quiet, and yet high-pitched.

"Know what?"

"You–you look just like I always thought you would," the woman said. Although her tone leaned toward the quiet side, her voice was now normal. "In fact, I'd say you look just like your father."

"My. . .father?"

The woman nodded.

Lisa gasped. "Are you saying you're–"

"Your mother!" The woman beamed with pride. "May I come in?"

Lisa faltered then said, "Of course. Let me unlock the door." She closed the door, unbolted it, then threw it open. "Please come in."

"Let me look at you," the woman said, stepping inside.

She eyed Lisa from head to toe. "You're beautiful, Margie–just beautiful."

"Margie?"

"Yes, that's your real name. Don't you remember being called Margie?"

"How could she?" Bronson stepped into the living room, carrying a cup of steaming coffee. He set it down on the end table. "She was just a baby when you gave her up for adoption."

The woman gasped, but quickly recovered. "Not so little. Margie was a toddler when I had to give her up."

Bronson tapped his forehead. "Well, of course, she was. How silly of me to forget. So tell me, Ms. . .uh?"

"Rogers–Emily Rogers and you're. . .?"

"Harry Bronson." He offered her his hand. "Tell me, Ms. Rogers, are you this little lady's real mother?"

Emily's eyes went toward Lisa and stopped there. "Oh yes, most definitely."

Lisa smiled.

"Well, in that case, you two must have a lot of talking to do. I'll be on my way." He moved toward the door, then abruptly stopped. "Plumb forgot my coffee," he said. "I'll take the cup back to the kitchen."

"Don't bother," Lisa said. "I can do that."

"I insist," he said. He was gone and back in a second. As he started to walk out for the second time he said, "Lisa, you take care of yourself, and I'll be back to check on you." Then he turned toward Emily Rogers. "Ma'am, it was nice seeing you again."

The statement took Lisa by surprise. "You two have met before?"

"Oh yes, of course," Bronson said before Emily had a chance to respond. "At the adoption agency."

"But–"

Bronson immediately stopped Lisa from continuing. "You see, your adoptive parents–they couldn't have a child. So naturally, they came to me. I steered them toward the adoption agency. That's when I met Ms. Emily here. She was just a kid herself then. She was–what?–sixteen, maybe seventeen?" He stared at Emily.

"I was fifteen."

"Uh-huh–and as I remember, very frightened." Bronson took off his glasses, breathed some air through his mouth onto the left lens, wiped it with his handkerchief, returned the handkerchief to his pocket, and put the glasses back on. He continued, "She wasn't sure she wanted to give you up."

Big tears covered Emily's eyes. "I didn't." She turned to Lisa. "I swear to you, Margie, I didn't want to give you up. But my parents. . ."

"Your father came with you." Bronson's eyes were now glued to Emily's face. "He forced you to sign those papers."

Emily stared at Bronson through wide, startled eyes.

"Didn't he?" Bronson's tone sounded harsh.

"I'm. . .not sure." Emily rubbed her fingers together.

"He did. Don't you remember?" Bronson took a step toward Emily.

She wet her lips and inched backwards.

"Remember?" Bronson repeated and took yet another step forward.

"Yes, yes! He forced me. I didn't want to do it, but he forced me." Emily's sobbing came from deep inside, each sob wrenching her body, making it seem as though someone had grabbed her and was ripping her apart.

Lisa stood in numb shock. She felt her face pale, her lips tremble. She stared first at Bronson, then at the woman who claimed to be her mother.

"He even held your hand over the pen to make sure you signed," Bronson said.

"Yes, he did." Emily sobbed. "It hurt so much, I had bruises for days."

The door to the bedroom opened and five-year old Tracy stepped out. She stood by the door. "Mommy?" She ran to her mom who placed a protective arm around her.

Emily took two small steps, her eyes glued on Tracy.

"I–I have a granddaughter?"

Tracy cowered behind Lisa.

Bronson stepped between them. "Ms. Rogers, ma'am, it's best that you get going now."

"But I just got here. I came to be reunited with–"

"No, ma'am. I believe you've made a mistake. This lady here is not your daughter. Those things I said, they never really happened. Now did they?"

Emily's eyes danced with confusion. "Oh yes, they did, just like you said. I remember so well."

Bronson shook his head and took several steps forward, forcing Emily to step backwards. "No they didn't, ma'am. None of it ever happened."

Emily's eyebrows knitted slightly in puzzlement. "They didn't?"

Bronson shook his head.

"But I remember. . ."

"No, ma'am, you don't."

Emily's body went slack. Suddenly she seemed to be an old woman, forgotten and defeated. "Lisa's not my daughter." It was more of a question than a statement.

"No, ma'am. I'm afraid not."

"Where's my Margie then?" She hugged the empty air. "I want my Margie back. She left when she was little, you know. I want her back. Where's my Margie?" Her face crumpled.

"I don't know, ma'am."

"I've searched for my Margie all over." She turned toward Lisa. "She had beautiful blond hair, just like yours. You're sure you're not my Margie?"

Lisa didn't answer, but Bronson did. "She's sure."

"Will I ever find her?"

"I hope so, ma'am. Just remember, Lisa is not your daughter. You leave her alone. I'm her uncle, and I'll be watchin' her. Leave her and the child alone."

Emily stared into Bronson's eyes for a long time. But if she found something there, she kept it a secret. She sighed, nodded and hunched over in a sign of defeat. "Margie," she whispered and strolled out.

"How did you know she wasn't my mother?" Lisa asked, once Bronson had closed the door behind Emily.

"At first I didn't," Bronson answered. "I reckon you could say I took a shot in the dark and my aiming was good. There was something about her, something that made me want to question her." He reached out and held her hands. "And, Lisa, I'm afraid she'll be the first of many."

"What do you mean?"

Bronson released her hands, walked over to the kitchen, and picked up his coffee cup. Lisa followed him. "Well, ma'am, there's these habitual confessors who seem to pop out of the woodwork all the time."

Lisa frowned. "Then how will I know when my real parents come forth?"

Bronson drank the last of his coffee. "I suppose you'll just know somehow."

"But when this woman came in—"

"You let your emotions rule you, not your mind."

Lisa nodded. She'd be better prepared for the next time. "You don't think she'll come back, do you?"

Bronson opened the refrigerator and helped himself to some apple juice. "Well, that's hard to say. She just might. That's why I told her to stay away. Anyway, most of those habitual confessors are harmless." He opened the top cabinets searching for some glasses. "Care for some juice?"

"I do," Tracy said.

Lisa shook her head. "What about this Emily Rogers?"

Bronson shrugged as he poured two glasses of juice. He handed Tracy one glass and drank from the other. "Let's just hope we saw the last of her." He looked up at Lisa with an expression that said, "But I doubt it."

Chapter 8

Because of his prominent position in society, at the snap of his fingers, James Johnson received what he wanted when he wanted it. Not only did he expect this treatment, he demanded it. With this in mind, James had cultivated friendships and done favors for people he knew would one day be in a position to help him.

Today, he would cash in on one of those debts. He took out his cellular and dialed.

"*Dallas Morning News*," said the voice over the phone.

"James Johnson here. Let me speak to Wayne." He sat inside the blue Toyota he had just rented and gazed at the Dunkin' Donuts shop across the street. Hunger pangs rumbled in his stomach. He shook himself and forced his attention back to the woman who had answered the phone.

She said, "Hi, Mr. Johnson. Wayne's in an editorial meeting, but I know he'll want to talk to you. It'll be four, five minutes, though. Would you like to hold?"

James knew the procedure. Wayne would never refuse to speak to him but would always keep him on hold for a few minutes, not long enough to aggravate him, but the few minutes were supposed to make James recognize Wayne's importance. What a pompous ass.

"Tell him to call my cellular." He hung up, walked over to the Dunkin' Donuts, and ordered two glazed doughnuts and a cup of coffee.

He had almost finished his first doughnut when the phone rang. James let the phone ring five times before he picked it up.

"Hey, James, sorry. I couldn't get back to you right away, but this big meeting–well, you know how it goes," Wayne said.

"Don't worry. What I need is so small it can actually wait."

"No need to keep you waiting. So tell me, what can I do for you?"

"Your paper ran an ad about a woman looking for her parents."

"Amazing you would bring that up. That ad aroused several people's anger. You know, it's not your typical ad."

"No, I suppose not. Anyway, I need Lisa Littau's home address. Thomas saw the ad, thought what a knock out, and wants to meet her. You know how that goes." James felt he was over-explaining–something he never did. If he wanted something, he'd demand it be given to him. He never gave explanations.

If Wayne noticed it, he gave no indication. "That's no problem, James. I'll have that address to you in less than five minutes."

True to his word, Wayne had Jennifer from the billing department call James with the address. James wrote it down, thanked her, hang up, and finished his doughnuts and coffee.

He drained his cup and signaled for a refill. He wondered what the chances were that Lisa would recognize him. The waitress refilled his cup, and James handed her a five-dollar bill.

He watched her walk over to the cash register and ring the sale, but his mind concentrated on Lisa. Naturally, if Lisa gave the slightest hint that she recognized him, he would take immediate actions. Too much was at stake.

But James realized he shouldn't worry. After all, his face had appeared several times in the newspapers and on television. He'd been featured on the cover of several magazines, including *Time* and *Newsweek*.

Unless Lisa had been living in a cave, she must have

seen his face on television or in one of those magazine or a newspaper articles. If she were capable of recognizing him, she would have by now. But still, the thought gnawed at him, eating at his gut.

Worse yet, he feared that when he confronted her, his old, unwanted desires would surface. Thus far, he'd been able to successfully bury them. At times they would emerge, but he'd drown himself in work, forcing his feelings aside.

James stared at his unfinished coffee, tired of all the brooding. He pushed the cup aside, fished the key out of his pocket, and headed for the rented, blue Toyota.

* * *

James parked the Toyota in front of Lisa's duplex, slumped down in the driver's seat, and stared at the house. She lived in a simple, square, reddish-brown brick house, very similar in color to the one he grew up in. If he closed his eyes, he could still see his older sister, Michelle, flipping her blond hair at him. Teasing him.

Father and Mother had gone out again and Michelle was supposed to take care of him. Normally, he liked this idea. He could stay up and eat whatever he wanted. He could even stay out way past the time when all eleven-year-olds were already fast asleep.

But today, Michelle was giving a party. That meant that he either had to stay locked in his bedroom or leave the house and not come back. Little choice there, he thought as he grabbed his stack of trading cards and carefully stashed them in his already overstuffed overnight bag.

He glanced around his room, making sure he hadn't forgotten anything. He decided he had everything he needed. Although he knew it wouldn't be necessary, he'd stop by his sister's bedroom and say bye to her.

He stuck his head in her bedroom. "I'll be staying at Mike's, if you need me."

Michelle set the hairbrush down and rolled her eyes. "Who cares?" She shook her head and her blond hair flew every which way. "Just hurry up and get out of here. My friends will be arriving real soon."

James focused his eyes on her hair. He willed himself not to touch it.

Michelle studied him with a knowing look. She approached him and stood very close to him. "You like it, don't you?" She touched her lips with her tongue. "What's the matter? Don't you get any of this?" She cupped her hand and placed it between his legs.

A bolt of electricity ran up his body. He gasped. He bolted out of the room, her laughter clinging to him long after he had left the house.

* * *

"She's a bitch." Mike popped a potato chip into his mouth and grabbed the remote control.

Rage, like a volcano ready to erupt, boiled in the pit of James' stomach. "She's my sister. You take that back."

"What's the matter? Truth hurts?"

"Fuck you!"

"Nah, it's your sister who does that." Mike giggled and stuffed a handful of potato chips in his mouth.

"Shut up. She does no such thing."

Mike shrugged. "Want some?" he asked. When he noticed that James didn't answer, he said, "Suit yourself." Then, after a small pause, he added, "Look, man, all I was doing was repeating gossip."

James bit his tongue. He knew there was talk, and he really didn't want to hear it, but today, for some reason, he had to know what they were saying. Lately, when he approached a group of students, they would stop talking. And he knew. They'd been discussing his sister. Feeling the bile stuck in his throat, he asked, "What do they say?"

"Shit, man, you don't know?"

James looked down and shook his head.

"They talk about her parties." He turned on the T.V. and pretended to be engrossed in the show.

He didn't fool James. "What about her parties?"

Mike shrugged and stared at the T.V.

"What about the parties?" James repeated.

"They talk about the drugs, and the booze, and the sex—you know, normal stuff." Mike's eyes remained on the T.V. and not on James.

"That's a lie!" James' mouth went dry. "A damn lie!" The air seemed to be sucked out of him. He ran out of the house.

"Wait! Where are you going?"

James didn't bother to answer. He continued to run, not knowing where he was heading.

He stopped only when he realized that he stood in front of his own house.

He looked at his watch. The party had been going on for over an hour. He should turn back, he knew. He had never walked in on one of her parties. He had always respected her privacy, but today he had to know.

He sucked in a deep breath and threw the front door open. The stench of marijuana attacked his nostrils. Opened bottles of booze and beer cans were scattered throughout the deserted living room. Stale cigarette smoke attacked his nostrils.

Laughter, coming from upstairs, mocked his pounding heart.

Fighting back tears, he dragged himself up the stairs. He could hear the laughter stemming from the first bedroom to his right—that would be his parents' room.

He hesitated a second before throwing the door open. The first thing he saw was his sister's blond hair, bouncing up and down. She was naked and four guys, also naked, lay beside her.

"Hey, kid, what are you doing here?"

The voice, which came from behind him, startled him. He pivoted and stared at another naked, blond-headed girl holding an armful of beer cans. She stood directly under the door's arch, blocking his exit.

"That's my brother!" Michelle said. "He wants to join us. Strip him."

James bolted toward the naked stranger, hoping to intimidate her, but she stood firm. From behind him, a youth with a linebacker's build, grabbed him.

James squirmed and screamed. "Noooo!" He kicked, he clawed, he spit, but by now the three guys who had been with his sister, held him down, while a fourth one removed his pants and underwear.

"Ohhhh, look at his little weenie!" Michelle threw her head back and laughed. She knelt down so that her blond hair covered his face. "How do you like it, little brother?"

"Pl. . .please, M-Miche. . .lle. Let me go." Sobs raked his body.

"What did you say?"

"Pl. . .please."

"Did you hear that, guys? He's begging for it. Take him over there to the bed and bend him over."

Her laughter echoed in his ears.

Chapter 9

James clinched his hands into fists and pounded them against the steering wheel. He turned to stare at Bobbye's duplex. "Fool," he said aloud. "What the hell am I doing here?" James reached for the key in the ignition.

His hand held onto the key when the door to the duplex opened. James held his breath. Bobbye stepped out and stood on the step as though waiting for something to happen. He immediately recognized her. That blond hair–the same as when she was a child. The urge to punish surfaced. With both hands he grabbed the steering wheel until his knuckles turned white.

Drive away. Forget she ever came back. Do it now before it's too late.

As James once again reached for the key, from the corner of his eye he saw a little girl step out. She wore a soft, frilly white blouse, and a bright blue jumpsuit.

The little girl had blond hair.

So Bobbye had given birth to a blond-headed demon. The thought filled him with a pain so intense, his eyes watered. He nodded in acknowledgment. He had no choice. He had to stop her. He had to cleanse the world of all blond-headed demons. It was his duty. His responsibility.

James never took his eyes off Bobbye and her little girl. He watched as the child reached for her mother's hand and smiled at her. Bobbye said something to her then bent down and gave her a kiss. Together, hand in hand, they walked away from the duplex.

James started the engine and slowly followed them.

* * *

"What's the name of this city again?" Tracy asked as they strolled toward the city park.

"Dallas."

"Oh yeah, Dallas. I forgot. Is it always like this?"

"Like how?"

"Dark, gray skies."

Lisa glanced up. The cheerless, gray sky threatened rain, and a haunting depression engulfed her. "No, of course not. Remember yesterday? It was nice and sunny."

"Oh yeah, I forgot. Were your parents really from outer space? Were they like E.T.?"

Lisa knew Tracy was referring to the last phone call she had received. It had been from a woman who claimed to be Lisa's aunt. According to her, space men had abducted, raped, and impregnated Lisa's mother. That's why Lisa had been put up for adoption. Disgustedly, Lisa shook her head. It seemed that weirdos certainly outnumbered the normal people.

"Well, were they?" Tracy repeated.

"No, of course not."

"Then why did that lady say that?"

Lisa glanced down at her daughter. She hadn't realized that Tracy had been listening. She'd have to be more careful.

"Why, Mommy?"

"I don't know, honey. There are a lot of confused people in the world. Maybe she was just confused." They got ready to cross the street. "We're almost there."

Tracy squealed with delight. "Oh, Mommy, look! It's got monkey bars. Can I go, huh, Mommy, huh?" Tracy jumped up and down.

Lisa nodded. "Just be careful. I'll sit on that bench over there and watch you."

Even before Lisa had finished talking, Tracy was already skipping toward the monkey bars. Lisa shook her head as she watched her daughter gracefully swing from one bar to another.

"She will make a beautiful ballerina some day," Lisa heard a male voice say. She glanced up and felt her breath taken away. She had seen this man before. But where? Overall, he was a very attractive, older man, maybe in his fifties. His broad shoulders and firm stomach told Lisa that he spent several hours a week in the gym. What seemed to have once been solid jet-black hair now contained traces of gray which added to his distinguished looks. He wore an expensive brown suit and two large diamond and gold rings.

Lisa followed his glance and noticed that this stranger referred to Tracy. "Well, thank you very much," she said. "That's my daughter."

"Your daughter? You have a lot to be proud of." He glanced at the bench. "Mind if I join you?"

"Of course not." She scooted over.

"Your daughter reminds me so much of my grandchild," the stranger said.

"Oh? How old is she?"

"She's not." And his voice went quiet, his features blank. "She's dead."

"Oh, I'm sorry." Lisa could see the anguish in this man's eyes. She felt sorry for him.

After a short, uncomfortable silence, he asked, "Do you come here often?"

"It's our first time." Lisa watched Tracy slide down a bar. "We just moved in. Tracy loves parks, so I'll probably bring her every day, or as often as I can." She stopped. Why did she tell him this? Normally, when a stranger approached, her guard went up.

"If you're here tomorrow and if I can make it, would you mind it terribly much if I brought a ball so I could play with your daughter? That used to be my granddaughter's favorite pastime."

His anguish touched Lisa's tender side. Normally men wouldn't allow their vulnerability to show. Then a warning bell rang inside Lisa. Why would a stranger do this? Because Tracy brought back recent painful, yet wonderful memories, she told herself. Lisa could tell by the way he stared at Tracy. The hunger in his eyes revealed it all. Should she whisk Tracy away and forbid this stranger from ever seeing her daughter again?

No, that's something David would do. He claimed that Lisa was gullible, but then she believed that David was paranoid. She could see no reason to deny this kind stranger the pleasure of Tracy's company. After all, Lisa would be right here. She wouldn't leave them alone. Still. . .

"Please?" He seemed to have read Lisa's thoughts. "All we'll be doing is playing ball, but of course if you don't want me to, I'll understand. It's just that she's so much like my granddaughter." His eyes pleaded with her.

Lisa felt her doubts melt away. She smiled. "Sure, why not?"

"Why not indeed!" the stranger said, slapping his knees joyously. "Now I'll finally have something to look forward to tomorrow. Thank you very much." He smiled briefly at Lisa, before his eyes rested on Tracy. He sighed, shook himself, and stood up.

* * *

As he walked away from Lisa toward his blue, rented Toyota, James couldn't help but smile. He felt a delightful rush of excitement, like awakening to the promise of a new day. And why shouldn't he feel that way? After all, he had made contact.

Chapter 10

The next day proved to be as hot and oppressive as the weatherman had promised. But the weather had nothing to do with Lisa feeling depressed. The constant ringing of the phone, each new call promising some good news, each one a disappointment, caused Lisa to consider giving up.

Lisa slammed the phone down and Tracy looked up from her coloring book. "Was it another one of those calls from strange people?"

Slowly, Lisa nodded. "This ad thing isn't working at all."

"Oh, oh," Tracy said and turned her attention to her coloring book.

Lisa picked up a piece of blank paper and one of Tracy's crayons, went over to the desk, and got to work.

Filled with curiosity, Tracy went to her mother's side. "What you doing, Mommy?"

"I'm drawing a memory."

"Huh?"

"When I was a little bit younger than you, in the front yard of the house I lived in, there was this beautiful and unusual fountain. I'm trying to draw it." She continued to put her thoughts on paper as Tracy watched.

By the time Lisa finished, she had drawn a pile of ornamental rocks with cascading water. A small pool collected the water, then recycled it back up through a pipe, thus creating the waterfall. All around its edges flowers grew abundantly.

"I used to love this place." Lisa showed Tracy her work,

amazed at how easily the memory of the fountain had come. Why should she remember a fountain, but not her parents? The answer came like a glacial whisper. She had often been afraid and the fountain–not her parents–had been her sanctuary. What had made her so afraid, she wondered?

She wrapped her arm around her daughter. "When I felt afraid, I'd sit by the gurgling water and listen to the waterfall. The tiny murmur of the cascading water took my fears away." She gave Tracy a squeeze. "Do you know what? I've always thought it was a dream, but now I know better."

Lisa reached for the telephone book and thumbed through its yellow pages. She carefully read each of the real estate ads and settled for one that sounded large and important. She wrote down the address and phone number, told Tracy to hurry and put her shoes on, then together they rushed out of the house.

"Where we're going, Mommy, will there be swings?" Tracy asked once inside the car.

"No, sweetheart. That's why I told you to bring your coloring book."

"I like coloring."

"I know."

"Did you like it when you were a little girl?"

"Yes, I think I did."

"Were you ever a little girl like me?"

"Yes, of course."

"I wish I could have known you then."

"Me, too."

"Yeah, then we could have played with our dolls. Did you like playing with dolls? What was your favorite doll's name?"

Lisa sighed and switched to automatic responses, inserting the appropriate "Yes, of course" and "Sure, sweetheart," whenever needed. Even though Tracy always asked the same questions, Lisa enjoyed her constant chatter. It made time go faster. Before she realized it, she found the address listed in the phone book.

* * *

"This may be the most unusual request you've had," Lisa told the real estate agent. "I'm Lisa Littau, and I'm Mr. Hoffman's secretary."

The real estate agent, an elderly, plump woman with almost solid-white hair, raised her eyebrows as though asking, who's that?

"Oh you know," Lisa said, waving her hand as though dismissing the subject. "The Hoffmans–the Texas oil millionaires."

The agent's eyes brightened up and Lisa relaxed. She had no idea if the Hoffmans existed, but at least the realtor seemed impressed. "Anyway," Lisa quickly continued, "it seems that Mrs. Hoffman–she's a bit of an eccentric, but please keep that just between you and me." She placed her index finger over her lips in a conspiratorial hushing motion.

The realtor eagerly nodded and smiled, agreeing to keep the secret.

"It seems that Mrs. Hoffman saw this one particular house for sale, and she's willing to pay whatever amount it takes. Unfortunately, other than knowing that it's in Dallas somewhere, she doesn't remember where, nor does she seem to be able to describe this house."

"Oh dear."

"But there's hope."

"Oh?"

"Mrs. Hoffman said that a few blocks away from her dream house there's another house that she can identify. Now, she still doesn't know where it is, but she was hoping you could find it just from a description."

"That's a pretty big order, but tell me about this other house."

"It's a big house, at least two stories."

"That narrows it down from three million houses to around a million houses."

Lisa smiled. "There's more."

"Well, good. Shoot."

"The house in question is at least thirty to forty years old and it's got a fountain out front."

"What kind of a fountain?"

"It's like a waterfall—a whole bunch of rocks piled up together with a cascade of water flowing over them. All sorts of brightly colored flowers grow around its base."

"That is unique."

"Yes, yes. That's probably why she remembered it so well." It surprised Lisa how comfortable she felt in her role as Mr. Hoffman's secretary. "If you could just find this house for her, I'd be able to drive Mrs. Hoffman to it, then she'll be able to lead us to the house she's interested in purchasing."

The realtor leaned back in her chair. "I can't guarantee anything, but I'll certainly ask around and maybe we'll get lucky."

"I'd appreciate that." Lisa stood up, opened her purse, and handed her a piece of paper. "This is my home phone. You can reach me there anytime."

The realtor clipped it to her stack of important-looking papers and made a notation.

Lisa tried to read it, but her upside-down reading skills needed polishing. She gave up and handed her a crispy, new, fifty-dollar bill. "This is for your trouble."

"Oh no, I couldn't possibly—"

"Call it gasoline money. You see Mrs. Hoffman is very interested in locating this house." Lisa signaled for Tracy to join her. She had been sitting in a chair in the waiting area of the realtor's office, coloring in her book.

As Lisa left the real estate office, she felt good about what she'd done, for it brought her one step closer to being reunited with her biological parents.

"Are we going to the park now? You promised," Tracy said as she put the seat belt on.

Lisa nodded. "I did promise, didn't I?"

Less than twenty minutes later, they reached the park. Even before Lisa parked the car, she spotted the same gentleman whom she had spoken to yesterday. He sat ramrod straight, his hands clutching a bright red ball nestled in his lap. For a second Lisa hesitated.

"What's the matter, Mommy? Aren't we going to get out?"

Lisa eyed the stranger speculatively, then decided he was harmless. "Of course we are. Come on; let's go," she said opening the car door. Holding onto Tracy's hand, they approached the friendly stranger. "Hi there!" Lisa said.

When he saw her, he stood and faced her. A wide smile formed on his face. "Hi! I'm glad you made it. For a minute there, I thought that maybe you weren't going to come."

"Mommy, can I go to the swings?" Tracy asked.

Lisa cast her glance toward her daughter, then back up at the stranger.

"Oh, please, don't stop her on my account. We can sit and chat while she goes to the swings. Then maybe afterwards the three of us can play ball."

Lisa nodded and Tracy took off running. Lisa and the stranger sat on the same bench as the day before. "I was thinking that after I leave the park," the stranger said, "I won't have much use for this ball. Would you mind if I give it to Tracy?"

"That would be nice, Mr., uh. . ." Lisa looked at him expectantly.

He opened his mouth as though to answer but nothing came out. He closed it again. He cleared his throat, buying time. Another second went by before he answered, "It's James Johnson."

Lisa gasped. "From Johnson Enterprises?"

He nodded.

Lisa snapped her fingers. "Of course! That's where I've seen you before–in the newspapers and magazines. Yesterday it kept gnawing at me that somehow I knew you, but I just couldn't place you." She sighed. "That's a relief–knowing who you are. It really was kind of bothering me."

"I'm glad that's cleared up," James said. "I don't want

to upset you. I only want to be with Tracy as long as you're here in Dallas. You're not planning to move, I hope."

"Actually, yes. I'm only here for a short time, hopefully no more than two weeks. Then I'll return to my home in San Antonio."

James' eyebrows rose in an arch. "Two weeks? That's not enough time–to get to know Tracy, I mean. I was really hoping to become her adopted grandpa. I guess I'd better enjoy her while I can. This being the case, would you do me the honor of having supper with me tonight?"

"Well, I–"

"My wife is out of town–Europe, in fact–and I have one of those dreadful business supper meals that I'm supposed to attend. Please provide me with an excuse. If you're leaving in a couple of weeks, I want to spend as much time as possible with Tracy. She's so much like my little granddaughter." He sighed deeply and a genuine, depressed look haunted his features. "You probably think I'm an old, sentimental fool."

"No, of course not," Lisa quickly said.

"Does that mean you'll come?"

Lisa considered it, and then nodded.

James smiled triumphantly. "Let's go play ball," he said. He looked at Tracy and an old familiar feeling stirred inside. It must be the blond hair, he thought.

He forced his feelings to scurry into the far recesses of his mind.

Chapter 11

James Johnson squatted so that he could be eye-level with Tracy. "So, what would you like to eat for dinner?"

Tracy put the tip of her middle finger on her nose and gently pushed, thinking. "Hmmm, let me see. I know! Pizza!" She bounced several times. "I want pizza. I want pizza." Bouncy. Bouncy. Up and down.

Just like his sister. Always bouncing so that her golden hair moved in every possible direction. Always teasing. Always taunting. He wanted so much to bury his face in that rich, blond hair. He quickly straightened up. Why had Bobbye come back to torment him like this?

Ever since Kathy's death–ever since he sold Bobbye–he had fought temptation. Often, the feeling of wanting to grab the little blond-headed demons and punish them overwhelmed him so much that he became physically ill. But still, he resisted.

Would he be strong enough to resist this latest temptation? If only Bobbye hadn't waltzed into his life, bringing with her this five-year old blond-headed she-devil. He was an old man now, much too old to want to resist.

He knew that it was time again.

Time to punish.

But this time, punish the right person: Bobbye. No more substitutes. That had never worked.

"James, are you all right?"

Startled, James shook himself and forced his eyes to rest on Bobbye–no, on Lisa. He must keep the two separate, at least for the time being.

"You look so pale," Lisa said. "Can I get you something? A glass of water? Anything?"

"I'm fine," James said. "It's just that the way Tracy answered was the exact way my granddaughter would have answered. I miss her so much." The urge to run his fingers through Bobbye's golden locks left him breathless and shaking.

He turned away. "I'm fine." He fought for control. "Let's go get that pizza."

* * *

After they had consumed two medium sized pizzas and emptied two pitchers of Pepsi, James handed Tracy a twenty-dollar bill so she could play the video games and the other carnival-type games that drew the crowd to the pizza house—certainly, it wasn't because they had the best pizza.

Afterwards, they went to Toys R Us. Tracy walked out with two new doll outfits and a complete set of toy dishes. Lisa watched Tracy's bright smile as she struggled to carry her packages. She shared her daughter's joy, but at the same time, that seed of doubt needled at her. "I really feel bad about all this money you're spending on Tracy," Lisa said.

If you think you feel bad now, wait until later, James thought. Aloud he said, "When you have as much money as I do, money doesn't really matter. What matters is happiness. Tracy has brought back the granddaughter I love so much and has re-introduced me to a world of pleasure. A world I had forgotten about. I know she will continue to add to this pleasure." *But not quite the way you think*, he added silently.

They got in the rented car and drove off.

* * *

In his private study at home, James wrinkled yet another letter and threw it on the floor. That made the sixth letter he had started and destroyed. All of these damn letters sounded like a business proposal.

What he needed was an emotional letter, something written by a man with feelings. Yet, ever since Kathy's death, he hadn't felt anything. Not when he sold Bobbye, not at his second wedding, not even at the birth of his son. Nothing. Just a void.

That was the only way he could control his urges. He had become a machine, a money-making robot.

It worked.

Then why in God's name was he sitting in this cold, empty office stuffed with expensive rugs and first class editions of books, fine furniture, and meaningless expensive nick-knacks? Why was he attempting to write this stupid letter?

If he did it–and he knew he shouldn't–he'd be bringing back the old James, a man who loved, who cared.

A man who killed blond-headed women.

He crumpled the blank paper in front of him and cast it on the floor with the others.

Walk away, his logic told him, while you still can. Forget Bobbye ever entered your life again. She'll never find you. Feeling disappointed, she'll go away and naturally, she'll take that she-devil brat of hers with her.

And Tracy will go unpunished.

And so will Bobbye.

She's the one who should suffer, he thought. Not me. Not anymore. I have deprived myself of living a full life–a life radiant with emotion–just to keep her alive. I owed Kathy this, but that debt has been paid in full over and over again.

I'm an old man now. I need to experience life to its fullest at least one more time. After all, Bobbye was the one who made the decision. She waltzed into my life. I never asked her to.

She must pay the consequences.

James took out another piece of paper and glared at it. It demanded warmth and love, not cold, empty business words. It should be written with the compassion that a woman would pour into it. An idea occurred to him. He knew exactly how to say what needed to be said.

Chapter 12

The speed limit signs posted on Clark Avenue read thirty-five miles per hour. The grayish-brown compact car's speedometer read sixty-one. By the time it made a right-hand turn onto Stephens Street, it had slowed down to a mere ten miles per hour.

Lisa lived on Stephens Street, two blocks up from where the car turned. When it reached the intersection near Lisa's duplex, the car came to a complete stop.

The driver quickly scanned the area. Two houses down, on the right, sat an old lady, rocking away her time. Catty-corner from that house, a chunky woman retrieved some grocery bags from the trunk of her car. Other than that, the neighborhood was deserted.

The driver liked that. A quiet neighborhood meant a better chance to observe Lisa and that brat of hers–what was her name? Oh yeah: Tracy.

The driver was about to take off when the door to Lisa's duplex opened. She stepped out, retrieved the mail, and glanced through it. Apparently one of the envelopes caught her attention as she suddenly stopped and opened it. She stood perfectly still, her hand at her throat, while she read the letter. Then she gave a little jump and ran back inside.

For a long second the driver sat there, staring at Lisa's duplex, then with sudden jerky movements, the driver turned the wheel and sped away toward the park.

Across from the park was a convenience store with a pay phone. The driver dropped a quarter and a dime in the appropriate slots and dialed Lisa's number by memory.

* * *

Lisa ran inside her duplex, set aside the water bill and the going-out-of-business advertisement brochure, and flopped herself down on the couch. She concentrated on the envelope the letter had arrived in. It had originally been sent to the postmaster general who, in turn, had written down her address. Other than that, it contained no other return address. A delightful rush of excitement flowed through her veins as she re-read the neatly typed letter:

> My dearest Lisa,
>
> I have re-written this letter at least twenty times and each time I've torn it up. Maybe this one will make it. First of all, I want you to know that I have never stopped loving you. You are the only part of my early life that I do not want to forget. I know you might not believe me, but it's true. I had my reasons for doing what I did. I know you'll understand when I explain everything later on.
>
> Lisa, it is so hard for me to write this. Right now, the way things are, I'm sorry to say that we cannot meet, but I'm working things out so that we can get together soon. When I do find a way, it's very important that you follow my instructions very carefully. I'm enclosing a picture of you when you were one-year old as proof that I am your mother. Sorry that all of the background has been cut out, but all the pictures I have of you are like that. Some memories are best forgotten. I'm looking forward to the day I can hold you in my arms again.
>
> Much love,
>
> Mother

Lisa's hands shook as she studied the image in the picture. Of course it could be a snapshot of somebody else, but Lisa doubted it. There it was: the same blond hair and sly smile she had seen in the pictures that her adopted mom had kept in the photo album back home in San Antonio. The resemblance between this picture and those she had of Tracy as a baby further erased any doubt Lisa might have had.

Lisa's concentration broke when the phone rang. She hurried to answer it. "Hello?" A silence followed and Lisa almost hung up when she thought she heard her name being whispered. She held the phone close to her ear. "I can't hear you."

The coarse whisper came back. "Lisa, I'm. . ." The whisper died away.

Lisa held her breath.

"Are you my mother?"

No answer.

"Father?" She felt the blood pounding at her temples. The line went dead.

* * *

Still shaking, the caller slammed the phone down and dashed toward the security of the grayish-brown compact car.

Fool! the driver thought. *What a fool I've been.* Without realizing it, the driver's fist had begun to pound against the steering wheel and had now turned a bright red.

"Lisa, I'm coming to get you."

Now it could be said. Back there on the phone it came only as a whisper–a whisper which Lisa obviously hadn't heard.

Filled with disgust, the driver sped off and didn't stop until reaching Pedro's Pawn Shop.

* * *

Pedro, an overweight green-eyed Mexican with a friendly smile reserved only for paying customers, possessed a unique talent. When a person walked in through his pawnshop's door, he could readily tell whether they were browsing or serious buyers, and for his buyers he always provided the goods.

Pedro heard the bell on the door ring, signifying he had a potential customer. He put down the Captain Marvel comic book he was reading and quickly surveyed his new customer. Immediately he knew this was a paying customer. "May I help you?" Pedro asked, flashing his widest smile.

"I'm looking for a hand gun."

Pedro knew he was about to make a huge profit. This customer wanted a handgun now and would not want to wait the required time. That meant Pedro could charge any amount of money and the customer would have no choice but to pay.

"No, problem," Pedro said and smiled.

Chapter 13

Thomas Johnson quickly skimmed through the stack of papers and briefly reviewed the various memorandums, advertising campaign ideas, statistical projections, and experimental program notes. He placed them in neat piles, arranged not only by categories, but also by order of importance.

He stole a quick glance at the decorative clock hanging on the wall behind his desk. "Jesus!" he said, grabbed the papers and hurried out of his office.

As he went by his secretary's desk she said, "Mr. Hagerman from Greenland is on line two."

"Hagerman. Hagerman." Then it dawned on him. "That's the branch having all those internal problems," Thomas said.

Liz nodded.

"My father is an expert at handling those kind of situations. Have it transferred over there, and that's also where you can reach me." He headed toward his father's office located down the hallway and around the corner to the right.

He stepped inside his father's office and saw his father's secretary busily typing. "Hi, Stacey," he said as he went past her desk.

She continued to type. "Hi, Thomas. Don't bother going in. He's not there."

Thomas came to a sudden stop. "What?"

"Mr. Johnson left about ten minutes ago."

"Where did he go?"

"He wouldn't say."

"Damn him! He knew we had this meeting. It's not like him. What's going on? Has he told you anything?"

Stacey shook her head. "No, he hasn't, and I'm concerned about him."

"What do you mean?"

"As long as I've worked for Mr. Johnson—and I'm going on my eleventh year—he's been a workaholic. Regardless of the time of day or season of the year, he's always working. Even his leisure activities are business related. But lately he seems to be very preoccupied. I know this has happened before, but it's always been with some kind of business problem. But not this time. He's hardly in his office anymore. Is there something wrong?"

"I don't know, Stacey, but I'm going to find out." Still carrying all the papers he had intended to discuss with his father, he started toward his office.

"Thomas."

He stopped.

Stacey pointed to the phone. "Liz had that phone call from Greenland transferred over here. What should I tell him?"

"I'll take it," he said.

* * *

Thomas Johnson's throat felt tight and raw. Oblivious to the office's opulence, he leaned back in his leather-covered chair. Johnson Enterprises had too much at stake and too much to lose if his father suddenly developed other interests.

He glanced at the complex communications system next to his desk. It consisted of several telephones, most with direct lines to the company headquarters around the world. Thomas ignored the telephones and instead reached for the intricate intercom system. "Liz, get me Tony Sheridan at security," he said.

Tony Sheridan was not head of the company's private security system, but he was a reliable man. On several occasions, Thomas had hired him to handle delicate matters.

Tony always did his job, discreetly and expertly.

And above all, he reported only to Thomas.

* * *

Less than forty-eight hours later, Tony had a report ready for Thomas. Tony waited until Thomas finished signing some letters and until Liz walked out of the office before speaking. "It seems that your father is having an affair."

"An affair?" Thomas gasped. Out of all the possible scenarios he had imagined, an affair was something he had never considered. He wiped his brow and stared at the security guard. "Are you sure?"

"Yes, sir. Her name is Lisa Littau. She's a divorcee from San Antonio and has a five-year old daughter, Tracy. Ms. Littau, by the way, is twenty-eight years old."

The news hit Thomas like a tidal wave. "Twenty-eight? Jesus, she's only five years older than me. What's her game? Is she a gold digger?" The questions came in rapid succession. He never had his father's love, but at least he had his money. Now. . . now. . . "What does she want?"

"It's hard to tell at this point, sir. If you want me to, I can work up a detailed report on her."

Thomas inwardly frowned. He had to have time to think. "That won't be necessary, but keep yourself open for the possibility." He stood up and walked around his desk. "I'm sure I don't have to say this—"

"No, sir, you don't. I won't say a word. You can count on me." Even though Thomas walked around his desk signifying that the meeting was over, Tony remained glued to his spot.

"Is there anything else?" Thomas asked.

Tony set down an eight-by-ten Manila envelope on top of Thomas' desk. "I thought, sir, you might want to see her picture."

"Yes, as a matter of fact I do. Thank you for a job well done." He handed Tony an envelope containing ten one hundred-dollar bills. "I would really like to see what kind of a woman it takes to evoke some kind of emotion from my father."

"I agree. Your father, if you pardon me for saying this, is the most unemotional man I've ever known. It's almost as if he has no feelings, not even for you. He's always business, business, business."

A touch of sadness settled in Thomas and sparkled the flames of jealousy and hatred toward this woman. "I know. That's why this idea of an affair is hard for me to accept. Are you sure that's all there is to it?"

"Have I ever let you down?"

"No, Tony, you haven't. You've always been very dependable. It's just that I have this feeling that something much deeper has to be going on." He looked up as though he had just remembered that Tony was still there. "I'll call you if I need you again."

Tony took the hint and left. As soon as Tony closed the door behind him, Thomas reached for the envelope. It contained three pictures: in one, his father played Frisbee with a little girl (a *little girl*?) Didn't his father hate little girls? As far as he could remember, his father ignored them and considered them a general nuisance. Yet, this little girl apparently brought him happiness.

That, if nothing else, reinforced the feeling that he needed to dig deeper for that piece of the missing puzzle that would provide the overall picture. He knew that missing piece would lead him to where secrets lie. Maybe if he studied each picture.

The second one showed his father, the same little girl and a woman. They were sitting down–the little girl between them–enjoying some ice cream. (Good ol' dad had never taken him for ice cream.)

The third picture focused on the woman's face and Thomas found his eyes glued there.

Thomas stared at her for a long time. Quite an attractive woman, he thought, not necessarily movie-star material, but nevertheless, pleasing to the eye. Her ice-blue eyes blended perfectly with her blond hair and light, milky complexion. If she had stolen his father's heart, he could hardly blame him.

But he still wasn't convinced–

Like a bolt of lightning. Thomas shot up to his feet. He had seen this woman before. Images flashed through his mind like an out-of-control slide projector.

Suddenly he remembered the ad in the newspaper.

And he remembered his father's state of mind after he had seen the ad for the first time.

Thomas reached for the telephone.

Chapter 14

Several days had passed since Lisa had originally heard from her birth mother. Surely, any day now, she'd call. The jingling of the phone interrupted her thoughts and sent her pulse racing. *Mother,* she thought.

She ran to the phone and answered it on the second ring. "Hello?"

"Lisa."

Lisa's heart fluttered with both disappointment and satisfaction. Hearing David's voice still reminded her of the pain, the anger, and the love she felt. Would she ever get over him? "How are you, David?"

"I'm fine. I was just wondering how. . .Tracy is. Is she doing all right?"

What about me, Dave? Why don't you call just once and ask how I'm doing? Aloud she said, "She's fine. There isn't a day that passes by that she doesn't ask for her daddy."

"I miss her, too."

And me? Do you miss me? Do you think of me as often as I think of you? "She's playing in the bathtub. If you give me a second, I can go get her."

"In a minute. Let her play for now. I know how much she likes that." He cleared his throat before asking, "Have you had any luck?"

"Oh yes! I've found her, Dave. I've found her!"

A startled silence followed, then, "Tell me all about it."

Lisa found herself telling him everything from that first compulsive confessor, Emily Rogers, to Detective

Bronson's—or as he called himself, "Uncle Harry's"—visit, to the numerous crazy calls she had received, to the meetings with James Johnson and finally the letter from her mother. They talked like old friends and more than ever, Lisa felt the vast hollowness David had left when he walked out.

"Lisa, I'm proud of you. You probably accomplished the impossible. You actually made contact with your biological mother." He sounded sincere, happy.

"But I haven't talked to her yet. Oh, Dave, what if she backs out? I don't even know who she is. It really worries me."

"Don't worry. She contacted you once. I'm sure she'll contact you again."

"Then why did she leave the address off both the letter and envelope?"

"She probably doesn't want you to visit her."

"See what I mean?"

David laughed. "Oh, Lisa, you silly gal."

David's joking brought a smile to Lisa's lips. It was almost as if she had gone back in time. Her smile faded when David's tone turned serious. "Lisa, what does that man—James Johnson—want with our daughter?"

"Nothing, Dave. He just misses his granddaughter. That's all."

"That seems too coincidental. Are you sure he's not after something else?"

"Oh, Dave, if you knew him, you wouldn't say that. He's just a sweet, lonely, elderly man."

"Who's after Tracy."

Lisa smirked. "You make him sound sinister."

"He probably is."

"Dave, he's one of the most respected figures, not just in Dallas, but in the entire world. He's powerful and rich."

"Precisely. You'd be surprised at the secrets the ultra-rich hide. I'd be leery of him. I want you to promise me that you won't see him again."

"Dave, I can't. He's taking us to dinner tonight."

"Oh? You didn't tell me that you two were dating."

Had she detected a trace of jealousy in his voice? Lisa smiled. "We're not dating. He just wants to spend time with Tracy, and he knows I'd never leave her alone. I'm just the tag-along."

"Don't put yourself down, Lisa. You're a very attractive woman. He'd be a fool not to see that. Are you sure he's not using Tracy to get to you?"

This idea appealed to Lisa. She didn't know why, but she found herself wanting James Johnson to like her. To accept her. She didn't love him. She had no interest in starting an affair. She just wanted him to accept her. Lisa shook herself. That was weird. Absurd. She probably felt sorry for the old man. He had everything, yet it seemed to her, he really had nothing at all. "He's married," she said.

"But he's wealthy enough to afford a mistress."

"Oh, Dave, I've already told you. It's nothing like that."

"All right, all right. It's just that I have this–" He paused momentarily. "–feeling. Maybe it's got nothing to do with James Johnson, but with your mother. Maybe I just feel helpless. I don't know. I wish there was someone over there I could trust." He paused again as though thinking. Then, "Hey, what about Harry Bronson?"

"What about him?"

"You said he was taking care of you, right?"

"Yeah, so?"

"So I want you to do something for me."

"Name it."

"Show him your mother's letter and see what he thinks."

"David, I can't. I kind of got the feeling she's hiding something. Hopefully, it's something as simple as trying to keep her family from learning about me." Then she found herself voicing the fear she had not wanted to admit, even to herself. "Or she might be running away from the police."

"Which would make her dangerous."

"Not to me. She's my real mother."

"Lisa, the parents who loved you and raised you and

cared for you are buried here in San Antonio."

Lisa's heart hummed with the pain and memory—and perhaps a bit of guilt—at the thought of her dad and mom. But she had come this far, there was no turning back. If only David could understand that. "In my heart, they will always be my parents. But I have to find my roots. Besides, I promised Mom before she died that I would do this, and a promise made is a debt unpaid."

"I understand. Anyway, if you hadn't promised, your stubbornness would have forced you to continue." The comment had been made off-hand and Lisa took no offense at it. David continued, "Lisa, I have a couple of sick days that I can take. I'm coming to Dallas."

Lisa's hopes soared. He was concerned about her, not just Tracy. "Where will you stay?"

Silence. Then, "I don't know."

"My place here is small, but you're welcome to stay—for Tracy's sake."

"Thank you, Lisa. I'll keep that in mind. I'll call you as soon as I have my airline schedule."

Lisa felt the tingling of excitement as she lowered the phone to its cradle. Soon she'd meet her mother and David was coming to visit. Things were looking up for her.

At that moment, Tracy stepped out of the bathroom, a towel wrapped around her. She was dripping-wet, and a small puddle had formed where she stood. "Who was that on the phone?"

"Daddy."

Tracy's face fell. "I didn't get to talk to him."

"I know, sweetheart, but I've got good news. He's coming to visit us!"

Tracy's face brightened again, and she ran to hug her mother. "Oh, Mommy, that's wonderful!"

Lisa hugged her tightly. "I think so too. Now get dressed. Mr. Johnson is probably already at the park waiting for us."

* * *

Twenty minutes later, Lisa found herself playing kick ball with Tracy as well as James Johnson. She was totally unaware that the driver of a grayish-brown compact sedan had parked across the street and hunched low in the seat in order to avoid being seen. Nor was she aware that the driver's right hand gently stroked the loaded gun kept under the windbreaker resting in the passenger's seat.

Lisa never realized that the driver's eyes were glued on her, and that only occasionally did they stray around the park. During the few times when they wandered off, it was only to glare at Tracy.

The driver hunched even lower and swallowed hard. It was easy to hate Tracy with such an intensity that it seemed to ooze out of the pores of the skin until it encompassed Lisa as well.

The driver continued to pet the gun, deriving a sensual satisfaction from its cool metallic touch. Then the hand abruptly stopped and the fingers wrapped themselves around the handle and slowly began to raise the gun. Just as the index finger found the trigger, a voice–possibly coming from the driver's own lips–spoke: "No. It doesn't feel right. Lisa can't die so quickly and so alone. Where's the pain? The suffering?"

The driver shrugged, returned the gun to its original hiding place underneath the windbreaker, started the engine, and sped away.

"Tomorrow," the driver said, "maybe tomorrow it will feel right."

* * *

It had been a long time since Lisa played kick ball and she wasn't used to the strenuous exercise. Her side began to ache. "I give up," she said. "I'm going to go sit on the bench for a few minutes and catch my breath."

"Me, too," James said. "I'm not so young anymore." He patted Tracy on the head and joined Lisa. Tracy frowned, kicked the ball a few times, then carrying the ball with her, she headed for the swings.

Lisa glanced at her watch.

"Are you in a hurry?" James asked. "I noticed you've been looking at your watch constantly."

"Not in a hurry–just impatient, I guess." Lisa sighed. "I've been expecting a very important letter and everyday I look forward to the mailman's arrival. In fact, he should be arriving any moment now."

Lisa watched Tracy until their eyes met. She waved her over. "Tracy! Time to go."

Tracy protested but nevertheless let the swing slow down until it came to a stop.

James stood up. "I hope your letter arrives today. May I offer you and Tracy a ride home?"

Lisa smiled. "No, thanks. Walking is good exercise."

"That's a good attitude to have." James smiled back.

Lisa offered Tracy her hand and the two of them began their journey back home.

"Oh, Lisa."

Lisa stopped and waited for James to catch up. "I've got a real busy schedule for tomorrow and I might not be able to get away. Hopefully, I can cut the meetings short, and I can meet you and Tracy here again, but don't count on it."

"I understand," Lisa said. "We'll see you the day after if we don't see you tomorrow."

"Of course," James said, "but since I know you plan on leaving, I don't want to miss a single day with Tracy." He handed Lisa his business card. "In case you need me for anything," he said.

Lisa looked down at it and noticed he had hand written his personal phone number. She stuffed the card in her pants pocket. "Thanks," she said.

"You're welcome," he answered and brushed the tip of Tracy's nose with his index finger. "And you, young lady, be good to your mommy. I'll see you soon."

Tracy giggled.

* * *

Lisa reached into the mailbox and retrieved its contents.

The first two pieces of mail were advertisements that she quickly discarded. The third envelope, however, held her interest. It was identical to the one she had previously received. She checked for a return address, found none, then tore the envelope open.

It read:

My Dearest Lisa,

Can we meet on Thursday? I know it's awfully short notice, but please, try to be there. There's an adult cocktail lounge called The Journey, located on 2311 68th Street. As you step in, the bar is off to your right. I'll be there at one-thirty. To make it easier to find me, I'll be wearing a bright yellow dress.

Lisa, please make sure you come alone. If you bring anyone, I won't reveal myself to you. I'll simply remain hidden in the shadows. I'm really looking forward to this Thursday. I hope you are too.

Much love,

Mother

Lisa put the letter down and closed her eyes. Thursday. Tomorrow. In her mind's eye, she could picture it all: Her biological mother wearing her bright yellow dress, would look up and immediately recognize her and Tracy. She would open her arms to them. She and Tracy. . .

Tracy! My God! Lisa didn't like the idea of exposing her five-year old to a cocktail lounge—especially an "adult" cocktail lounge. Just what exactly did her mother mean by an adult cocktail lounge? Weren't all lounges intended for adults only? Then a disturbing thought crept into her mind. Did it have nude dancers? Were the bar maids clad in almost nothing? If so, that was even more of a reason not to take Tracy in.

Why, from all the places, had her mother chosen a place like this to meet? Lisa frowned. She had no control over this aspect of the arrangement. What she needed to do was concentrate on the things over which she did have control.

Like finding a babysitter. Her mind spun with different possibilities as she headed back inside the house. She found her daughter playing with a Barbie doll. "Sweetheart, tomorrow we get to meet Grandma."

"The new grandma or the old grandma?" Tracy spoke without looking up.

"The new one, honey. The old one went to live with God in heaven, remember?"

A sad veil covered Tracy's face. "Yeah, I remember, but I want it to be the old one. Will the new one be as nice?"

"I'm sure she will, dear. But we have a problem."

"What?"

"When I go get Grandma, where are you going to stay?"

"I'll go with you."

"That's just it. You can't. I'm meeting her at a place where little children don't belong. Would you like to stay with Mr. Johnson? Maybe, I can call him."

"Yeah! That be good. I like Mr. Johnson."

Tracy retrieved the business card from her pants pocket and dialed the number. On the fourth ring, the answering machine picked up. "State your business," it said.

The brief, curt message surprised Lisa. She had thought of James as a caring, loving person. Before the machine disconnected, she quickly said, "Hi, James. Lisa. Tomorrow I'm meeting someone at The Journey at 1:30. I know you said you had meetings, but you also said you might be able to get out of attending them. If you're available, I need a sitter. If I don't hear from you, I know you're busy and I'll understand." She paused, then quickly added, "Thank you." She hung up.

She waited for an hour before considering other alternatives. The most obvious choice was the daycare centers. Lisa looked them up in the telephone book. She tried each of them, but each required that she'd bring Tracy's updated shot record. Unfortunately, she hadn't even thought about bringing the medical records with her.

Next, she tried individual baby-sitting services, but none had an opening on such short notice. Disgustedly, Lisa slammed the phone back into its cradle. There had to be someone. Who? Detective Bronson! She took out his card and dialed the police phone number.

"I'm sorry," the voice at the other end of the line said, "but Detective Bronson will be out of town for a couple of days. Can someone else help you?"

Lisa's last hope faded. He and his wife were finally taking that much-needed vacation Bronson had promised his wife. Well, good for them, but that left Lisa still without a sitter.

"Sweetheart, I can't seem to find anyone to take care of you."

"Good!" Tracy mumbled. "I don't need anyone. I want to go with you."

"Sweetie, I told you. You can't come. What about going next door?"

Tracy wrinkled her nose. "She doesn't like little kids. Can't I just wait in the car? Please, Mommy?"

Lisa considered the possibility. She could run in, get her mother, and run back out. Tracy would be alone–what? Two, three minutes at the most?

Her only other choice involved taking Tracy inside the bar. It would only be long enough to spot her biological mother, then the three of them would step outside. But the letter had specifically requested that she come alone. But what harm could a child cause?

Lisa bit her lip as she put herself in her birth mother's place. Assuming there had to be extreme secrecy, a child could unintentionally blurt something out. This realization would scare her off.

No, Lisa couldn't take that chance. Besides, what could happen in the two, three minutes it would take Lisa to find her biological mother and explain her dilemma? Tracy would be safe alone in a locked car. It wouldn't be for long. Lisa would make sure of that.

"Okay," she said. "I guess it'll be okay for you to stay in the car while I run in, get her, and then we'll all go to McDonald's."

"Could I go to the playground in McDonald's?"

Lisa smiled. Things were going to work out after all.

Chapter 15

"Hurry up, sweetie. We've got to go meet our new grandma."

"Can Ms. Muffet come?" Tracy clutched the doll her father had given her two years earlier. Above all dolls, she loved Ms. Muffet the most.

"Yes, of course, dear, let's just get going," Lisa glanced at her watch. It read twelve twenty-four, a little early, Lisa realized, but she didn't want to keep– Lisa stopped as she reached for her purse. Here she had an appointment to meet the woman who gave her life, but she didn't even know her name. She sighed and followed the roads she had memorized by studying the Dallas city map.

The closer they got to the bar, the greater Lisa's apprehension grew. "While I'm out getting Grandma, what are you supposed to do?"

Tracy frowned and said monotonously, "Wait in the car until you get back."

"And?"

"And don't open the doors to any strangers."

Lisa bit her lip. She didn't like leaving her alone like this. If the place looked decent enough, she would take her inside. On the other hand, if she had to leave her alone in the car, it would be for such a short time. "You're sure you'll be all right?"

"Yes, Mommy."

"That's my girl." Lisa reached over and squeezed Tracy's knee.

Lisa spotted The Journey Lounge. Its advertisement

lured customers in with the words *Naked Dancing Girls!* Damn! She had no choice. She had to leave Tracy in the car. Time froze and doubts flooded her mind, causing her to almost drive by the parking space across the street from the lounge. She slammed on her brakes.

The car behind her–a grayish brown compact–almost ran into her car, then with squealing tires swerved around Lisa's car. As it whizzed past her, Lisa looked at the driver. When she made eye contact, she planned to nod an apology for almost causing an accident. She shouldn't have bothered. The driver turned away from her.

Lisa shrugged. She was feeling good, and she wasn't about to let this driver–or anyone else–ruin her day.

She parked and sneaked a look at her watch. Why did she insist in getting here so early? It was only fourteen minutes past one. "We're a bit early," she said and silently added, might as well take advantage of the circumstances. "See if you can help Mommy spot a woman dressed in bright yellow, then maybe I won't have to go in there and leave you alone."

"It's okay, Mommy. I don't mind waiting in the car." Tracy straightened out Ms. Muffet's dress.

"I'd rather not do that," Lisa answered but by one twenty-eight, it was obvious she had no choice. To keep the car cool, she cracked the windows about an inch on both sides of the car. She was thankful for the overcast skies. That would help keep Tracy cool. She kissed her and stepped out of the car and headed toward The Journey, leaving Tracy alone in the locked car.

* * *

Tracy watched Mommy disappear into the building across the street. She wasn't worried though. She had Ms. Muffet with her, and she had to show her how brave she was.

She leaned back on the seat and placed Ms. Muffet on her lap. She straightened out her doll's new outfit. "There's no need to be afraid, Ms. Muffet," Tracy told her doll. "Mommy is just inside that building. We're going to be okay. Do you know why Mommy went there? Because we're going to meet our new grandma. But this is a different grandma—not the one we know. She died. Did you know that, Ms. Muffet? Mommy says—"

A sudden tapping on the window brought her to an abrupt stop. Tracy looked up and saw a huge hand flattened against the window pane.

She gasped and felt as though someone had sneaked up on her and whacked her bottom for doing something she shouldn't have done. "Mommy!" she murmured. She felt the sting of fear well up in eyes. She clutched Ms. Muffet tightly and shut her eyes, trying to block the image of the gigantic hand.

"Tracy."

Upon hearing her name, Tracy opened her eyes and let out a sigh of relief. It was only Mr. Johnson. Mommy said not to open the door to strangers. She never said not to open to friends like Mr. Johnson. So it was okay to open the door, wasn't it?

Tracy smiled, waved, and reached for the door handle.

Chapter 16

Lisa's eyes absorbed every detail in the bar. Resting against the back wall were three popular video game machines which were somewhat hidden by the small round tables covered with red and white checkered tablecloths. These tables seemed to have been randomly placed about the room with no regard for symmetry. Two couples sat quietly around the farthest table.

In front of the games were four pool tables. A group of five men sat engrossed in their game and stopped only long enough to sip their beer.

The longest bar Lisa had ever seen took up the right hand side of the room. One lonely man sat at its far end, his head hanging low in an obvious posture of defeat. Adjacent to the bar stood a small empty stage. Lisa supposed the naked, dancing ladies were taking a break. Lucky for her.

She looked around and surmised that The Journey Lounge was neither a luxurious place nor a dump. At best, it could be classified as an "average" club that was clean and unlike most bars, adequately lit. She wondered how the atmosphere would change once the dancing ladies did their thing.

As far as she could tell, she had now surveyed the entire bar and had checked out each of the bar's customers. No one wore yellow—not even a shade close to it. That meant that Mother had not yet arrived, but there was one more place to check: the ladies room.

The small, Lysol-smelling bathroom was neat and

empty. Maybe by now her mother had arrived. She hurried out of the bathroom and back to the saloon area.

She scanned the room one more time, hoping to spot anyone wearing yellow. The more she stared, the more she changed her mind. This place wasn't really "average"—it was a dump. Lisa wrung her hands and watched the round clock on the wall mark the passage of yet another minute. She had now been searching for three minutes. That was long enough.

She would wait outside with Tracy. From where she was parked, she could easily see the lounge's entrance. She just wished Mother would hurry. She was about to head out when she heard the bartender say, "Hey, Lady."

She turned. He was a youthful-looking man who was probably working his way through college. "Seems to me you're looking for someone."

Lisa's spirits lifted. Her mother had left a message. "Yes, as a matter of fact, I am. I'm looking for a woman dressed in yellow."

"That's it?"

Lisa's spirits dropped. She nodded.

"Well, in that case, I can't help you. I haven't seen anybody dressed in yellow that I know of—and I opened the place today."

"Thank you," she said and stepped outside. She quickly stole a quick look to her right, then to her left, each time hoping to catch a glimpse of someone wearing yellow. It was then that she saw her car–her *empty* car.

She's sitting on the floor, playing with Ms. Muffet. Please, dear God, she's sitting on the floor. She wanted to run to the car, but her legs, as though encased in cement, refused to obey.

Move! she ordered herself, and suddenly she was staring into the empty car.

Chapter 17

Six Flags Over Texas bustled with the noise and activity of people. A tired mother with one wailing child and another one clinging to her shoulder occupied most of one bench. Families and friends jabbered nonstop to each other as they went from one ride to another. Leggy girls with short shorts and skimpy tops teased the male population. Tourists snapped roll after roll of scenic pictures, usually with these leggy girls in the background. Small boys darted between the trees and benches, often creating traffic jams on the crowded walkways.

All of these activities seemed to awe Tracy as she drew closer to James Johnson. He noticed that she held onto his hand rather tightly. "You're sure Mommy won't be mad at us?"

"She knows we're here. She called me and asked me to take care of you."

Tracy squinted and her brows knitted and pulled into a tight little frown. She remembered Mommy calling, but Mommy hadn't said anything. Adults sure were confusing sometimes.

James noted her hesitation. He smiled kindly at her and led her toward an ice cream stand. He ordered an ice-cream sandwich, found a park bench, and sat down. He handed Tracy the ice cream. She thanked him and sat beside him.

While Tracy enjoyed her snack, James let his mind wander. He had never returned the call, and of course, Lisa had no idea where Tracy was, which was exactly what he wanted. His only regret was that he hadn't been able to be standing next to Tracy's car when she got there and found Tracy gone. What had she done? Had she screamed? He hoped so. By now, feeling very lonely and lost, she was probably surrounded by police.

He noticed Tracy's frown. "Your Mommy is busy with her friends, and she's happy. Let's be happy like her. Tell me, Tracy, what would make you happy?" Unable to stop himself, he reached down and ran his fingers through her golden hair.

Tracy shook her head. He removed his hand. She looked around. "The Ferris wheel," she said. "I love the Ferris wheel!"

James reached down and wrapped a strand of Tracy's hair around his finger. Its soft texture gave him a tingling sensation. He released it. "In that case, let's ride the Ferris wheel," he said. They stood up, and he maneuvered her through the crowd.

When they reached the line for the Ferris wheel, he squatted down so he was eye-to-eye with Tracy. "You wait here in line. I'm going to see how long we'll have to wait. Don't move from here."

"I won't, Mr. Johnson."

James walked straight toward the Ferris wheel attendant. "Young man," James said, "I need for you to do me a favor."

The teenage boy gave him a weary look. "Depends, mister. What do you want?"

"It's my granddaughter," he said. "She loves the Ferris wheel and would be just thrilled if the Ferris wheel stopped while she was at the very top." As he spoke, James reached into his wallet and took out a twenty dollar bill. "It would really make her happy."

The teenager's eyes remained glued to the bill. "Yeah? Well–"

James held the bill out closer to the attendant. "Do you think that would be possible?"

The teenager's hand plucked the bill with the speed of an animal taking food from a human it didn't quite trust. "Sure," he said. "I think that would be possible."

James smiled. "You won't forget now?"

"Oh, no, sir. I won't forget."

As James made his way back to Tracy, he wondered what it would feel like to be falling from the top with nothing to stop you. What would a five-year-old's thoughts be? Would she call out to her mother and would Lisa somehow hear her daughter's desperate cries?

As they climbed into the Ferris wheel basket and the teenager strapped them down, James winked at the teenager. The youth nodded as though saying, "I remember."

Seconds later the Ferris wheel was on its way up. "Lean over, Tracy," James said, "so you can see how pretty it looks down there."

Tracy leaned over.

"Don't be afraid," he said. "Lean over some more so you can really see."

Tracy did.

And the Ferris wheel stopped.

They had reached the top.

Chapter 18

Officer Loyce Guthrie was new to the force, this being only her fifth week. But in that short time, she had already shown a lot of promise. She was filled with compassion, but believed in strictly following each rule she had been taught. Officer Guthrie studied Lisa. "Now let me get this straight." Her forehead wrinkled in a frown. "You left your daughter alone, locked in a car, while you went drinking at that bar across the street."

"I didn't go in to drink. I just went in to pick up my mother."

"And where is she?"

"I don't know. She hasn't shown up yet."

Guthrie made a notation in her spiral notebook. "How does she get along with your daughter?"

"She doesn't know her. Look, she's my biological mother and I was going to meet her for the first time. She doesn't even know Tracy exists. I went in to pick her up, and she wasn't there. So I came back to the car to wait for her. I was gone for no more than three, four minutes." Five minutes. An eternity. What difference did it make? Tracy was gone. It was her fault. She should have never, never left her alone. "Please help me find my little girl."

"That's our job and we'll do it, but we wouldn't have to do this if you hadn't left her alone." Officer Guthrie stormed off to join the other policemen who were already conducting a block-by-block search.

Feeling worthless, Lisa paced the sidewalk. She

wanted to scream, to hold her little girl. A tremor ignited deep inside her as fear gnawed at her insides.

When she saw two policemen heading toward her, she anxiously ran to them. They shook their heads and neither would meet her eyes.

"Oh, God! Where is she?" Lisa's eyes filled with tears.

"She's got to be around here somewhere," the taller of the two policemen said. "There were no signs of forced entry. That's good news. She left of her own free will. Maybe she got thirsty."

"I told her not to get out of the car."

"Does she usually mind you?" Officer Santos asked. His partner had gone back to the police car and had picked up the microphone to call in.

"Always." Lisa's lips were dried and she wet them. "Always."

By now Officer Guthrie rejoined them. "We will keep patrolling this area, but you better go back home, just in case Tracy is trying to reach you. Some detectives from the Missing Persons Department will stop by. You'll have a lot of accounting to do for your actions."

Lisa stared down the street. "Tracy?"

Guthrie's features softened. "I too am a mother. I can imagine what you're going through. I promise you we'll keep looking for your little girl and won't stop until we find her. Okay?" She smiled reassuringly.

Lisa nodded. "Thank you."

"Best thing for you to do is go home. Officer Santos will drive you. We want your car here just in case Tracy is still around, she can see it. Later, you can pick it up."

Lisa nodded, removed the car key out of the key ring and handed it to Officer Guthrie. Lisa searched the area just one last time, hoping to see Tracy come running to her. A lump in her throat the size of a lemon made it hard for her to breathe.

She climbed inside the police car.

* * *

Bronson stormed into his office with the speed of a fleeing criminal. Loyce Guthrie had contacted him as a standard procedure about the child's disappearance. Under normal circumstances, he would have made a notation, let his partner work the details, then join him after his vacation was over. He had three more days to relax and he had promised his wife that this time they would take the entire week off and enjoy their time together. It had been five years since his last real vacation.

Then the call came. Guthrie told him about the woman who had left her child alone in a locked car. Bronson stroked his forehead. How could anybody be so stupid? He frowned and admonished himself. *Get the facts first*, he told himself. "Fill me in," Bronson said.

"The child, Tracy, is five years old. The mother claims—"

"Back up!" Bronson found it hard to catch his breath. "Tracy? Please tell me it's not Tracy Littau."

Guthrie's hesitation told Bronson everything he needed to know. He closed his eyes and reached for his wife's hand.

"I'm sorry, Detective Bronson," Guthrie said. "I didn't know you knew her. Is there anything I can do to help?"

"As a matter of fact, there is." He barked a set of instructions, hung up, reached for his wife, and told her about Lisa and Tracy.

Two hours later—record time, even for Bronson—he was back in his office. "Did you get the list of incoming calls Lisa's received since she got here?' Bronson asked Guthrie.

"The fax came in less than ten minutes ago." She handed him the paper.

"So you haven't had a chance to follow up on any of these calls?" Bronson asked.

Guthrie brushed her short brown hair back as though it interfered with her sight. "No, I'm sorry." She shifted her weight from one foot to the other. "I'll get on it right away."

"I'd appreciate that." He glanced down at the list. One phone listing jumped at him. It came from San Antonio and not from his daughter, either. Must have been from David. That was expected, he supposed.

Years in the force had taught him that a vast majority of this kind of disappearances often involved family members. Fortunately, his daughter was Lisa's best friend. She'd know what kind of person David was. It wouldn't hurt to call.

From Donna, Bronson confirmed what he already knew. David was a decent kind of fellow. No way would he ever do anything like that. Still it wouldn't hurt to follow through.

Bronson called David at work, but was informed that he was not there. The receptionist told Bronson that it was against company rules to give out any private information, so Bronson requested to speak to David's boss.

After Bronson had filled in Mr. Alire as to what had happened, Mr. Alire said, "David is not here because he took some personal time off."

"Do you know where I can reach him?"

"No, I don't, but I do know that it would be a lot easier for you to reach him than for me to try to do so."

"Why is that?" Bronson asked.

"I drove him to the airport early this morning. His flight landed at the DFW International Airport several hours ago."

Bronson thanked him and hung up.

So David's flight had landed several hours ago. Yet Lisa had not heard from David.

Interesting.

Chapter 19

Lisa sat rigidly on the sofa, her hands neatly folded on her lap. The clock hanging on the wall marked the passage of yet another hour. Four hours had gone by since Tracy. . .

Since Tracy. . .

The little courage Lisa had left evaporated, and she felt as though she would collapse. She heard her name being called. Startled, she shook herself.

"Lisa! Lisa, are you all right?" Detective Bronson bent down toward her, a worried frown evident on his face.

For the first time since the incident began, Lisa felt a spark of hope. "I'm so glad to see you. I thought you were out of town."

"I was, but when I heard what happened, I turned to my gal and she said, 'Yeah, let's go home.'"

"I'm sorry I messed up your vacation."

"Minor detail," Bronson said. "How are you holdin' up?"

"I'm fine. I'm just worried about Tracy."

"Of course you are, and I want you to know that we're doin' all we can."

"I know."

Bronson frowned and shook his head. "Lisa, Lisa. You know you're in a heap of trouble."

"That doesn't matter. I feel terrible about leaving her alone. I should've known better." Straight ahead of her, on top of the television set, the framed picture of Tracy filled her with a sense of longing. Unable to move her eyes away from it, she spoke to Bronson without looking at him. "What happens now?"

"As far as Tracy is concerned, we wait and pray. As for you, young lady–"

A new fear set in Lisa's heart. "They're not going to take my Tracy away, are they? I'm a good mother. I only left her for a few minutes." She raked her hair with her fingers. "Oh God, I'm so sorry."

"Fret not about that now, ma'am. I know a couple of people who owe me favors, but don't you ever–"

"Oh, no, don't worry. I've learned my lesson. I just want her back in my arms." She wrapped her arms around herself as tears ran down her cheeks. "Thank you for helping me."

"Don't mention it, ma'am." He fidgeted with his shirt collar and cleared his throat. "Now, let's talk about David."

David! She should contact David. Divorced or not, he was still Tracy's father. "He's in San Antonio," Lisa mumbled.

"I see." Bronson smacked his lips. "He never mentioned to you that he was comin'?"

Lisa felt her eyebrows arch in surprise. "Why, yes. As a matter of fact, he did mention it. I talked to him–"

While Lisa searched her memory, Bronson turned the page of his notebook back to a previous page. "Monday," he said. "You talked to him Monday."

Lisa stared at Bronson in amazement. "Yes, it was Monday, and he did mention it."

Bronson scratched his chin. "My daughter tells me that David is a decent sort of person."

"He is." Why was he talking about David? It was Tracy who was missing. Then it dawned on Lisa. "You don't think David–"

"The thing that bothers me is that David flew out of San Antonio this mornin'. Did you know that?"

Lisa bit her lip and shook her head.

"He's here in Dallas, somewhere. His plane landed almost five hours ago."

The bottom fell out of Lisa's world. "Why hasn't he contacted me, then?"

"My question precisely, ma'am."

Lisa searched Bronson's face, but all she found were his analytical eyes. "Of course, if Tracy is with David–" *God, please let her be with David.* "–then she's safe, and he'll bring her back. He's just trying to teach me a lesson."

"Uh huh. It's lesson time. May I ask what kind of lesson?" As Bronson spoke, he cast his eyes from object to object as though absorbing and categorizing every detail.

"I met a man in the park who took quite an interest in Tracy."

Bronson's eyebrow raised as he looked down at Lisa. "Go on." He reached into his pocket, retrieved a small spiral notebook, clicked his pen, and wrote something down. "And this man–his name is. . ."

"James Johnson."

Bronson gazed up from his notes. For a moment, he was quiet. Then he said, "Of Johnson Enterprises?"

Lisa nodded as the apprehension ate at her. What good was this line of questioning doing? Why was Bronson here instead of out there looking for Tracy? She–

The front door opened, and James Johnson stepped inside holding Tracy's hand. Behind them were the same two officers Lisa had originally talked to, Santos and Guthrie. Lisa dropped to her knees as she stretched out her arms toward her daughter. "Tracy!" she cried. "Oh, Tracy."

Tracy released James' hand and ran to her mother. Lisa's body shook with deep-felt sobs. "Oh, Tracy, darling. I was so afraid for you." She hugged her daughter tightly. Then she looked up at James.

Although James Johnson had always impressed Lisa as being a very secure man, now she noticed that his confidence seemed to seep out of him like water in a leaky glass. He took several steps back and wet his lips. "Li–Lisa," he stammered. "I told my secretary to call you and let you know I'd be picking up Tracy at one-thirty in front of The Journey. When I saw Tracy alone in the car, naturally I assumed. . . ." He shrugged and looked away.

Lisa glared at him. "If you told your secretary to call, why didn't she?"

"She swears that I told her to remind me to call, but I didn't say that. I told her to call. It was just a big misunderstanding. The bottom line is neither of us called and I'm sorry. I'm awfully sorry. I didn't mean to make you go through this horrible ordeal." He seemed on the verge of tears. He looked up at the ceiling and exhaled noisily. "On the bright side, Tracy and I had a very nice time. We went to Six Flags Over Texas."

Lisa broke the silence that followed. "How dare you take my daughter."

"Like I said, Lisa, it was just a big misunderstanding. Nobody's at fault here." His voice was thick with emotion. "Remember, you did call me asking me to baby sit. I thought I was doing something nice for you."

Lisa took in a deep breath. Part of her wanted to see the situation from his point of view. The other part–her mother instinct part–wanted to lash out at him.

"Will you be pressing charges, ma'am?" Bronson asked Lisa.

She considered the possibility. If she did, what purpose would it serve? He was rich and famous. He'd be out in less than an hour. The worst thing that would happen was that he'd be publicly humiliated or maybe, because of all of his money, his lawyers would find a way to turn this around and make her look like a bad mother. After all, she had left Tracy alone in a parked, locked car. She might even end up losing Tracy.

Besides, Lisa could see that he was sorry, and all of this had just been one huge misunderstanding.

Tracy was home, safe.

"Well?" Bronson asked and Lisa realized she still hadn't answered.

"No, I won't press charges," she said and glared at James, "but if you ever–"

"No, don't worry. I won't." James looked relieved. Once again his air of confidence seemed to return. "From here on, I'll make sure I talk to you personally."

Bronson signaled for Santos and Guthrie to head out. "Well, seeing how you're not going to need us anymore, I suppose we'll leave. I'll have Guthrie drive your car back home."

With a wave of his hand, he dismissed the officers, but he made no attempt to leave. Instead, he walked toward James. "Mr. Johnson, I've seen your picture in the newspaper many, many times." He offered him his hand. "It's a pleasure to meet you, sir. And, gee, listen, I'm sure sorry about your granddaughter. You must have loved her a lot."

"Yes, I did, Mr.–"

"Bronson. Detective Harry Bronson."

"Yes, Detective Bronson." He turned away from Bronson and faced Lisa. "Thanks, my dear, for being so understanding. I will never do anything so stupid again." Like a true gentlemen, he kissed her hand. He winked at Tracy and turned to leave.

"Mr. Johnson."

James stopped. "Yes, Detective Bronson." His tone was laced with irritation.

"It's nothin' really important. I was just going to say that Tracy sure has a nice smile."

A frown formed on James' face. "Yes, I suppose she does."

"Just like yours."

For a fraction of a second, James hesitated and stared at Bronson. His forehead wrinkled. "Thank you," he said and walked out.

* * *

As James opened his car door, he pondered Bronson's odd comment. Had he been trying to say something? No, of course not. He was just being paranoid. There was no possible way anyone could ever connect him to Lisa.

And speaking of Lisa–that had worked out beautifully. When he had walked in with Tracy, Lisa had seemed ready to collapse. Her complexion was the shade of a vanilla shake and perspiration had beaded on her forehead. Her hair was ruffled and her shoulders were hunched forward. She was devastated, and that had pleased him.

As far as he was concerned, he had given an award-winning performance during his apology. They had all swallowed it–Lisa, the police, and especially that stupid Detective Bronson.

He had accomplished what he set out to do. For several hours, he had made Lisa's life miserable. And he would do it again soon, but this time it would be something completely different–and of course, more daring. More dangerous. More deadly. Little by little, he was going to pay her back for all the misery she had cost him.

He smiled as he formulated his next plan.

Chapter 20

Lisa waved as the last policeman left. She closed the door behind her and leaned against it. She hadn't realized how tired she was, how drained she felt.

"Doin' okay?" Bronson asked.

Lisa opened her eyes—she hadn't realized she had closed them. "Yeah, I'm okay, now. Thank you very much for all you've done."

"Oh, I'm just glad it turned out this way. I wish all my cases ended like this."

Lisa nodded and wished he'd leave so she could lie down. She was still weak and shaking.

Instead, Bronson sat down. "So, I see you've become good friends with this Mr. Johnson."

"I wouldn't exactly say 'good friends.' His granddaughter died, and Tracy reminds him of her. That's all."

"I see," Bronson said rubbing his chin. "So Mama never showed up."

Mother! Damn! Lisa had forgotten all about her. How could she possibly get in touch with her now?

When Lisa frowned, Bronson smiled reassuringly. "If I were you, Lisa, ma'am, I wouldn't worry. I'm sure that if she was there, and she saw what happened, she'll call. In fact, I bet ya a cup of coffee that even if she wasn't there, she'll call back again."

"I thought gambling was illegal in Texas." Lisa winked. "Besides, what's going to happen if I win?"

"Then I'll have to come over so you can teach me how

to make a good cup of coffee. Then I'll treat you to a cup."

"With my own coffee which I helped you to make?"

"Sure, why not? This way I don't really lose the bet. Either way, I get my good cup of coffee."

Lisa smiled. "Would you care for a cup of coffee now?"

"Uh, no thanks." He rubbed the back of his head. "Gee, I can't believe that I'm actually turning down a cup of coffee. That must be a first. But, you see, there's Carol–that's my wife. Oh, but then you knew that. Right? You have met my Carol?"

Lisa nodded. "Once, just briefly."

"Isn't she just wonderful?"

"She seems to be."

"Well, take my word for it. She is–except when it comes to times like this. She's preparing a special dinner for me, and she'll be awfully upset if I'm not there to eat it." He stood up and walked toward the door. "She's real fussy that way."

He started to leave, then stopped. "But if I can, just one more question." Then he continued without giving Lisa a chance to answer, "This James Johnson–you've known him for how long?"

"I met him when I arrived here in Dallas, a little over two weeks ago."

"Aha, and when you met him, you immediately recognized him."

"Well, not really. When I first saw him, I thought he looked familiar, but I couldn't quite place him. Later, when he told me his name, I realized why I felt I knew him."

"I see. Well, that's how it usually goes with those famous people. You try to place their faces, but they elude you, unless of course, they are very, very famous."

Bronson opened the door and with his hand still holding onto the knob said, "Lisa, I'm glad everything turned out just fine for you. You just watch that little girl of yours, and watch yourself too."

"Detective Bronson–"

"What happened to Uncle Harry?" he asked.

"Uncle Harry, you don't think he did this on purpose, do you?"

"What's important is what you think."

"I think–" Lisa paused to collect her thoughts. "I think Mr. Johnson was just trying to help, and after all, no real harm was done. He thought he was doing the right thing. He assumed his secretary had called."

"And you think that's how he runs his business. By assuming?"

For a second, the question floored Lisa. "I suppose not. But it was an honest mistake."

"That's exactly what I was thinkin' too," Bronson said as he stepped outside. He took a deep breath. "I wonder if his secretary ever reminded him to call. Have a good evenin', Ms. Lisa, ma'am."

Bronson's observation struck a nerve hidden somewhere in Lisa's memory. For some reason, she felt something was just out of reach. She fumbled over his words again, trying desperately to unlock her gut feelings. Had his secretary reminded him to call? If so, he would have known she hadn't called. If she hadn't, she wasn't very efficient. James wouldn't hire someone like that. "Wait, Detective Bronson–uh, Uncle Harry." But by now, he had driven away and couldn't hear her.

Lisa went back inside, closed the door, leaned against it, and put her hand over her eyes. "Oh, God," she whispered, then in a much louder voice she added, "Tracy, get in here right now, young lady."

Tracy peered through the bedroom doorway. "You mad at me, Mommy?"

"I want to know exactly what made you open that car door."

"Mr. Johnson said to open the door, and he's not a stranger. You said not to open the door to strangers, but Mr. Johnson is not a stranger. He's my friend." Tears streamed down her cheeks. "Besides, he said you knew where I was."

Lisa squatted so she was eye-level with Tracy. "It

doesn't matter what he said. What matters is what I said, and I told you not to leave that car."

The buzzing of the doorbell interrupted her. Lisa glanced at her watch, noticed that it was past six and wondered who would possibly be ringing her doorbell this late in the afternoon. "Wait here," she said. She peeped out of the front window, and her heart fluttered with both delight and confusion. "It's Daddy!" she said.

In less than a second, Tracy dodged around Lisa and threw the door open. "Daddy! Daddy!" She squealed with delight as she opened her arms for him.

David set down his suitcase, a large brown bag, and a package, then scooped Tracy up in his arms. He stepped inside.

Lisa felt her stomach tighten when she stared at David's suitcase. That meant that he hadn't checked into a motel–or at least not yet. Maybe. . .

Lisa smiled as David set Tracy down.

"Lisa, you're looking good," David said.

"You're not looking so bad yourself." She looked past David, toward the suitcase and the package.

David noticed it. "It's okay to bring them in?"

"Yes, of course." Had she answered a bit too fast? She didn't want to appear anxious. She moved to her left so David could come in.

"Whatcha got, Daddy?" Tracy's face lit up as she eyed the package her father carried.

"Well, now I've. . .uh, forgotten." David scratched the back of his head in mock forgetfulness. "But we can find out. Do you want to?"

"Yeah!" Tracy placed her open hands on her cheeks.

David handed Tracy the package, and she ripped it open. "Well, what do you know!" David said as Tracy produced a four-foot tall teddy bear.

Lisa watched as David stared at Tracy who squealed with delight as she hugged the stuffed animal. David's eyes contained so much love. If only he'd look at her that way too.

"Let's get some ice-cream," he said and the spell was broken.

* * *

When they returned David said, "Pumpkin, I want you to go take your bath now so I can tuck you in bed." He playfully pushed Tracy toward the bathroom. "Now go, go, go."

"But Daddy, I'm not tired."

"Go." He pointed toward the bathroom.

Tracy frowned and left.

David turned to Lisa. A spark ignited in his eyes and Lisa held her breath. "We, uh, need. . .to talk," David said and all the time, he talked to the floor.

A familiar stirring invaded Lisa's body. God! How she wanted David, and he wanted her too. She could tell, or maybe she was hoping. She stood perfectly still, willing him to rush to her. But of course he didn't, just as Lisa had known all along. She settled into the recliner.

David sat on the couch facing her. "I've been here for a little over six hours," he said. "I rented a locker at the airport, left my luggage there while I visited the mall. That's where I've been all of this time, except of course for going back to the airport to pick up my stuff." He reached out for Lisa's hands.

She stood up, walked toward him and stretched her arms in front of her. David wrapped his hands around Lisa's and stood up. "All of the time that I was at the mall, I was debating with myself." He looked tenderly into her eyes. "Lisa, if your offer about me staying here with you and Tracy still stands, then I'd like to accept."

Lisa gazed deeply into his eyes. "I'll make room–" She looked around the tiny duplex. "–somewhere."

"Don't worry. The couch is fine, unless–" He moved an inch closer toward Lisa.

"Daddy, I'm ready for bed," Tracy said as she burst through the door. "Are you going to put me to bed?"

David nodded. "Of course I am." He turned to Lisa and whispered her name. He winked and released her. "Come on, Pumpkin, let's go to bed," he told Tracy.

"Dave."

He turned.

"After you finish with Tracy, I need to tell you about our misadventure today."

"Oh, Mom, do you have to?"

Lisa nodded.

Tracy frowned and reached for her father's hand. She led him into her bedroom. "Promise me, Daddy, that you won't get mad at me."

"Oh, oh," he said.

"On second thought, Tracy, I want you to stay up," Lisa yelled from the living room.

"Weepee!" Tracy bounced around her dad. "I get to stay up! I get to stay up!"

"That weepee may be a bit premature," Lisa said.

Tracy stopped bouncing. "Huh?"

"The three of us are going to sit down while I tell Daddy what happened."

"Nooo, Mommy." Tracy faked a yawn. "I'm tired. I'm going to bed now. Good night."

"Tracy Katherine Littau! You get your little budinskey back over here."

Tracy covered her face. "I don't like it when you call me by my full name, Mommy."

"Then get over here."

Tracy did as told. She sat next to her dad, held his hand, and smiled at him.

David beamed until he realized Lisa was glaring at him, then he straightened himself up and said, "Let's hear what you did, young lady."

Tracy released his hand and pouted.

"You remember I told you about James Johnson," Lisa began.

David's body stiffened as a frown formed across his forehead. "Go on," he mumbled.

Lisa swallowed hard and told him everything beginning with the letter she had received from her birth mother. She spoke quickly and looked him directly in the eye, except for the part when she told him about leaving Tracy alone in the car. Lisa concluded her narrative with Bronson's help and comments.

When she finished, the room remained as quiet as the eye of a hurricane. Lisa opened her mouth, but she found she had nothing to say and felt somewhat relieved when David stood up and walked toward the window, his back to them. His body was as rigid as steel pipe.

When he turned around, he fixed his eyes on Tracy. "I'm very disappointed in you, young lady."

Tracy's pout moved up and down, and her eyes glistened with tears.

"What do you have to say for yourself?"

"Mommy said not to open the door to strangers. Mr. Johnson's my friend. He took me to Six Flags. He bought me ice cream and toys. He plays with me at the park. He took me to the Ferris wheel. He's not a stranger. He's my friend!"

"That's not the point, Tracy." He squatted in front of her so that he was eye-level with her. "You left without Mommy's permission. You know that's wrong, don't you?"

Tracy nodded. The tears ran down her cheeks. "I'll never do it again. I promise, Daddy." She wiped the tears with the back of her hands.

"Make sure you keep that promise. Now get to bed."

Tracy jumped out of the couch and ran to her bedroom. At the doorway, she stopped. "Are you still going to tuck me in?"

"Later. Right now Mommy and I are going to go sit on the step outside and talk about what we should do about this. When I come back inside, you better be in your bed."

"Yes, sir." She disappeared into her bedroom.

David signaled Lisa to follow him outside. No sooner had she closed the door behind her than David began, "Lisa, what were you thinking?"

"I know. I know I did wrong. I just didn't think–"

"That's exactly right. You didn't think. Does finding your

birth parents mean that much to you? You're willing to put our daughter's life in danger?"

"David, she wasn't in danger. She'd be alone for only–"

"She wasn't in danger? For God's sake, she was kidnaped. I don't trust this Mr. Johnson, and I don't like him."

"You don't know him either."

"What's that supposed to mean?"

"He's kind and gentle with Tracy and. . .and, oh God, David, I really messed up, didn't I?"

David's features softened. "Yes, you did. Why didn't you call me? I would have come to be with her. As it turned out, I could have been here if I'd come straight over from the airport. I could have been here for you. I'm sorry I failed you."

"Oh, Dave, I'm the one who's sorry. So very sorry." She began to sob and her body shook.

David wrapped his arms around her, and she buried her face in his broad shoulders. She let herself cry, releasing all of her pent up anguish. She cried for her mother's death, she cried for what could have happened to Tracy, she cried for her stupidity, and she cried for her broken marriage.

* * *

It had been several hours now since the commotion at Lisa's house had died away. All of the police cars were gone, and the street had settled back to its normal routine. Almost, but not quite.

A solitary sedan, a grayish-brown car, remained parked across the street and down the block from Lisa's duplex. Inside the car, the driver sat intently watching Lisa and that young man of hers. How dare he touch her that way! Only lovers shared such special intimacy. The fury the driver felt filled the entire car with a burning, suffocating anger.

The worst part was not being able to do anything about it, but time would come when things would change. They say time heals all things. And speaking of time, here it was, way past eleven and the man still held her in his arms. He appeared he had no intention of leaving any time soon.

And that meant trouble, for it could easily be that when

he left, he would take Lisa with him. This called for immediate plans. Time ceased to be a luxury.

Tomorrow, for sure, Tracy, Lisa, and maybe even this new guy—whoever he was—would die.

Yes, tomorrow for sure. And if tomorrow proved to be impossible, then the next day. But for sure, very soon.

Very, very soon.

Chapter 21

James Johnson mulled over the possibilities in his mind. Out of the three candidates he was considering for the job, Albert Henderson, alias Big Al, seemed to be the best prospect.

He had been arrested four different times for domestic violence which, considering what he had done to his live-in wife, was the polite way of phrasing it.

Less than two weeks ago, his wife, Louise had taken him his usual cup of coffee and set it down on the night stand. She had been careful not to spill it, so she wouldn't burn herself.

Big Al opened his eyes when he heard her enter the bedroom. He frowned. What a repulsive sight so early in the morning.

She wore her usual tent-type dress which gave her as much sex appeal as a sack of potatoes. Her left cheek remained slightly swollen, and her eye hadn't yet opened up all the way. However, most of her bruises had faded to a soft mauve.

That was one of the beatings Big Al had been arrested for. James paid her five thousand dollars to drop the charges.

She was about to leave the room, when Big Al said, "Strip."

She stopped, considering the alternatives.

"What? Are you hard of hearing? What do I need to do, woman? Cut your damn ear off so you'd have a reason for not hearing me?"

He'll do it. She turned and quickly dropped her dress. She glanced at the coffee. It would get cold. "Y. . .your co- coffee."

"Fuck the coffee. I said strip!" He swung his feet out of the bed. The leer in his eyes was an icy tentacle on her skin.

She stepped out of her panties and removed her bra. She wished she was anywhere but here. She folded her arms in front of her. Big Al stood up and walked toward her. She let her arms drop. Big Al's gaze traveled up and down her naked body. He moved on and stood behind her.

She intertwined her hands, then she separated them. She attempted to fix her hair. Why did she always have problems deciding what to do with her hands?

"Bend over, bitch."

No, not from behind. That always hurt and made her feel—

Big Al pushed her with such force that she went flying. Luckily for her, she landed on the bed. He yanked her by her hair and turned her over.

She gasped when she felt him inside of her. She bit her lip to keep from screaming. He pounded and thrust, and when he finished, he shoved her to the floor. He kicked her twice.

He took a sip of coffee. He spit it out. "It's cold! The fucking coffee is cold." He glared at her. "You know I hate cold coffee." He reached for his belt.

She rolled herself into a tight little ball, trying to protect as much of her body as she possibly could. Big Al laughed as he whipped her.

Such was the man James Johnson had decided would be perfect for the job.

* * *

Big Al took a drag off his cigarette, then gulped down the last of his whiskey sour. He wanted another one, but his ride should be arriving any minute now. Well, fuck 'em. Let him wait. If he wanted another whiskey sour, he'd order another one. He signaled for the bartender, and just as he was about to order, Big Al spotted the white Cadillac pulling up in front of Joe's Bar. "Shit!" he said. He crushed out his cigarette and walked out.

"You're three minutes late," Big Al said as he got in the back seat.

"I'll make up for lost time," the chauffeur answered and even before the big man got a chance to settle down, he sped away.

* * *

James Johnson frowned when he saw the white Cadillac approaching. He knew Big Al was coming. He had, after all, set up this meeting, but that didn't remove the sour taste in his mouth he felt every time he was forced to deal with the man. He was a brute, and James hated having to conduct business with him.

But at times it was unavoidable, and those few times he had to deal with Big Al, he took every possible precaution. That's why he had set up this meeting in the middle of nowhere. There was almost no chance of them being seen together, and as soon as business was concluded, he'd be able to leave and not worry about having Big Al hang around.

James sighed. He might as well get it over with. He reached over and opened the limousine door and signaled for Big Al to join him. "I have a very special job for you," James said as Big Al climbed in and slammed the limousine door shut.

"Yeah."

James frowned. What kind of an answer was that, he wondered. "There's a certain woman I want you to frighten."

"Yeah." He picked his back teeth with his pinkie fingernail.

"I want you to rape her. And I want her to suffer, mentally and physically, for a long time."

"No problem." He smiled and wiped his finger on the car seat.

James noticed it, inwardly cringed, but otherwise tolerated it. "However, under no circumstances, is she to be permanently damaged. I'm not through with her, and I don't like damaged goods. Is that understood?"

"Yeah." He began to work on the other side of his mouth.

"If I find out that you didn't follow my specific instructions. . . Well, I don't need to say what will happen to you."

"Yeah, I got it," he answered off-handily as he wiped his finger, length-wise, on his shirt. "I just have two questions."

"What's that?"

"I'm suppose to rape and torture some broad."

"That's right."

"And I'm suppose to let her live?"

"That's also right."

"To do this properly, this broad is gonna have to see my face. What's going to keep her from identifying me?"

"Nothing."

"What the—"

James raised his hand and waved it. "Just make sure nobody else sees you. Wear gloves so there's no fingerprints. Then leave the rest up to me."

"What do you plan to do?"

"I'll provide you with an alibi. There'll be twenty, thirty people in the bar who will swear you were there at the time of the alleged rape."

Big Al smiled. "I like it. So who's the dame?"

"Her name is Lisa Littau."

Chapter 22

Lisa's peaceful dream came to an abrupt end as a ringing sound jangled her awake. Still half asleep, she rolled on her side and thrashed at the nightstand like a drowning swimmer. The persistent ringing continued. Startled, Lisa realized it wasn't her alarm clock ringing, but her phone.

Suddenly wide-awake, Lisa remembered the last time the phone had rung at two in the morning. Katie had informed her of her father's sudden death. Her fear became a cramp in her gut as she half-stumbled, half-ran toward the living room. She grabbed the phone and mumbled a frightened, "Hello?"

There was a pause, accentuated by heavy breathing. It was followed by a hoarse voice that said,   "Lisa, I want you."

As though she had been burned, Lisa dropped the phone. It wasn't so much what he said, but how he said it that terrified her. She was about to bend down to retrieve the phone when she realized she wasn't alone. Someone inched toward her. Lisa held her breath.

"Who was it?" The voice belonged to a man.

Lisa let out a sigh of relief as she recognized David's voice. She hesitated. "It was just some damn kid playing a joke," she said as she bent down to retrieve the receiver. She screamed into the phone, hoping that bastard was still there before she slammed it down. "Sorry it woke you," she said, suddenly conscious of her lacy mini-gown.

David seemed oblivious to her concern. Instead, he seemed to be concentrating on the phone call. "Has this happened before?" His tone was laced with concern.

"No," Lisa said. "It was just a random call." *Probably got my name and phone number from the ad I placed in the newspaper.* This, she kept to herself.

David nodded. Now that the panic was over, he looked at Lisa, really looked. He let out a wolfish whistle.

Immediately, Lisa felt the blood rush to her face.

"God, Lisa, I can't believe that after all of this time, you still blush. You're absolutely beautiful!" He swept her into his arms. He kissed her, his tongue urgently seeking hers. Then abruptly, he pulled away. "Lisa, I'm sorry."

"For what? Kissing me? Don't be. I enjoyed it."

David shook his head. "I enjoyed it too, but we made a mistake once. Let's not do it again." He smiled, not seductively as he had before, but sheepishly. "Good night," he said. He winked and returned to the couch.

Lisa went to bed but couldn't sleep. She lay awake watching the black of night turn into the gray of dawn.

* * *

Louise half-crawled, half-dragged herself out of the bedroom and toward the bathroom. She tried to wash herself but she could barely move. She didn't think Big Al had broken any of her bones—this time.

Behind her, Al quietly dressed. He hummed softly as he slipped into his light blue jogging suit. He took out a pair of dress pants, a plain white shirt, and dress shoes and stuffed them inside of a bag.

Louise knew he was on the prowl again. He would find some poor woman out there. By the end of the day, he would rape her. She should call the police, she knew. But before the police would react, he would kill her. Let him go. At least when he was out prowling, he wasn't home torturing her. She half-cried, half-laughed.

She had become such a pathetic little nothing.

* * *

He cruised slowly by Lisa's house. He knew she was home because the car was parked in the driveway, but he didn't know if she was alone. Big Al drove a block past Lisa's house and parked. He sat quietly, surveying Lisa's duplex through his side mirror.

Within five minutes he began to squirm. He tried sitting up straight. That didn't work. He sat sideways on the seat, his back to the door. Too uncomfortable. He moved the seat as far back as it would go. That wasn't much better. Finally, he gave up, swung the door open and stepped out. He jogged one block past Lisa's house, turned around and did it again.

During the eighth round, he noticed Lisa's door swing open. Immediately, Big Al bent down to tie his shoe.

A man and a little girl–probably Lisa's daughter–stepped out. Soon a dame followed. Man, he hoped that was Lisa. She was none too bad looking. In fact, not bad. Not bad at all.

Big Al watched as Lisa hugged and kissed her daughter good-bye, then resumed his jogging until he was within listening distance. Making sure that his face remained hidden, he stopped to fiddle with his shoe again. While pretending to focus his attention solely on his shoe problem, he concentrated on listening to the conversation between these three people.

"Bye, Mommy. I'll miss you," Big Al heard the little girl say. He looked up only long enough to notice that the brat was wearing a bright red dress.

"I'll miss you too, sweetheart," Lisa said, "but you enjoy your movie."

"And ice-cream. Daddy said we could go get some ice-cream after the movie, didn't you, Daddy?"

"I sure did, Pumpkin." The man–"Daddy"–turned his attention to the dame. "Lisa, are you sure you don't want to join us?"

Lisa nodded. "Don't tempt me. I really rather go than stay and clean the place."

Big Al didn't hang around to hear the rest of the conversation. He heard all that he needed to know. This dame was Lisa, and she was going to be alone for several hours. Man, oh man, it wasn't that often he was this lucky.

Immediately, Big Al resumed his jogging. When he

reached his van he changed into his dress pants and white shirt. He picked up the latest copy of *Playboy* and turned it straight to the centerfold. Ten minutes later, he drove his van to the front of Lisa's duplex, parked it, and got out.

Chapter 23

Lisa watched David and Tracy leave. She had wanted to go with them, but now, more than ever, she realized she had to let David go. This would be a good time to begin. She had made cleaning the house an excuse, one that David had not swallowed, seeing the expression in his face.

No matter. Lisa sighed and went inside.

She looked for a dust rag. Unable to find one, she settled for one of Tracy's blouses which was getting to be too small for her. Armed with the blouse and a spray can of furniture wax, Lisa reached for the plain, straight back kitchen chair and placed it under the fan so she could clean its blades.

She started to climb on the chair when the doorbell rang. "It figures!" she muttered.

She looked around for a convenient place to set the wax down. The doorbell rang again. "Ooooh," she snapped. She ran to answer the door. She swung it open and stared at a monster of a man. He was, no doubt, the largest man Lisa had ever seen. And he was solid too, as though he had been carved out of a single piece of wood.

"Mrs. Littau? Are you Lisa Littau?" the man asked in a thunderous voice.

Lisa nodded. "Yes?"

"I am Detective Albert Smith." He showed her his badge, but with such quick movements that Lisa didn't really get to see it. She was surprised that such a big man could be so agile. She looked past him, at his van. What did the police want with her?

"Are you Tracy Littau's mother?" the man asked.

"For a moment, time came to an abrupt stop. *Tracy! Had something happened to Tracy?* Lisa wanted to scream. Instead, she numbly nodded.

"Was she wearing a bright red dress?"

Was? Oh, God! Again, she nodded.

"In that case, may I come in?" Albert aggressively pushed his way in.

"Is she–" Lisa stepped aside so he could come in. "Is Tracy all right?"

Albert headed toward the back of the living room. "Please sit down, Mrs. Littau." He pointed toward the couch.

"Why?" She closed the door, but didn't lock it. "Tracy–is she–"

"Please, Mrs. Littau, sit down."

Lisa felt the weight of despair slow her down. She would never be able to reach the couch. "Please, is Tracy–"

He stared at her and didn't answer.

Lisa slumped down on the couch. If Tracy was hurt or worse. . . She felt the tears at the edge of her eyes.

Albert smiled–a wide toothy smile filled with malice–and advanced toward her. "She's fine, I guess, but you won't be."

Lisa sprang to her feet. Her mind ordered her to run, but her legs refused to obey. "Wh-what do you want?"

"Lisa, I want you."

A cold wave of despair washed over Lisa. She recognized the voice, the phrase. It came from the same hoarse voice she had heard last night on the phone.

Keep him talking. Stall him. Think of something. "Who are you?"

"Your friendly neighborhood fucker." He laughed, a deep guttural sound. "There's no place to run, so you might as well give in. Make it easy on you. Otherwise, I'm afraid I'll have to use this." He produced an eight-inch switchblade and waved it threateningly in front of her.

Lisa felt the world closing in on her. Somehow this–this man had gotten between her and the front door. If only she could get around him, she could reach the main door which, thank God, she had left unlocked. Once outside, she would call for help. Surely, someone would help her. She took a step backwards and to the side.

"Freeze, sweetheart. You ain't going nowhere."

Fear gnawed at her and forced her to clutch the spray can of furniture wax tighter. She made another attempt to get past him.

"I told you to be still, bitch!" He slapped her with his free hand.

The powerful blow sent Lisa smashing backward, her head bumping against the bookcase. Blinding lights exploded inside her head. The pain made her want to float into darkness.

No! Don't give in. Fight him. You can do it. She attempted to get up but wasn't able to. She had to move. Move fast.

Albert lunged toward her. She rolled over, but her movement was impaired.

Albert grabbed her legs, flipped her over, and dragged her to the middle of the living room. He straddled her, reached down, and tore her blouse open, exposing the soft pink, semi-transparent bra. His lips spread awkwardly in sharkish anticipation.

Lisa held back the tears of repulsion. She felt she was going to be sick, but she knew she had to remain calm if she was to think clearly. She had been holding the spray can of furniture wax. Where was it now? She glanced around and spotted it. It lay six inches beyond her reach to her left. If she stretched, surely she could grab it.

Summoning every ounce of courage and self-control she had, she waited until he was close enough for her to feel his hot, rancid breath on her face.

Letting out a scream, in one swift movement that even surprised her, she reached for the can, pointed it at his startled face, and sprayed. He bellowed, reaching for his eyes and rubbing them furiously.

Lisa didn't waste any time. She called on all of her reserved energy and pushed him off her.

"You bitch! You fucking bitch!" he screamed, still rubbing his eyes. He squinted and began to blindly deliver blows.

Lisa was caught unaware, and his right knuckle connected with her left temple. Little droplets of blood formed and ran down her face. The fear seething within her brought out a violent nature she was not aware she possessed. She kicked him in the groin as hard as she could.

Albert's breath escaped from him as his eyes bulged out with pain. He fell backwards, into a sitting position. His knees clamped together.

Lisa scrambled away from him. She knew she could neither outrun him nor out fight him. Her only chance lay in using logic. Desperately, her gaze flicked over the objects within reach. A decorative pillow on the couch, worthless. A magazine, a newspaper. One of Tracy's fairy tale books. Heavy, but not heavy enough. The kitchen chair she intended to use as a stepping stool. Possibly.

Albert rubbed his watering eyes and focused them on Lisa. She realized he was regaining some of his sight. The thought sent more adrenaline pumping through her body.

She scanned the rest of the area. The room next to the living room, the kitchen. Too far away. The chair would have to suffice. She wobbled to her feet, reached for the kitchen chair, and with all her might, swung it. The chair broke in two when it crushed on Albert. He crumbled to the floor.

Lisa raced out of the duplex, screaming louder than she had ever screamed before.

Chapter 24

"Now, Lisa, ma'am, I know it's hard on you, but I want you to tell me exactly what happened." Detective Harry Bronson handed Lisa a glass of water.

She accepted it gratefully and drank most of it before beginning, "A policeman forced his way in and tried to. . .rape me. I let him in because he said–or at least I think he said–that Tracy was hurt. Ouch!" She jerked back as the paramedic applied an antiseptic swab to the corner of her cut eye.

"Did you open the door because maybe you recognized him?"

Lisa shook her head. "No, I've never seen him before."

"Don't answer so quickly. I want you to think about it carefully. Was there anything about his voice, his manner, his face–anything at all that will help us identify him?"

Lisa bit her lip, trying to remember. "When he first came in, he gave me his name, showed me his badge. His name was something very common." She clucked her tongue against her teeth. "Jones? No, that's not right. Smith? Yeah, that's it. Albert Smith."

Bronson wrote the name down. "Did you actually see his badge?"

Lisa was about to answer, then stopped herself. "He flashed it at me so fast." She shook her head. "I should have made sure it was a badge, huh?"

"You weren't thinking right. You were worried about Tracy, and under the circumstances, I don't blame you."

"Thank you for saying that." She felt her mouth go

suddenly dry. She turned to the paramedic. "Mind if I get some more water?"

"Tell you what," Bronson said. "Let me leave you alone with the paramedic so he can finish with you. In the meantime, if you don't mind, let me make a couple of calls, but first, mind if I pour myself a cup of coffee? You do have coffee left from this mornin'?"

Lisa nodded.

"Ah, good." Bronson disappeared into the kitchen. A few minutes later he reappeared carrying a cup of coffee. He picked up the phone, dialed, and spoke in a low tone so that Lisa couldn't hear what he said.

In the meantime the paramedic, whose name tag read "Hollins," checked on the worst of Lisa's bruises, took her blood pressure, pulse, and respiratory rate. He asked her for her medical history, whether she had consumed any alcohol or drugs, and if she had any allergies to any medicines.

Bronson returned the phone to its cradle and asked, "You about finished?"

"Not quite," Hollins said as he continued to check the deep cut in Lisa's forehead.

"Ah, well, you won't mind if I talk to her, do you? I won't get in the way this time. Promise." Then before Hollins could answer, Bronson turned to Lisa and said, "Just got off the phone, ma'am, and seems like there's a small hitch. We don't have an Albert Smith working for our department." He took a sip of coffee. "Ah, good coffee. You've got to teach my Carol how to make a good cup of coffee. Now, about that name. Are you sure that's what he said?"

Lisa nodded. "Fairly sure, but I was so worried I could have gotten it wrong." She flinched and Hollins frowned. "Sorry," she said. Then turning her attention back to Bronson she said, "Maybe he works for the Fort Worth Police Department or the Arlington Police Department or. . ."

"No, I don't think so. I checked with them too."

Lisa frowned. A coldness touched the nape of her neck as a glimpse of the thug flashed before her. She tried to grab the image, but it vanished before she could verbalize her thoughts. "He'll be hard to find without a name."

"Maybe, maybe not. We can go by other things."

Relieved, Lisa drew in a deep breath. She certainly didn't want to encounter that big goon again–or read about another woman meeting him in some dark alley. "Like what?"

"Was there anything distinctive about the way he was dressed? Was there anything at all that gave you a hint as to his real name? Was he wearing an initial ring–anything like that?"

Was Bronson kidding? She hadn't even noticed if that monster was wearing a ring. Still, she tried to focus her attention on his brutal hands. No images came to mind. "I'm sorry," she said. "I just can't recall." A sharp spasm shook her body as his image slowly took shape in her mind.

"Please, Mrs. Littau," Hollins said, "stop moving, or I won't be able to finish dressing your wounds."

"Sorry, doc. I believe that's my fault," Bronson said. "I'm afraid I'm the one askin' all of these questions." He turned to Lisa and said, "Lisa, I want you to try to relax and think. I want you to start all over again, this time from the moment you heard the doorbell. Do you realize you haven't even mentioned what he looks like? Close your eyes and concentrate. Relax. When you're ready, start all over again from the moment you saw him."

Lisa felt drained. He had to be kidding. Didn't he realize all she wanted to do was put the experience–the nightmare–behind her? She couldn't possibly–

"I know I'm askin' the impossible," Bronson said as though he had read her thoughts. "And to be truthful, this isn't proper procedure, but I reckon you know I'm not one to follow procedure. I'll get you a rape counselor, if that's what you want, but I really would appreciate it if you'd put up with me. In my many years' experience, I've noticed that if the victim tells the story a second–a third time–he starts rememberin' details that didn't seem important the first time. It's these details I'm lookin' for. So Lisa, please, if you don't mind. But if you don't want to, I'll understand. We can do this later, and we can do it the proper way too. Your choice."

Lisa drew a deep breath. "I'd rather get it over with now."

"That's my girl!" Bronson said patting her on the shoulder, and in so doing, he accidentally got in the paramedic's way. "Oh, sorry," he said.

Hollins gave Bronson a dry smile, then turned to Lisa. "Are you sure, Mrs. Littau, you'd rather not go to the hospital?"

"I'm fine," she said, "just a bit shook up."

"And bruised and cut," Bronson added.

"You'll have to sign an A.M.A.," Hollins said.

"A what?" Lisa asked.

"It's a release form. It stands for Against Medical Advice."

"Oh, I see. I'll sign it."

The paramedic shrugged and began to gather his equipment.

Lisa turned to Bronson. "The doorbell rang and I went to answer it." A shiver radiated through her, as she began to remember. "There was this big man–"

"Good, Lisa. You said he was big. How big?"

"Very big. Huge."

"Six foot? Taller?"

"Taller, I guess. He was huge. Football type." Images flashed before her. She had seen him–God, she had seen his face. What did he look like? Her mind, trying to protect her, had shut down like a broken engine. She wouldn't allow it to. She was calm when she first opened the door. It wasn't until later that the panic set in. "He was an average-looking man, I guess."

Bronson scratched his chin. "Average, huh? Define *average*."

"You know, brown hair, brown eyes. Not ugly. Not good-looking. Just average." Lisa searched her memory, forcing her mind's eye to see him again.

"Did he have a mustache? A beard? A scar, perhaps?

Was his face burned? Did he have a glass eye?"

The questions came at a fast pace. Lisa's mind couldn't keep up with them.

The paramedic handed her a paper. She signed it, thankful for the break. "I saw him. I should recognize him, but I can't describe him. Maybe later, when I've had a chance to calm down."

"Would it help if you look at the mug files?"

"Yes, of course, that would be a tremendous help." Lisa felt relieved. She'd be able to identify him then.

"When you're ready, I'll take you to the station," Bronson said, "and maybe while you're there, you can talk to Charlie."

"Who?"

"Charlie. He's our police artist–computer graphic expert. Whatever you want to call him. You'll like him. He's a real joker. Very nice person. Young too. Anyway–" He momentarily paused. "What was I sayin'?" Bronson tapped his forehead as though he could remember by doing that. "Oh yeah, Charlie. He can help you remember what this jerk looked like. You'll choose different face shapes, noses–that kind of thing. Before long you'll remember every feature, and Lisa, ma'am, don't worry. This happens all of the time. You're under a lot of stress. It'll come to you."

Lisa smiled at his kindness. Unable to stop herself, she threw her arms around him and cried.

He held her in his arms, much the same way her father would have done. She felt lonely and lost.

Bronson led her to the couch, refilled her glass of water, and finished his coffee. "Are you all right?"

The doorbell rang and Lisa jumped up.

"It's probably the police," Bronson said. He gently pushed Lisa back down to the couch. "I'll handle them." He walked over to the door and swung it open. Two plain-clothes policemen stared at Bronson. "What the hell are you doing here?" asked Detective Reede. "You're out of your jurisdiction."

"I know that." Bronson nodded several times,

resembling a bobber at the end of a fishing line. He wrapped his arms around both men and led them out. "You see, Ms. Lisa and I–we go back a long way, and I was sort of in the neighborhood when I heard the call. You know how it goes. I felt I had to be here."

"We're here now," Reede said. "We'll take over."

"I got most everything wrapped up."

"It figures," Reede smirked.

"Hold on, Aaron," Reede's partner said. "This may not be a bad deal." He looked at Bronson. "Who does the paper work?"

"I do," Bronson said.

"Who gets the credit?"

"You do," Bronson mumbled.

"In that case, continue. We'll just hang around until you're finished."

Bronson looked up over the detective's shoulder and noticed that David and Tracy were driving up the driveway. He motioned for the detectives to go inside, then went out to meet David. Bronson waited until he rolled down the window.

"Bronson, it's good to see you," David said. "How have you been?" His voice trailed off and his eyes narrowed as he studied Bronson's face. "What's wrong?" David's face was enveloped with concern.

"Some jerk tried to force his way in," Bronson answered very quietly so Tracy couldn't hear. "Lisa's fine. She's inside. Go to her, David." He looked at Tracy. "How you doin', sweetheart?"

Tracy smiled and waved.

David ran out of the car, not bothering to close the door.

Chapter 25

As Bronson drove toward the police station, he made mental notes. Some animal out there had tried to hurt Lisa. Why? Was it just a weirdo who had randomly chosen her? Uh uh. He didn't think so. Something bigger was happening, and he aimed to find out what it was.

He gunned his VW and made an illegal U-turn to prevent being stuck in at least ten minutes worth of traffic jams. He'd avoid the heavy traffic congestion by turning down Lincoln Avenue and not using Main at all. This would enable him to reach the police station much faster.

Less than half-an-hour later, he parked his car, glanced at his watch, and ran up the stairs.

"Bronson, get your ass in here."

Bronson glanced up at the ceiling. He knew what Captain Porter wanted. There had been a series of disappearances with a possible drug connection. He was supposed to be devoting most of his time to this case. So far, he'd spent less than an hour working on it.

"Well?" Captain Porter folded his arms and glared at Bronson.

"I'm working on it. I'm following a couple of leads. I should have somethin' very soon."

"See that you do." Captain Porter turned his attention to his pile of paper work.

Bronson flopped down on his chair. He planned to concentrate on his case. He read through his notes and thought about Lisa. He shook himself and forced his mind back to the case. He shuffled some papers, then pushing with his feet, he rolled away from his desk. His eyes focused on the far corner of the wall. "What the hell," he mumbled, rolled back toward his desk, and reached for the phone.

After an exchange of pleasantries, Bronson said, "Juan, I need a favor."

"Shoot–anything for you, buddy," said Officer Juan Saenz.

"I know you're off duty and you're probably sittin' at home relaxin', and since this is personal, I can't ask my men to do it. And, by the same token, if you don't want to do it, I'll understand."

"Like I said, anything for you," the officer repeated.

Bronson told him about Lisa.

Saenz said after Bronson finished, "Sounds like she's had a hard time. I don't know her, but I'd like to help her, especially since she's so close to your daughter."

"Yeah, she's almost like family."

"So tell me, what can I do?"

"I'd like you to check out the neighborhood. You know, talk to her neighbors, the mailman, anybody who might have seen somethin'. Think you could do that?"

"That sounds like real police work," Juan, who was still a rookie, said. "I'm tired of this school crossing duty and shit like that."

"We all have to start at the bottom," Bronson said.

"True, but I'm anxious to prove I can do more. Yeah. I'd love to do that for you."

* * *

For the past two hours, the grayish brown sedan had been parked three houses down from Lisa's duplex. Its driver yawned. It was boring as hell, but it was necessary to keep surveillance. In a way, it was, well, inspirational. Except for today. Two long hours had dragged by and nothing. Not an idea. Maybe a change of scenery would do wonders. It was almost time for Lisa to take her brat to the park.

The park!

Of course. That was it. Her car would become a weapon. It was a brilliant plan. The problem was, after it was over, no one would recognize the genius behind the master plan. Not unless someone was notified. Someone, like Bronson.

The driver reached for the notepad that was always kept in the glove compartment, then retrieved a pen, and began to write:

Dear Detective Bronson:

I am writing this to you because I have noticed that you have taken deep interest in Lisa Littau.

By now, as you know, she is dead, apparently the victim of a hit and run accident. However, I want you to know that it was no accident. I know because I'm the one who ran her over. For the last couple of days, I have been watching Lisa and memorizing her schedule. I knew that she always took her daughter to the park and that they always walked.

I noted with interest how, in order to reach the park, they had to cross the intersection of Pendleton and White. Keeping this in mind, I waited for them down the block, then as they crossed the street, I floored the gas pedal. Just as I expected, Lisa was too stunned to move. I ran her over, just as I planned.

But that's not all. After I killed her, I purposely drove my car head-on into the wall by which you found my car. That, I hope, resulted in my death. I wanted you to know this so that you wouldn't be sad about Lisa. She's with me now where she belongs.

The driver re-read the letter and felt pleased. Tomorrow the letter would be mailed. Depending on the mail service, the next day or the one after that, Bronson would receive it. By then, both Lisa and the driver would be dead.

The letter was sealed. All was set. Tomorrow would be a good day.

Chapter 26

At a quarter past ten, Harry Bronson attempted to open his eyes. But no matter how hard he tried, sleep's gooey embrace summoned him back to slumber. He forced himself to sit up and plant his feet flat on the floor.

"Up," he said to no one in particular. "You gotta get up. You gotta get up in the   mornin'." He rose slowly and walked over to the window, then drew the drapes aside. He could see Carol through his second floor bedroom window. She was working on the flower garden, and he was sure she was humming a tune only she could recognize.

Bronson smiled as he stepped away from the window. He was lucky to have such a wonderful woman. He had gotten home last night–or should he say this morning?–at four-thirty, and she hadn't even complained.

Carol had simply kissed him good night and rolled over and returned to sleep. Somehow, she had known he didn't feel like talking. That happened every time he had a rough day.

Bronson, still wearing his striped pajamas, moved away from the window and sat by the phone contemplating whether he should call Juan at home or at the office. He decided to try his house first.

"Hello?" came the sleepy voice over the phone.

"Juan, gosh, I'm sorry. Did I wake you? It is past ten."

"I stayed up late last night."

"Not because of me, I hope."

"Nah, buddy, don't worry.   It wasn't you.   Your

assignment took only a few minutes. I had other stuff I needed to get done. But getting back to last night, I did come up with something that might interest you." His sleepy-tone left him, to be replaced by the enthusiasm of doing "real" police work.

"Oh?"

"The lady down the street from Lisa's duplex complained that there has been a dirty, grayish-brown compact car parked in front of her house at rather frequent intervals."

"Ah ha," Bronson said as he reached for his pocket notebook and scribbled down the information. "Did she happen to mention just when it was parked there?"

"Well, Harry, you've got to understand. She's an old lady, and getting any information from her was no easy task. But as best as I can pin-point it, yes, the car was there on the day of the attempted rape as well as on the day the little girl was reported missing."

"That little ol' lady—she didn't by any chance get a license number."

"She did, but I haven't followed up on it. I'm not officially on the case, you know. And to be truthful, the captain doesn't like policemen like me sticking their noses in detectives' work."

"No need to apologize. You've done a heck of a good job. I'll check on that license plate myself."

Bronson jotted the license number on the same piece of paper where he kept his collection of notes on Lisa. He thanked his friend, told him to go back to sleep, and hung up. Even as Bronson returned the phone to its cradle, he was reaching for his shaving items.

Forty-five minutes later, he sat at the police station. As he keyed in the information he wanted, Matthew, one of his colleagues, walked by and tapped him on the shoulder. "Hey, that's my computer you're using. Take good care of my baby."

"Yeah, sure," Bronson answered. He could never understand how somebody could get so attached to a simple machine. He smirked and finished typing the information.

Seconds later, the information he saw on the screen confirmed his suspicions. The car was registered to Emily

Rogers–the same woman who insisted that she was Lisa's long, lost mother.

Bronson reached for his handy notebook, flipped the pages until he found Lisa's phone number, and dialed. He tapped his desk with the bottom of his pencil while he waited for someone to answer. He let the phone ring a long time then slammed it down.

Bronson returned to the computer and fed it the name Emily Rogers. The database informed him that whenever a child disappeared, Emily Rogers claimed responsibility for the child's disappearance.

A couple of paragraphs further down on the monitor, he read:

> MAGGIE ROGERS: daughter of William and Emily Rogers. Died at age two while riding her tricycle. Emily Rogers failed to see her daughter playing behind the family car when she backed out of the driveway.

Further on down, Bronson read an excerpt from Emily's confession: "I never saw my Maggie. I only heard the crushing of bones and that last, desperate wail."

Bronson leaned back in his seat and shook his head. "No wonder."

Chris Hamilton looked up from his own computer and asked, "What did you say?"

"This lady here–" Bronson pointed to his computer. "She accidentally ran over her own kid and apparently, she never got over it. It seems that she has spent her entire life searching for her dead daughter. I suppose that's her own self-punishment."

"That's a tough break. When did this happen?"

Bronson looked back up at the monitor. "It happened twenty-six years ago. Had the girl lived, she would be about Lisa's age. No wonder Emily Rogers thinks Lisa is her daughter." He reached over and turned off the computer.

"See ya," he said.

"Hey, where are you going in such a hurry?" Chris asked. "We're supposed to be working on those missing people reports. Remember?"

"Gee, Chris, I know that, and I feel real bad about that. But this thing with Lisa. Poor lady doesn't even know her life may be in danger. Someone's got to tell her, you know?"

"Yeah, yeah. I know. But why you?"

"I promised my daughter I'd keep an eye on her. You know how that goes."

Chris frowned and waved him away. "Sure, I understand. Go. You've covered for me many times. I guess it's my turn. So go on, before the captain sees you sneaking out again."

"Thanks. I owe you."

"You better believe you owe me, you dumb ass. You owe me big time."

Bronson heard Chris say something else but couldn't make out what. The door was already closing behind him.

Chapter 27

David rolled the ball past Tracy toward Lisa. Tracy tried to grab it, but Lisa was quicker. She caught the ball and threw it back at David. David dove for the ball and tripped, but not before pushing the ball back to Lisa. All three started laughing.

Behind her, Lisa heard the phone ring. She glanced toward the duplex and decided to ignore it. Instead, she picked up the ball just before Tracy grabbed it. "It's mine!" Lisa said and rolled it to David who was busy dusting himself off.

The phone continued to ring. Lisa squinted, wondering who would let the phone ring that long. "Phone's ringing," she said as she ran inside.

She picked up the phone just in time to hear the party on the other end hang up.

"Who was it?" David asked once Lisa had rejoined them.

Lisa shrugged. "Beats me. They hung up before I got a chance to answer." She looked at her daughter. "Too bad it disrupted our game."

"It's okay," Tracy said in a somewhat sad voice. Then she brightened up. "Hey! Maybe we can go to the park?" She turned to look at her father. "Mommy and I always go to the park." She began to run circles around David.

"You want to go to the park, we'll go to the park." David managed to gently swat Tracy as she ran by him.

Tracy giggled. "Betcha can't catch me," she said.

"Oh, I could catch you all right, but then we wouldn't get to the park," David answered.

Tracy seemed to consider this for a minute, then quickly said, "Betcha I'll beat you all inside the house." She took off running.

David and Lisa looked at each other, smiled, and made an attempt to beat Tracy inside the house.

They lost.

* * *

Another thought brewed in Emily's mind. Why wait until tomorrow? After all, waiting had spoiled lots of good plans. How did that saying go? Never put off for tomorrow what you can do today.

But today had a big drawback. That darn letter. If she acted on her idea today, she wouldn't get the chance to mail it. Then what?

She thought for a minute. If she left it out where it could be seen, the police would notice it. Eventually they'd give it to Bronson, and that's what she wanted. It didn't matter whether she mailed it or not, as long as he got it.

She folded the letter in quarters, and using large block letters, she wrote Bronson's name. She dug into her purse, found a roll of tape, tore a piece, and taped the letter to the front passenger seat.

She smacked her lips in anticipation, and then settled back to wait for Lisa to start her daily walk.

Emily didn't have long to wait. Within five minutes, she saw the door to Lisa's duplex swing open. Emily sat up straight. She reached for the keys hanging from the ignition.

Lisa and Tracy—and that bothersome man—were on their way to the park.

This was it.

It was actually happening.

Emily was ready.

* * *

The traffic on the freeway came to a sudden stop. "Damn!" Bronson said, slamming his open hand against the steering wheel. He wondered how long this traffic jam would delay him.

He stuck his head out the window. All he could see were other impatient drivers. He sighed. Probably somewhere in front of him there had been some horrendous accident that caused this back up.

He'd try calling Lisa again and warn her, just in case. He reached for the cellular that he kept in the passenger seat for emergencies like this. Damn! The phone wasn't there. He searched the floor and under the seat. Then he remembered. He'd been in such a hurry to leave the office, he had neglected to pick it up.

Might as well not fight it. Anyway, there wasn't much he could do except turn off the engine, settle back, and relax. It looked like he'd be stuck here for quite a while.

Chapter 28

Emily's fingers were wrapped so tightly around the steering wheel that her knuckles turned white. She stared at them for a second, then turned her attention to the intersection. Emily placed her right foot on top of the gasoline pedal but didn't press down. She was ready for Lisa–no! She was ready for Maggie to cross the street.

Emily leaned forward, eagerly anticipating what was to come.

* * *

Tracy, who had been skipping ahead of David and Lisa, came to an abrupt halt. She turned and looked at her parents. "Mommy, Daddy, I like playing keep-away. Can we play that again in the park? It'll be fun. There'll be lots and lots of places to run."

"Sweetheart, we didn't bring the ball," Lisa answered.

"I'll run home and get it. You and Daddy can wait for me right here. I'll run. Can I go get it? Please?"

Lisa and David exchanged looks. "Why not? We're not in any hurry," David said.

"Yeepee!" Tracy began to run back, but David stopped her.

"Young lady, how do you expect to get inside? I've got the keys." He jingled them in front of her.

"Oh, yeah," Tracy said. "I need the keys." She reached out for them, but David dropped them into his pocket.

"We'll walk back with you," he said.

* * *

The longer Harry Bronson sat in the car, the more the anxiety gnawed at him. All doubts had now left him. Emily was dangerous, and right now she was probably parked in front of Lisa's house—or worse. . .

If he waited another minute or two, that could make all the difference in the world. He opened his door, stepped out, and walked toward the wreck.

An eighteen-wheeler had overturned and landed sideways, blocking the entire east bound lanes of the freeway. It had apparently been heading toward a construction site as it was carrying a full load of pipes, which, along with the broken glass, lay scattered everywhere.

A bald man sporting a gray beard leaned on a police car. He seemed disoriented and bruised, but not seriously hurt. Bronson spotted the officer in charge and headed toward him.

"Sir! Excuse me, sir." Bronson heard someone behind him say. He turned and noticed a youthful-looking policeman rushing toward him.

"Excuse me, sir," the uniformed policeman repeated, "but you'll have to get back to your car."

"I'm afraid I have an emergency, son. Now don't get excited. I'm just going to reach in my back pocket and get my ID," Bronson said as he reached for his wallet.

The policeman took a precarious step back.

"It's just my wallet," Bronson said as he opened it to reveal his badge. "I'm Detective Bronson and—"

"Harry Bronson?" The policeman's eyes popped like two, huge brown buttons.

"Uh, yeah."

The policeman broke into a wide grin. "It's a pleasure to meet you, sir. I've heard so much about you. You're a legend among us rookies."

Bronson felt the blood rush to his face. "That's just gossip, and you should never listen to gossip."

"Yes, sir." The policeman looked as though he wanted to salute the detective.

Bronson spotted the squad car parked on the other side of the overturned eighteen-wheeler. "Where do you keep your key to your car?" he asked, turning his attention to the rookie.

"My key, sir?" His eyebrows furrowed in confusion.

"Yes, your key. Where is your car key?"

The rookie fished it out of his pocket. "Right here, sir."

Bronson grabbed the key and tossed him his own keys. "If you walk down this row, about eight or nine cars back, you'll find a white Volkswagen bug, BGY 347. That's my car." He began to walk away from the rookie, toward the patrol car. "We'll exchange cars at the police station."

"Uh, sir, you can't–the car. My partner–"

Bronson ignored him and, as he headed toward the patrol car, he heard the rookie say, "Oooh shit!"

Bronson smiled and sped away. He drove at a speed that brought curious stares from passersby. He could use the siren, he knew, but he'd been pushing his luck with the chief lately. Better save it for the real emergency which he knew would come.

After what seemed to be an eternity, he turned onto Lisa's street. He strained his eyes, trying to catch a glimpse of the grayish-brown sedan. As far as he could tell, the car was not parked in front of Lisa's duplex.

Well, that was peachy-cream. What was he supposed to do now?

Chapter 29

Emily frowned, and her eyes squeezed shut with frustration. Through clenched teeth, she hissed. She would have preferred to have screamed, but under the circumstances, of course, she thought it best not to.

Maggie, her little girl, and that man had turned back. They hadn't crossed the street, after all. What was she going to do now?

Emily reached for the gun still wrapped in the windbreaker lying on the floor by the passenger's seat. She unwrapped it and checked to make sure she had at least two bullets. She planned to use one for Lis–uh, Maggie and the other for herself.

Emily took a deep breath, raised the gun, and noticed that her hand trembled. For a long second, Emily watched Maggie walk back toward the duplex. She had her arm intertwined in that man's arm. Both were smiling, obviously happy.

Emily sighed. It was no good. She couldn't possibly shoot Maggie as long as she was that close to that man. Not that she cared if she killed him or not. It's just that if she shot him accidentally, Maggie might take off running like a scared rabbit, then Emily would never be able to catch her. No, she would wait until Maggie stood all alone.

Emily watched as the little girl went inside the duplex while Maggie and her man waited out front. A few seconds later–an eternity to Emily–the little girl returned, bouncing a ball. Then the three of them turned back toward the park.

Smiling, Emily put the gun away and got ready to follow them once more.

She would wait until Maggie reached the middle of the street. Emily would then accelerate, and Maggie would have no place to run. Emily's car would surely hit her. It seemed inevitable.

* * *

"Is that your neighbor?" David asked as he nodded toward the grayish-brown compact sedan parked across the street.

Lisa turned in time to see the driver look away, but that one second was all Lisa needed. She looked like–like what's her name? That lady who first claimed to be her mother. But Detective Bronson–"Uncle Harry"–had specifically warned her to stay away.

"Lisa? Are you all right?" David asked as he followed her glance. "Do you know her?"

"No, uh-uh." The answer came much too quickly. An involuntary chill spread through Lisa's body. She pretended that she hadn't recognized her so as not to worry David, but she felt the fingers of concern squeeze her. Lisa planned to keep an eye on her. "Come on," she said, grabbing David's hand. "Let's go to the park and enjoy our daughter."

In spite of Lisa's gallant efforts, the magic spell had been broken. They walked most of the way to the park in silence.

"Lisa, are you sure nothing is bothering you?" David asked after a lengthy silence.

"Yeah, I'm sure." Lisa glanced at Emily's compact. It was barely rolling along, a block away.

"Is she following us?"

"I. . .I don't know." Lisa recognized the fear in her voice.

"Well, let me find out." David turned to head toward the car, but Lisa stopped him.

"No, David, please. Let her be. She's just a confused

old woman, but she's harmless. When we get back home, I'll call Harry Bronson. In the meantime, let's enjoy Tracy."

"I thought you said you didn't know her." David's eyes shone with anger or concern. Or both. Lisa couldn't tell.

She knew she should apologize or explain, but later. Right now she had to concentrate on Tracy. Her heart jumped to her mouth. Where was Tracy?

By now Tracy–who was usually half a block ahead of her parents–had reached the corner, and Lisa opened her mouth to scream to wait for them. However, before she could get it out, Tracy automatically came to a stop and waited for her parents. She bounced the ball, oblivious of the threatening car, her mother's anguish, or her father's guarded concern.

David and Lisa soon joined her. They put Tracy between them as they stepped down into the street.

* * *

Bronson slowed down as he drove past Lisa's duplex. All seemed quiet. Maybe he had reached the wrong conclusion, but his gut feeling told him otherwise.

Be alert! Think like Emily. Bronson tapped his forehead. What would Emily do? She'd follow Lisa wherever she'd go, he reasoned.

Bronson sat up straight as he spotted the grayish-brown sedan slowly creeping toward the people crossing the street. Bronson sucked in his breath when he realized it was David, Lisa, and Tracy.

In seconds, he perceived Emily's plan. It had been a car that had originally stolen Maggie's life. In Emily's warped mind, it was only appropriate that a car end it all.

Yet, he was too far away to help.

* * *

Lisa clenched Tracy's hand so tightly that the girl protested. "Mommy you're hurting me."

But Lisa wasn't paying attention. Instead, she kept her mind busy registering each separate detail. The wailing police siren a block behind the speeding car Emily drove. Both were rushing toward her.

Toward them.

The policeman yelled something as he drew his gun and fired at the grayish-brown car's tires. One must have pierced the tire, as the car careened off to the side and ran over the curb, heading straight for them.

Without a second's delay, Lisa shoved Tracy away from her, grabbed David's arm, and both lunged forward, the car missing them by less than a foot. The three of them lay on the street staring at the car.

Feeling as though she'd been drugged, Lisa raised herself in time to see the speeding car crash against the corner brick house.

"Are any of you hurt?"

Lisa looked up. It was Bronson. Anxiety gnawed at her as she turned to stare at David and Tracy. Tracy began to cry, and David scooped her up in his arms. Only then, did Lisa allow herself to breathe again. "We're fine. A bit shook up and bruised, but otherwise okay."

Bronson nodded and ran toward the wreck. Lisa got up, but the pain in her ankle almost made her tumble down. She stood on one leg until she regained her balance. "I'll be back in a second," she told David.

He reached out for her. "Stay."

Lisa shook herself free. "I have to, Dave. I have to go to her. I'll explain later."

"If it's that important to you, go ahead. I'll stay with Tracy."

Lisa threw him a kiss and headed toward Emily's body that had been thrown out of the car. When she reached the body, Lisa averted her eyes from Emily's body and directed them toward Bronson.

He nodded once, stood up, and ran toward the patrol car. In the background, she could hear him using the police radio to call for an ambulance.

Lisa knelt down when she noticed Emily's eyes slowly open.

Emily, gasping for air, managed to smile. "Maggie,

you're. . .alive." She breathed through her mouth. "I'm so sorry. I didn't see you. I didn't know you were behind the car. All I could hear were your pathetic little screams. Then I felt the wheels run over your little body. Oh, God. I'm so sorry, baby." She closed her eyes and gasped for breath again.

All the anger and hatred Lisa felt toward this woman who had tried to kill them evaporated like small clouds disappearing in the sky, leaving only pity and sorrow.

Emily grabbed Lisa's arm with unbelievable strength. When Emily opened her eyes again, they seemed clouded with confusion. "You. . .you're not. . . .Maggie, are you?" Her body stiffened, waiting for the answer.

Lisa took in a deep breath. "Of course I am. I'm Maggie." She wrapped her hands around Emily's.

Emily smiled and released Lisa's arm. She reached out and stroked Lisa's cheek. I...love you, Maggie I'm so glad...you're...alive." Emily's smile faded as her life slipped away.

Chapter 30

The voice on the other end of the phone sounded harsh. "This is the third time I've called, Mr. Johnson, and your father has not returned any of my calls. If he doesn't think our internal problems are any of his concern, then I believe we can pull out. Anyway, Rome would be better off not having an American parent company."

Thomas leaned back and rubbed the bridge of his nose. "No, Mr. Spattoni, there's no need to do anything so drastic." His eyes quickly scanned the office as though searching for an answer. "My father hasn't totally neglected you. In fact, he's authorized me to transfer ten million dollars to the Rome branch. He's also working on some other angles, and he will personally notify you as soon as he works out all of the details. Expect to hear from him in a day or two."

"That is wonderful news. I knew you'd come through. Now tell me, how are you and your dad doing?"

Thomas sighed. He forced some cheerfulness into his voice. He knew etiquette called for the exchange of pleasantries. As soon as he could, he ended the conversation and pressed the intercom button. "Liz, get me my father."

A few minutes later Liz buzzed Thomas. "He's not at his office, and Stacey has no idea how to reach him."

"Damn it, Liz! What is that man doing? He's hardly here anymore. Now, where am I going to get the ten million dollars I told Spattoni about?"

"Sir?"

"Never mind." He opened his side drawer, emptied it,

felt around for the false bottom, released it, and retrieved a different ledger than the one the accounting department maintained, opened it up, and glanced through its pages. "Let's see. Ten million dollars." He tapped his fingers as he studied the figures.

Suddenly he looked up, slammed the book shut, returned everything to its proper place, and ran out of his office.

As he entered his father's work area, Thomas saw Stacey filing some papers. She looked up at Thomas. "He's not in, Thomas. I thought you knew that."

"Yes, I did, but I'm working on this delicate matter and my father has all of the notes from our brainstorming session. They should be right on top of his desk. Would you mind if I go look?"

"No, of course not."

Thomas gave a curt nod and leisurely strolled past Stacey and toward his father's inner office. Once inside, he immediately locked the door behind him and headed directly for his father's desk.

At first, the lock on the desk offered resistance, just as he had expected it to, but eventually the lock gave in to his strong hands and solid letter opener. Thomas didn't waste any time looking any place else. He reached for his father's side drawer and emptied it just as he had done in his own desk.

It came as no surprise to Thomas that his father's desk also contained a secret compartment. He searched through his father's contents and found highly classified company records, a ledger, and correspondence—all work related. "Shit!" Disappointment ate at him.

He was about to put the items back when he noticed something unusual about the emptied area. Something seemed to be different. It wasn't as deep as it should be. He reached down, played around with the bottom of the drawer until, as he had suspected, a second compartment opened.

A leather-bound scrapbook stared back at him, daring him to open it. Thomas swallowed hard and grabbed it.

Neatly glued to the first page was a twenty-eight year old newspaper article dealing with the disappearance of seventeen-year-old Vanessa White. Next to the article was some blond hair neatly held in place with aged, yellowed tape.

The next page contained another article–this one dated seven months after the first one. Like the other one, it also dealt with a disappearance. This time the victim was fourteen-year-old Laurie Walker. Again, there was blond hair taped next to the article.

The third page contained a slight deviation. There were two articles taped, one right next to the other. The one on the right dealt with the disappearance of sixteen-year-old Janet James. The adjacent clipping reported the finding of Janet's body. She had been repeatedly stabbed, and her hair had been chopped off so much that she was almost bald. The police had no clues. A strand of blond hair separated the two articles.

With trembling hands, Thomas turned the page. Another disappearance, similar to the previous three. The only differences in the crimes were the cities. The fourth, fifth, and sixth pages–all contained similar articles.

Thomas slammed the book shut. He sat motionless, staring at nothing. Then mechanically, he reopened the book. The first disappearance occurred on February 18, 1973, in New York. The second one was on September 1, 1973, in Los Angeles. He scribbled down the dates and names of the cities. He did this for the remaining of the articles.

He pressed the intercom button. "Stacey, how far back do we keep company records?"

"Forever. Your father insists on it. Says that the rich and powerful are always being accused of misappropriating money. Should that happen to him, he wants us to get hold of the records immediately. Why? Is there something in particular you're looking for?

"Yes. I'm doing some research on travels done by top corporate officials. I'll need the records for the last thirty years." He leaned back, stared at the scrapbook, stashed it away, and waited for Stacey.

Minutes later she handed him several computer printouts. "Is there anything else I can get you?" she asked.

"No, this is all I need," Thomas answered. He waited until Stacey stepped out before he settled back to examine the records.

On February 18, 1973, his father had been in New York. On September 1, 1973, he had been in Los Angeles. With a sinking sensation, Thomas continued to match the dates and places with his father's business trips, each a perfect match.

Thomas retrieved the scrapbook, opened it, and counted the newspaper clippings. There had been a total of seven disappearances. Of these, only two bodies had later been found.

According to the newspapers, both of those young ladies had died from multiple stab wounds. The first article quoted an expert by the name of Couch who said that the wounds showed "patterns of rage."

Both articles mentioned that the girls' blond hair had been chopped off, almost to the point of leaving them bald. None of the missing hair was ever found.

The last disappearance had occurred twenty-two years ago. Then suddenly, there were no more clippings. Why? Had the killer–

The killer!

His father!

Feeling numb, Thomas replaced the scrapbook. As he did, he spotted a large, brown envelope lying in the compartment. Without hesitating, he reached for the envelope, opened it, and discovered three more newspaper clippings. The first was an article reporting the death of Kathy Johnson, his father's first wife.

Thomas had long suspected that his mother wasn't his father's first wife. He had picked up bits of information from conversations here and there. He had once dared to ask, but the answer came in the form of a glacial glare. Thomas never mentioned it after that.

He studied the words in the article, but their meanings made no sense. He couldn't concentrate. Too much was happening. It was too much to absorb.

His eyes kept drifting toward the picture of his father's wife. She had been a beautiful woman who reminded him of someone he should know. But who?

He forced himself to read the article. It contained the usual information. Mrs. Johnson had devoted her time to many charitable organizations and was apparently well liked. She had been killed in a car accident. Survivors included her husband, James Johnson, and their three-year-old daughter, Bobbye Johnson.

Their daughter?

Thomas had never known this. Had never even suspected. A little girl.

Had she been blond?

Quickly, Thomas moved on to the second article. Another death. This time, a drowning. The victim was none other than Bobbye Johnson. She had out lived her mother by less than a month.

Another death.

Quickly, Thomas moved on to the third piece, a recent advertisement. Lisa Littau asked the readers: Are you my biological parents?

Thomas remembered the ad. His father had been riding the stationary bicycle when Thomas walked in. The newspaper had been opened to Lisa's ad. Thomas had read something in his father's face. Shock, perhaps?

Or was it fear?

Thomas recognized Lisa's picture. This was the woman with whom his father was supposedly having an affair. The longer he stared at the picture, the more he realized why he had recognized his father's first wife. The resemblance between Lisa and Kathy Johnson was uncanny.

Bobbye Johnson had not died.

She had grown up to become Lisa Littau.

And now she had returned, but why? Did she plan to

expose their father? How much did she know? How much would it take to keep her quiet? No matter what angle he took, Thomas would lose out. He had never had his father's love, and he'd be damned if he let her have even a single penny. She had robbed him of everything else. She would not rob him of his inheritance.

"If revenge is your game, I can't allow you to taint the name of Johnson Enterprises," Thomas said to the picture. "If people find out what Father did, the company will go broke. I will lose all of my money. All that work would have been for nothing. Then again, maybe you're not after revenge. You're here for your share of the money. Well, sister, either way, I think I'll have to make this obituary come true—twenty-odd years later."

He reached for his private line and dialed Sheridan's cellular number.

"Sheridan," came the voice over the line.

"Tony, are you still following that broad my father is having an affair with?"

"That's what you told me to do."

"I need to get into her house. When's the best time?"

"Right now. The old lady is out looking at mug shots, and her ex and their kid went out somewhere."

"Mug shots?"

"She was almost raped."

Thomas sat in stunned silence. Rape? What exactly was going on? Thomas shook himself. There would be plenty of time later on to digest this information. Right now, there were other more pressing issues to attend to.

"How long will they be gone?"

"I can't answer that."

"You're observing her house now."

"Just like I'm supposed to."

"Good. Give me directions on how to get there. If they show up before I get there, call my cellular."

"I don't like it. It's too risky."

"You're not being paid to like it. I need to get into her

house, and your job is to get me in."

"If you don't mind me saying so, you have no idea what you're doing. I'm a professional. Tell me what you want, and I'll get it for you."

"All I want is for you to keep an eye on the house. When I arrive, I want you to break into Tracy's house in such a way that no one will ever suspect we've been there."

"But—"

"Just shut up and listen." Thomas' anger rose. Employees now a days were insubordinate. If Tony wasn't so damn good at his job, he'd fire him. "Once you're inside, open up the back door and let me in."

"Yes, sir, Mr. Johnson."

The curt answer made Thomas realize that Tony was upset. Under any other circumstances, Thomas wouldn't care. But right now he needed Tony's expertise and shut lips. He may be arrogant, but at least he's reliable, Thomas thought. "Look, I have to do this myself, Tony. I don't even know what I'm looking for, but I'll recognize it when I see it. That's why I have to do this myself. Do you understand?"

"Yeah." He sounded somewhat calmer. He gave Thomas explicit directions.

Chapter 31

When Tony opened the door, Thomas barged in and glanced around. This home belonged to an organized person.

That meant that whatever he was looking for would be tucked away somewhere in a drawer. He surveyed the place. There was a corner desk in the living room. More drawers in the kitchen. Even though he hadn't gone into the bedroom, he knew there had to be some more drawers in there.

"Hurry up, man," Tony said, glancing out the window. "I've no idea when they're planning to return. Why are you standing there instead of doing whatever you're supposed to be doing?"

The disruption sent a bolt of anger through Thomas' body. "I'm thinking," he snapped. "I'm trying to approach this logically."

Tony threw his arms up in the air as though that was the stupidest thing he'd ever heard. "Just hurry up." He continued to keep a watchful eye down the street.

Thomas decided to start his search in Lisa's bedroom. He reasoned that if someone valued something, it would most likely be kept in a bedroom drawer.

He began his search with the dresser. The top drawer contained costume jewelry, hairbrushes, a blow dryer, and some make-up. Nothing that interested him. He slammed the drawer shut.

The second drawer held Lisa's underwear. He felt funny digging through her personal items, but he realized he had no choice. He reached under the panties and bras in hope of seeing something. Again, his search proved to be fruitless.

He went through the third drawer. It held her shorts, some pants, and a purse. He closed the drawer. He'd been wrong. It—whatever *it* was—wasn't in the bedroom.

The living room, then. It had to be in the living room. He headed directly toward the corner desk and opened its only drawer. It was jammed full of papers.

"Have you finished yet?" Tony asked as he directed his eyes away from the window and toward Thomas.

"I'll let you know when I'm finished," Thomas snapped. As he looked through the papers, he came across bills, receipts, expense accounts, and budget sheets. Nothing of interest there. He rummaged through the rest of the drawer. An envelope with Lisa's name caught his attention. He picked it up, then noticed another similar one. He also picked this one up and examined both of them. Neither had a return address. He took out one of the letters and began to read.

Tony interrupted him, but this time Thomas recognized the sense of urgency in his voice.

"Car's pulling up in the driveway!" Tony spoke in a stage whisper.

Thomas straightened out the mess he had made in the drawer and quickly shut it. He and Tony headed for the back door.

They closed the door behind them just as the front door opened.

Chapter 32

Lisa shifted positions and Bronson glanced up at her from his desk. "I'm afraid the police department's furniture isn't very comfortable."

Lisa nodded and turned her attention to the mug files. "I've gone through four of these things." Lisa pointed to the mug books. "I'm beginning to think that that creep isn't going to be here."

"Don't give up Lisa, ma'am. I want to nail that bastard."

Lisa yawned and rubbed her eyes. "Me, too," she said and turned another page.

Not there.

She massaged the back of her neck and moved her head from side to side. She turned the page again.

And froze.

"That's him!" She pointed to a picture of Albert Henderson, alias Big Al. Just looking at him filled her with terror.

"You're absolutely positive?" Bronson asked as he glanced at the picture.

Afraid of her own voice, Lisa nodded. Staring at his mug, she wondered how she could have momentarily forgotten that terrifying face. She knew that from now on, it would be forever embedded in her mind. A shiver ran up her spine.

Bronson wrapped his arm around her. "Don't shake, Lisa, ma'am, you're quite safe now." He gave her a fatherly smile, and Lisa responded with a smile of her own.

"How about some coffee?" he asked moving away from her.

"No, thank you. I think I just want to go home."

"To San Antonio, you mean?" Bronson nodded as though answering his own question. "I can't say I blame you. You probably have this terrible concept of our fine city, but really, Dallas isn't so bad. Unfortunately, you just got to see the worst of it."

"I'm sure you're right," Lisa said, "but I don't plan to leave Dallas. I just want to go home to my duplex here in Dallas. My biological mother contacted me once, and hopefully she'll do it again. I want to be there in case she calls."

"She'll call." Bronson rubbed his chin and his eyes narrowed as he focused them on Lisa. "If you don't mind me sayin' so, ma'am, you're one tough cookie." He took out his pen and filled out a form. When he finished, he glanced at his watch and back up at Lisa. "Listen, there's no use you hangin' around. Want me to take you home?"

"Please." The sooner she left the police station, the sooner she could put this in her past.

Bronson took out his car keys, and Lisa followed him.

"What happens now?" Lisa asked once they reached his car.

"Now we pick up Big Al, bring him in, and you pick him out in a lineup. We have a long rap sheet on him, but we've never been able to hold him. Your positive I.D. will be enough to put him in the slammer, and then we'll throw the key away. I hope." He stopped at a red light. "I hate to drive," he said. "Did I ever tell you that?"

Lisa shook her head.

"Yeah, well I do. I often threaten to get a partner and always make him drive. Are you interested in the job?"

"I'm afraid not. I don't think I could handle a life filled with so much adventure."

"Yeah? Me neither," Bronson said. The light turned green, and he drove off.

* * *

"It's been a while since you've heard from your biological mother," David said as he stepped into the kitchen.

"Do you really think she's going to contact you again?"

Even though Lisa had her head in the refrigerator, she still heard David's question, but she continued to search for the butter. She found it buried behind some leftovers on the second shelf. She grabbed it and let the refrigerator door close by itself. "I don't know, David." She sighed. "Each day I pray that she calls me."

"And if she doesn't?" David opened a can of frozen lemonade. "How long do you plan to stay here? We need to get back to San Antonio and get on with our lives."

Lisa was reaching for the eggs, but she stopped halfway to turn to gape at her ex-husband. "*We*, David? Did you really mean *we*?"

"Uh–" David's eyes popped open, becoming the dominant feature on his face. "Yes, you know, Tracy and me."

"I see." Lisa's voice sounded like a mouse's even to her own ears. She cracked the egg open, but she hit it a bit too hard and the top of the shell caved in. "Damn it!"

"Lisa."

She ignored David and instead focused her attention on separating the bits of shell from the egg.

David wrapped his hand around her arm. "Lisa, talk to me."

"What's wrong with me, David?"

David squinted. "I don't understand the question."

"It just seems that every time you say something nice to me, you immediately change your mind as though you're sorry you said it." In spite of her efforts, she found the tears sting her eyes.

"Oh, Jesus, Lisa, don't do that." He reached out for her and wrapped his arms around her. "That's not it at all. I'm sorry I gave you the wrong impression. Let me see if I can explain." He paused, as though searching for the right words. "Lisa, I'm. . .afraid. Nothing has really changed. We're still the same people. I know you long for money and for a fancy house, and I'll never be able to provide you with those. I'll always be just a car salesman."

"Couldn't we compromise?"

"We tried that once, and we failed."

Lisa nodded and looked down. A large sob raked her body. "I. . .want you, David."

David raised Lisa's chin with gentle fingers. "Oh, Lisa," he whispered and suddenly he found himself urgently kissing her. His hands traveled down Lisa's back and pulled the blouse out of her jeans.

His hands found the soft, smooth skin of her back. His lips traveled down to her neck, and when she threw her head back, he gently squeezed her breast.

His fingers found their way to the buttons on Lisa's blouse, and he began to unfasten them as his lips caressed her chest. He slipped his other hand inside her jeans.

"Tracy," she whispered.

"Let her find her own man," he answered as he exposed her breast.

"David!"

"All right, all right." He withdrew from her. "But we have to finish this." He scooped her up in his arms and carried her into the bedroom. With his foot he slammed the door shut.

He was ripping her clothes off even before she had landed on the bed.

* * *

An hour later, they were back in the kitchen. He continued to make the lemonade he had started fixing a while back. In the meantime, Lisa finished preparing the mix for the cake. "I've been meaning to contact Lucy," she said.

"Who?"

"Lucy, a lady at the real estate agency." Lisa whipped the eggs as she spoke. "Remember I told you that I often dreamt of a big, white house with a fountain outside?"

David poured water into the empty lemonade can, then poured it into the pitcher. "I remember," he said.

"I don't think that it's a dream anymore. I believe it's a memory, so I hired Lucy to help me find this house."

"Then what?" David stirred the lemonade.

"Then I can talk to the owners. If they're not my parents, maybe they will know who the previous owners were." Lisa measured two cups of flour.

David nodded. "That should work." He put the lemonade inside the refrigerator and the spoon in the sink. For a while, he helped Lisa with the cake, but she noticed that his eyes strayed to her body.

When they had finished with the cake and had cleaned the kitchen, David once again reached for Lisa. They kissed, long and passionately. Gently, he scooped her up in his arms and carried her back to the bedroom. This time their lovemaking was more relaxed, more fulfilling.

When they finished, she lay in his arms. He kissed her forehead and asked, "Are you sure those two letters you received from your mother didn't give you any hint as to her identity?"

Lisa shook her head as she snuggled in closer to him. "None at all. Why? Do you want to see them?" She could hear the television in the living room. Tracy had awakened from her nap and was watching cartoons.

"Yeah, I'd like to see them if you don't mind."

"Sure, no problem," she answered. "I knew this couldn't last forever, anyway." She got up.

David jumped out of bed and stood in front of her, blocking her way. "This time, let's make it last forever."

Lisa also wanted this, but she couldn't do it alone. "I can't give you a guarantee, Dave. All I can do is promise to love you like crazy, and I pray that's enough."

David reached out for her and wrapped his arms around her. "Sometimes loving one another isn't enough. Lisa, I have never stopped loving you, yet I couldn't make our marriage work. I'm. . .afraid." He held her tighter and buried his face in her hair.

"I know. Me, too," she said. "Having a successful marriage means work. Maybe we didn't work hard enough, and that's something we can change. Are you willing to work hard? Really hard?"

He nodded.

"Me, too," Lisa said.

He raised her chin to meet his lips. They kissed long and hard. "Welcome back," she said, and she could read the love in his eyes. She stepped back, breaking the magic spell that surrounded them. "I'll go get those letters."

As she reached for the desk's drawers in the living room, she turned to Tracy and said, "Hi, sweetheart. Did you have a good nap?"

Tracy nodded without looking up. "Where's Daddy?"

"Here I am," he said, entering the living room.

"Come watch cartoons with me."

"Sounds like a great idea." He lay down beside her on the floor.

Lisa rummaged through the opened drawer. She found the bill for the last ad, the checkbook, the papers where she had been keeping an account of all of her expenses, various receipts, pens, pencils, erasers. She even found the emergency money–close to three-hundred and forty dollars–she had stashed in the drawer. But no letters.

"David?" Lisa spoke from the living room.

"Yeah?"

"Have you seen the letters?"

"Not since that day when you first showed them to me." He looked away from the television, toward Lisa. "Why?"

"They're gone." She emptied out the drawer. "I can't find them."

"Would Tracy have them?"

"Have what?" Tracy asked.

"Mommy's letters."

She pouted. "Why would I have them?" She seemed hurt that her parents would consider the idea.

"We know you wouldn't take them." David corrected himself. "But maybe Mommy was reading them, then she went to tuck you in and accidentally left them in your bedroom."

"I don't think so," Tracy said, losing interest in the conversation. She turned to the cartoons.

"I'll go check anyway," David said. He stood up and headed toward Tracy's bedroom. A few minutes later, he returned empty-handed. "Did you take them with you that day you went to meet your mother at that bar?"

"No," Lisa said, but still she checked her purse. And the closet. And the pockets of her clothes. Next, she checked behind the desk. As before, her search remained fruitless.

"The car," David said.

"I'll check." Lisa looked on top of the dashboard and under and between the car seats. She checked the glove compartment. She even checked above the visors. But the letters were nowhere to be found.

Chapter 33

For the past six years, every Monday morning–including holidays–Thomas had sat down with his father to discuss the week's work agenda. The meetings began promptly at 7:30 and neither Thomas nor his father had ever been late.

However, today Thomas had gotten up a little later than usual and took his time shaving and showering. As he did, he wondered what he should say to his father. "Hi, how's the murdering business? Surprised that I know? So tell me all about my sister. What are you planning to do for her? Are you planning to take my money and give it to her? And why not? She's already got everything else. You have never loved me, have never even respected me. And now, you're going to take my money away from me."

The more Thomas thought about it, the angrier he grew. He should confront his father, but not once had he ever taken a single problem to him. Why begin now?

Thomas' stomach tightened into a hard knot. No use postponing the confrontation. As it was, his father would be furious with him for being late, and he still had to get the coffee and sweet rolls.

Thomas rushed through the rest of his morning routine, grabbed the list of the week's agenda, and left his bedroom.

Once in the kitchen, he placed two coffee cups on the tray along with two packages of Sweet 'N Low, the cream, two spoons, the percolator, and two doughnuts. Balancing the tray with one hand, he grabbed the stack of papers with his other hand and rushed down the hallway. He hesitated for a second in front of the closed door before he swung it open.

"Good morning, Father," Thomas said as he stepped into the joint office they shared. It was located in the front portion of their mansion, providing easy access to the world outside. "What will we be discussing today?" Let him think it's business as usual, he thought.

Startled, James Johnson glared at his son over the top of his newspaper, frowned, and quickly shoved the paper in the top drawer of his desk. As he slammed the drawer shut, deep, angry creases crossed his forehead. "What the hell are you doing here? Can't a person have any privacy in his own home?"

Thomas had been prepared for his father's wrath for being late–but not for intruding on his privacy.   Did he somehow know he'd been through his desk at work? Best to play it innocent, Thomas thought. "Father, perhaps you forgot that today's Monday," He set the tray and stack of papers down on the desk.

"I am well aware of what today is." James stood up and stormed out of the room, slamming the door behind him.

For a long second, Thomas stared at the closed door, then back at his father's desk. Violating a trust, he opened his father's top drawer and withdrew the newspaper.

He glanced at the paper, searching for the bit of news that had so obviously upset his father. The name "Lisa Littau" jumped out of the page, calling his attention to her ad. So that was it. Lisa again.

That bitch was always disrupting things.   Full of contempt, Thomas returned the newspaper where he found it, stormed out of the office, and fished the car keys out of his pocket.

Last Friday, while at the company's cafeteria, he had heard some of his employees discussing Lloyd Crestmont, an eccentric millionaire and a friend of his father–if indeed they had friends. Thomas sat down with his cup of coffee and buried his nose in his paper work, but in reality, his mind focused on every word being spoken at the table behind him.

"Seems that ol' man built Crestmont Hill Park. He grew up in West Virginia, and he missed the mountains so much that he decided to build himself a hill. Can you imagine anybody actually doing that?" Thomas recognized Laura's voice. She was probably one of the company's most knowledgeable female employees and had to let everyone know just how much she knew.

"So what's so special about this hill?" asked another employee whose voice Thomas did not recognize.

"Not much," Laura answered. "It's just there. Hardly anybody visits it, so it's a huge waste of money. The only way to reach it is by following a long, single-lane twisting road. Maybe that's why nobody goes there." She paused, perhaps to take a bite of her sandwich. The next time she spoke, it sounded like her mouth was full. "That'll take you to a small parking lot. From there, you'll see a steady, gradual footpath which leads up the hill.

"At the hill's crest, Mr. Crestmont ordered several trees planted, then he placed three benches under the largest tree. This way, weary climbers can rest there and catch their breaths before descending. It's really a nice park. Like I said, too bad nobody uses it. Maybe sometime we can have our company picnic there."

The conversation switched to the upcoming company picnic and Thomas stopped listening.

Now, a little over forty-eight hours later, Thomas drove his Porsche toward Crestmont Hill Park. If what Laura said was true, this park would be exactly what he needed.

An hour later, he brought his Porsche to a stop in the Crestmont Hill Park parking lot, a cleared-off area facing the hill. It accommodated six cars. As far as Thomas was concerned, the parking lot was plenty big. He was Crestmont Hill's only visitor. So probably Laura was right. The place was not often frequented. He liked that.

He started the timer on his watch and began his hike up

the hill. It took him eighteen minutes to reach the top and another fifteen minutes to descend it.

Assuming Lisa was in as good shape as he, that would give him a minimum of thirty-three minutes alone at the bottom of the cliff before Lisa returned to her car. That was plenty of time to get underneath Lisa's car and sever the brake fluid tube.

A flood of relief flowed through Thomas' veins as he stepped into his car. He had found a foolproof plan, and for the first time since this ordeal began, he felt confident. As he carefully maneuvered each sharp curve down the steep, narrow road, he whistled. Lisa would never see a single penny of his hard-earned money.

Now, the only detail pending was getting Lisa to go to Crestmont Hill Park. That shouldn't prove to be a problem.

As soon as he arrived home, Thomas headed for his private study, reached into the bottom of his drawer, and retrieved the two letters he had taken from Lisa's duplex. He re-read them.

He knew his father had sent Lisa those letters. The stationary matched the type the company used for very special occasions. Every once in a while it became necessary for Johnson Enterprises to send an anonymous letter to another company or an employee. In those rare times, plain white paper or the Untraceable Stationary—as they called it—was used. Now, once again, the demand for the stationary arose.

Thomas nodded with approval. His father had been very wise sending those letters as though he were "Mom." Everyone would be looking for a woman, and no one would be expecting a man.

Carefully imitating the tone of the two letters he held in his hands, Thomas began composing another letter.

Chapter 34

Lisa peeped out the window. The bright blue sky promised yet another beautiful day. Surely, this would be the day she'd been waiting for. She closed the curtain and went to check on Tracy. She found her sitting on the floor, crossed legged, fitting different hats, eyes, and noses on Mr. Potato Head. She giggled with each new creation, and Lisa smiled at her daughter's reactions.

The one that brought the most giggles from Tracy consisted of Mr. Potato wearing a blue hat in the place where his nose went. Lisa shook her head at Tracy's simple joy. Looking at Mr. Potato's blue hat reminded Lisa of the mailman.

She wondered if he had already come. Just as she stepped outside to check, she saw him pull up to the mailbox. She ran out to meet him. He nodded a greeting and handed her two pieces of mail.

"Thanks," Lisa said, glancing at them, wanting with all her heart to see the letter she so desperately expected, yet afraid to look and be disappointed again. She glanced at the envelope. The one on the top had a label addressed to Occupant. Lisa tore it in half and examined the second one. A tingling of excitement spread through her body as she ran back inside. Immediately, she ripped the letter open and read it:

My Dearest Lisa:

I've arranged a meeting for us. It might be a little inconvenient for you, seeing how far away our meeting place is from where you live. But I feel we need to meet there because I'll be safe from any roving eyes. (I'll explain what I mean when you get there.)

There's this place called Crestmont Hill. Park the car at the foot of the hill (you'll see a small parking lot). Then follow the fairly easy footpath up the hill. You'll see three benches. I'll be on the middle one.

Lisa, one more thing. As much as I want to meet your family this would not be a good time. Please come alone. I'll wait for you on Wednesday at 9:30 in the morning. Please be prompt.

Love,

Mother

P. S. I'm enclosing a map. Remember to come alone. I'm counting the minutes until our meeting.

Lisa held the letter close to her chest. Wednesday. Two more days. She glanced out the window and saw David. He had just finished washing the car and was rolling up the hose. She ran outside.

He smiled when he saw her. "What have you got there?" he asked when she waived the letter in front of him.

"Wonderful news," she answered. "Come, let me tell you all about it."

He wrapped his arms around her as they strolled toward the house.

Chapter 35

When Thomas pulled up into the Circle K parking lot, he saw Tony sitting on the hood of his Chevy truck, sipping a cup of coffee.

"Morning, boss," Tony said once Thomas had parked his car and started to get out.

Thomas nodded in response and asked, "Are you ready?"

"It depends. All I know is that I'm supposed to show up here so here I am. Now what?" He took another sip of his coffee.

"Get in my car." Thomas slid off the hood and got inside his car.

Once Tony was inside the car, he glanced over at Thomas expectedly.

"Do you remember Lisa Littau?" Thomas asked.

"Your father's mistress?"

Thomas smirked. "You could say that. I've arranged for her to go to Crestmont Hill."

"And may I ask, what is the purpose of this meeting?"

"Lisa is expecting to meet someone on top of Crestmont Hill. While she's busy waiting at the top, I'll slip underneath her car and sever the brake fluid tube."

Tony's eyebrows shot up in amazement. "You're playing with fire. What if something goes wrong? Say for example, she notices the puddle underneath her car before she drives off."

"I seriously doubt that. I have a feeling that by the time she's ready to leave, she will be rather upset. I'm counting on that to keep her from noticing anything unusual."

Tony remained quiet while digesting the information. Finally he said, "I'm not all that familiar with Crestmont Hill."

"The road leading down from Crestmont Hill is steep and filled with tight, dangerous curves. At first she won't notice anything wrong. In fact, her brakes will probably be good for two or three more uses. But as she continues to head down the hill, her speed will gradually build up and will continue to do so every time she takes one of those dangerous curves."

"I can see where this is heading." Tony drank the last of his coffee. "She will obviously lose control of the car, and eventually she'll fail to negotiate one of those curves. But what is my role in all of this?"

"I don't want the police to notice the severed brake line. What I'm counting on is an explosion to cover it up. There's a good chance that the car won't explode. If it doesn't, you make sure it does."

"What about witnesses?"

"I've been there several times during the day. Each time I went, I was the only one at the park. I'm hoping it'll be like that today again."

"And if it isn't?"

"We'll be the first ones at the scene of the accident." Thomas reached into the glove compartment and retrieved two badges. He handed one to Tony.

Tony looked down at the realistic looking police badge and put in his wallet.

Thomas did the same and said, "Do you know what I like about people?"

"What's that?"

"They're gullible. We'll show them our badges and tell them that we got everything under control, then ask them to move on. They will, then after they're gone, we'll go check on Lisa."

"And if she's not dead?"

Thomas glanced at Tony and smiled. "The accident will be fatal—one way or the other."

Chapter 36

Lisa started the car and rolled down the window. "I don't know how long I'll be," she said.

David leaned down. "I don't like you going off like this by yourself."

Lisa gave him a kiss. "You worry too much. She'll turn out to be a real neat person. After all, she's my mom." She kissed him again and smiled.

"For your sake, I hope she's one heck of a nice lady."

Lisa kissed Tracy, waved good-bye, and drove off.

Half an hour later, she left the congested traffic behind her and enjoyed the relaxed pace of the countryside. In spite of the anxiety she felt about meeting her biological mother, the scenery captivated her so much, she began to relax. The green hills came alive with beauty. The trees stood powerful and strong. In one quick glance to her right, Lisa tried to absorb as much of the serenity as possible.

She did this even though she was hesitant to take her eyes off the road. She found it challenging to maneuver the car through the tight, sharp curves. She didn't recall San Antonio having such a dangerous road and was not used to driving on one.

Because the hill was so steep, Lisa shifted to second gear. The car struggled to make it up the hill, but coming back down, Lisa knew she would have to ride her brakes.

For the twentieth time, Lisa wondered why her birth mother had chosen such an obscure place to meet. She really did seem to be going out of her way to avoid being detected.

Well, she didn't need to fear anything. The only reason Lisa wanted to meet her was to keep her promise to her adopted mom, and yes, maybe to get in touch with her past. That's all she wanted and nothing more.

Soon that moment would arrive. She concentrated on maneuvering the tight curves and to entertain herself, she hummed Buddy Holly's "Everyday."

When she saw the top of the cliff, anticipation tightened its grip on her stomach. For a fraction of a second, she even considered turning back. But of course, she really couldn't do that. She had endured too much to give up now.

Lisa slowed down as she took yet another curve. She wished that she had told David that it was okay for him and Tracy to come along. Lisa realized that he had wanted to come, had almost been afraid for her. But her biological mother had specifically asked that she not bring anyone, and like a dutiful daughter, she drove up this steep hill alone.

As she rounded the next curve, Lisa could barely make out a car in front of her. If it belonged to her birth mother like she assumed it did, it meant that they would finally meet. Lisa held her breath as she followed the curve. She'd been wrong. The car, a red Porsche, wasn't moving. Its driver had already parked it in front of the footpath. Lisa felt her heart catch in her throat. She had reached the parking lot.

The image of the large, white stucco, Spanish-style house flashed before Lisa's eye. She had been rich when she was a little girl, and her mother was still rich. The Porsche proved that. No wonder she had always dreamt of wealth. A smile broke out on her face, and she found she couldn't contain her excitement.

She parked her car, glanced at herself in the vanity mirror, swallowed hard, and stepped out. She knew her birth mother waited for her on top of the hill, ready to greet her.

Lisa eyed the footpath leading to the top. From where she stood, it seemed to be a fairly easy foot trail to follow.

Slowly, Lisa began her climb.

Although she tried to keep in shape, by the time she

had advanced three-quarters of the way up the hill, she gasped for breath. Often she stopped, glanced up, and hoped to catch a glimpse of her birth mother, looking down at her, smiling, waving. But not once did Lisa catch even a hint that she was up there waiting for her.

What kind of a woman was this? First, she stood her up when they were supposed to meet at the bar. And even if she had been there, how could she just stand around while Lisa was going out of her mind because Tracy– *the woman's own granddaughter*–had disappeared?

And now, she had arranged to meet in this. . .this desolate area and then forced her to climb this ridiculous hill. Lisa had half-a-mind to turn back and forget all of this silliness.

Following the impulse, she turned to look at her car, wondering how far she had already climbed.

That's when, from the corner of her eye, she caught a movement–a shadow–creeping toward her car.

Lisa froze.

* * *

Thomas lay perfectly still under Lisa's car, scolding himself. *Stupid! Stupid. Stupid!* He felt his heart jump to his throat as he stuck his head out far enough to see if Lisa had spotted him.

Damn! She remained perfectly still staring down at him. Cold, clammy fingers of fear tightened around his neck. Immediately, Thomas ducked his head back under. He tried to reason with himself. Surely, she had no way to see him. Then why did she remain so still, and why were her eyes glued to the car?

The worst part came with the knowledge that everything had started so perfectly. From the top of the hill, he had watched Lisa slowly ascend toward him. His biggest concern–whether or not he would find the place deserted–had been eliminated. He hadn't had to turn a single car back.

Anticipating Lisa's arrival, Thomas drove his car to the parking lot and parked directly in front of the path where Lisa would surely think that the Porsche belonged to "Mother."

Then he hid behind a cluster of trees where he knew he'd be safe from Lisa's eyes.

He watched as Lisa studied the Porsche, gave herself the once over in the vanity mirror, and stepped out of her car. Before beginning her ascent, Lisa's eyes followed the footpath all the way up. Thomas knew she was searching for her "mother." He wished he could tell her what a fool she was!

Once she was halfway up the trail, Thomas ventured out of his hiding place and began to creep toward Lisa's car. He kept low, just in case Lisa, for some reason, decided to turn to look back toward her car.

Not that Thomas expected her to. Her mind should be totally focused on reaching the top and meeting "Mother." But there was no use taking chances. He'd keep low so Lisa wouldn't see him.

He had almost reached the car, when in his excitement, he straightened up and continued to run in an upright position. Immediately, he realized his mistake. He dove underneath Lisa's car, but by then it was too late. Lisa had turned and stared straight at him.

Thomas felt the perspiration beads form on the top of his lip. He wanted to wipe them away but knew it would be better not to move.

He watched as Lisa scrutinized the area, focusing her attention on detecting the slightest of movements. Then she turned and glanced at the top of the hill, as though deciding whether she should continue going up or go back down and investigate. She seemed undecided, so she moved a few feet to her right, then to her left trying to get a better view. She shrugged, turned, and continued to climb.

Thomas let out a sigh of relief. He waited a few precious minutes before he decided it was safe to continue. He had wasted too much time already, but at least the hard part was over. Now all he'd have to do was reach for the brake line and sever it.

Moments later, Thomas had accomplished his goal.

Chapter 37

Tracy stared at her father. They sat facing each other, a game of Chutes and Ladder between them. David should have made his move a long time ago, but obviously his thoughts roamed somewhere else.

"Daddy, it's your turn." Tracy's voice was filled with anxiety. "You're not paying attention."

David shook himself as if waking from a bad dream. He wished he had been a bit more persistent in insisting that he'd go with Lisa. "I'm sorry, Pumpkin. My mind is on other things."

"You don't want to play?" Tracy's voice sounded small and disappointed.

"No, Pumpkin, I don't."

Tracy frowned.

Seeing his daughter's disappointment, David quickly added, "But let me tell you what I want to do."

Tracy remained quiet and continued to pout.

"Let's not waste the day. It's beautiful outside, so let's go have a picnic. We can take a ball and chase each other. It'll be lots of fun. How about it?"

As David spoke, Tracy's face brightened, but still she glanced at the game longingly.

"And I tell you what else," David added. "We can leave this game set up, and when we come back, we can finish it."

Tracy's eyes glittered with contentment. "Yeah!"

"And I get to win!" David added with a smile.

"No way!"

"Yes, way!"

She giggled.

David also laughed and ruffled his daughter's hair. "You go make us some sandwiches, and I'll call a car rental company."

"Me? Make sandwiches for us? Real sandwiches? Like the kind you eat? Wow!" She ran out.

David smiled and reviewed his options. He knew Lisa had been blessed with a trusting nature, but he had been cursed with just the opposite.

True, all of Lisa's misfortunes had been attributed to Emily Rogers, and Emily was dead. But for some reason, David didn't seem to trust Lisa's mother. Why had she chosen such an isolated area? He was thankful he had memorized the map and knew exactly where Lisa should be. But he couldn't get there without a car.

He opened the telephone book and searched for the number of the car rental agency. All they had available was a tan, Dodge Colt, and for an additional, small fee, they would deliver the car to him.

He took them up on both offers.

* * *

A big smile filled Lisa's face as she reached the top of the hill. "Hello?" She looked around. She spotted the three benches–the three *empty* benches. Like the leaves of fall, Lisa's smile drifted away.

She walked to the middle bench, flopped down, and shook her head in disgust. Didn't the letter specifically ask her to be on time? So, where was she?

Lisa surveyed the area. Only one foot path led to the top. If her mother was planning to show up, she had to use it, so why wait up here?

She had only descended several feet when she began to feel tired. She had thought coming down would be a lot easier, but already her breathing came at unsteady intervals.

She stopped to rest and once again noticed the Porsche parked next to her car. Who did it belong to anyway? As far as she could tell, she was here alone.

Or was she?

Maybe she had seen someone heading toward her car after all. But who and why? As a new worry set in, she continued to descend, increasing her pace with each downward step.

As soon as she reached the bottom, she stopped. Her car looked all right. There were no broken windows. She walked around it and kicked each tire. None were flat.

If there had been someone, that person would have probably been going toward the Porsche, rather than her car. The Porsche's owner was probably a hiker or maybe someone who had come to get away from the pressures of the city. For all she knew, the Porsche's owner had come to meet a lover.

Satisfied that she had come up with a logical explanation, Lisa sat on the car's hood. She glanced at the Porsche. Better safe than sorry, she thought. She jotted down its license plate number, folded the piece of paper, stuffed it in her purse, and waited.

And waited.

Soon, it became evident that she had been stood up again. With tears stinging her eyes, Lisa opened the car door, got in, started the engine, and drove off.

Chapter 38

As instructed, Tony waited close to the foot of the hill, watching for any approaching cars. Thomas had been right: this place was deserted. He shifted positions, yawned, and stretched.

The reflection of the sunlight caught his eye. He sat straight up in the cab of his full size pick-up. A car was coming his way, up toward Crestmont Hill Park. He squinted as he focused his attention on the curves below him.

At that moment, a tan Dodge Colt took a curve and became fully visible for a few seconds. Tony could see it was definitely heading his way, and it seemed to be in a terrible hurry.

Tony was about to reach for the cellular phone when it began to ring. "Hello?"

"Hey, Tony," said Thomas. "I–"

"There's a car coming," Tony interrupted, "and it's in a hell of a hurry."

"Can you see who it is?" Thomas' tone grew very serious.

"It's probably some teenage lovers looking for a quiet place to park." Tony said. "But the car–it's too far away for me to check"

"Think of something. You've got to delay their arrival. The car's already on its way down the hill, and we don't want these fools to be there when Lisa loses control. Think you can handle that?"

"Yeah, I'll manage. How long do you think I've got?"

"I'd say by the seventh curve, she'll be in trouble. That's

what, three, four minutes from now?"

"That soon?" Tony caught a glimpse of the approaching car.   "I don't think anything will happen until at least the twentieth curve."

"How about putting your money where your mouth is."

"How about fifty?"

"You're on and I'm off."

Tony hung up, started the engine, and positioned his truck in such a way that it blocked the entire road. He rolled out his spare tire, removed the valve stem, let the air out, and scattered his tools around the tire. He sat on the pavement, facing his truck, and waited for the Dodge Colt to arrive.

Chapter 39

"Shit!" David said under his breath so that Tracy wouldn't hear him. He spotted the truck blocking the road and immediately slammed on his brakes. Luckily, he was able to slow down in plenty of time.

David rolled down his window and stuck his head out. "Hey buddy! Do you mind moving your vehicle? I need to get through."

"Sorry about that," the man said without turning to look at him. He took his time standing up. "I was turning around when I blew a tire." He dusted himself off. "Good thing it didn't happen in the main highway, huh?" He walked toward David's car. "I'm pretty much finished now. I just have to gather my stuff up. I'll be out of the way in no time at all." He looked at David and his eyes flickered. "That's a mighty pretty girl you got there. Is she your daughter?"

"Yes, she is. Now if you don't mind, I'm in a hurry."

The man tapped David's car. "Sure. No problem. I'll just gather my stuff and get going." He turned to look down the road. "I can't imagine though why anyone would be in a hurry to get up there. It's just a park. It ain't gonna go away."

David glared at him.

The man threw his arms up in the air. "Suit yourself, but let me give you a piece of advice. Relax. Slow down. You're going to die from a heart attack or stress. The day is still young." He smiled. "Okay, now that I've had my say, I'll go get my tools and get out of here. You have a good day now, you hear?" He turned, slowly picked up his tools, and arranged them neatly in the toolbox.

He picked up the toolbox and since he had neglected to close it, all the tools tumbled to the ground. He looked up at David, flashed him an embarrassed smile, gathered the tools, arranged them, and locked the box. "I remembered to close it this time," he said. He set the toolbox on the back of the pickup, neatly covered it with a cloth he had, and strolled toward driver's side. "I'm out of here," he said. He started the engine and killed it. He stuck his head out the window. "It does that sometimes, you know. I just got to let it sit here for a minute or two. Then it'll start right up."

David tapped the steering wheel as he waited for the man to move his truck. Under normal circumstances, he would have found this character amusing. Today, he found him annoying.

As soon as the man cleared enough space for him to go through, David maneuvered his car around him and sped off.

* * *

Tony had barely made the first curve before he reached for the cellular phone and dialed Thomas's number.

"The car is coming through," Tony said once Thomas had answered the phone, "and it gets worse. That was her husband and her kid. There's no way we can do this without getting caught. Whatever happens to Lisa in that accident, happens. Best thing we can hope for is that it kills her, and the car is damaged enough where no one will know about that brake line."

"Damn it!" Thomas said and slammed the phone down.

Chapter 40

The more Lisa thought about it, the angrier she became. As far as she was concerned, that woman could go to hell. After all, she didn't need her. Everything that she could possibly want she had. She was blessed with a beautiful, healthy daughter. And it even seemed that maybe–just maybe–she and David would patch things up. No, she didn't need her biological mother at all. As far–

The tires squealed as she made a curve. Slow down, Lisa ordered herself. What are you trying to do, kill yourself? She stepped on the brake. The car slowed down and Lisa continued with her brooding.

But not for long. She noticed that even though she braked frequently, she didn't seem to be slowing down. Instead, the car gained speed–not much, only one or two miles an hour at a time. But still, it *was* gaining when it should be dropping in speed.

She stepped on the brake pedal again. She slowed down a bit, but not as much as she hoped to. What was going on?

She pressed her foot down on the brake pedal, but again the car did not respond. The speedometer needle continued to climb, higher and higher. She was now doing forty-five.

Lisa stepped on the brake again. This time harder, pushing with all her strength until she could feel the pedal pressed flat against the floor, but still the car would not slow down. She tried the emergency brake and stole a quick glance at the speedometer. She was doing forty-eight.

She swallowed hard and felt the panic wash over her like a tidal wave tightening her chest, making her head spin. She fought her fear and considered her alternatives. She could jump out, but she was going much too fast. Chances were that she probably would die in the attempt.

A morbid fear forced her to steal another glance at the speedometer. It had climbed past fifty.

Please, God, don't let me die.

Another curve lay ahead. She didn't know if she could make it. She felt her hands gripping the steering wheel so tightly that they began to ache. Her mouth felt as though it had been stuffed with cotton.

She reached the curve, but she over reacted and steered too far to the right. She tried to correct her mistake, but it only resulted in the car fishtailing.

Instinctively, she steered in the direction of the skid. For a fraction of a second, she felt relief. The back wheels straightened out. But she was far from being safe. The car continued to race down the hill. The speedometer climbed to sixty.

Desperately, Lisa searched her mind. Were there any extra-sharp curves that were particularly dangerous? For those, she could drive as close to the mountain as possible, even if it meant driving on the wrong side of the road. She'd honk her horn constantly, trying to warn drivers who might be heading her way.

Despair engulfed Lisa as she recognized the irony behind her situation. Just a little while ago, this same hill vibrated with beauty. Now it harbored death.

Or did it?

Was it possible to drive up the hill? On her way up, she hadn't remembered seeing any dirt roads, but the trees did seem to be spread out. At least there, she'd have a chance.

She forced her eyes off the road long enough to glance at the trees. There was an opening wide enough to allow her car to pass through. But she had no idea what the area was like further out.

Still that was better than the alternatives. She turned the wheel sharply to the left and drove into the grove of trees. Lisa held her breath as her car skidded, but she slowly let her breath out when she felt the front tires grasp the gravel.

As Lisa fought for control of the wheel, her eyes darted, desperately searching for the best path to take. The trees were much closer together than she had first thought. Everywhere she looked the trees surrounded her. Their branches, through the open car window, slashed her face, her arms.

Desperately, she turned right, only to be blocked by a large tree. Sharply, she turned the wheel to the left, but this wasn't much better.

At least I'm slowing down, she thought. She swung the wheel to her left again. Then, her worst fear materialized. She was surrounded by trees with no path wide enough to allow passage.

She tried to put the car in reverse, but the giant tree in front of her loomed up and Lisa knew with all certainty that she was going to crash.

God, please help me. She closed her eyes and bit her lip. Seconds later, she felt the impact and her body exploded in pain.

Thankfully, the pain subsided as the warmth of blackness closed in on her.

* * *

Thomas cursed under his breath as he watched Lisa's car enter the grove of tress. He had to give her credit. She was a smart lady.

But not smart enough. A sense of satisfaction filled him when he saw Lisa's car crash into the tree. The impact came like a thunderous roar that had to have been heard for miles around.

"You're dead," he said as he drove past the "accident."

* * *

When David saw the red Porsche drive past him, he barely gave it a second look. His thoughts dwelled more on

Lisa than his driving. For the hundredth time, he rethought his excuses for being here. He knew he would feel foolish when he saw Lisa safe and sound talking to a friendly, elderly lady. He would explain that–

Suddenly, he spotted Lisa's car folded into a tree. He slammed on the brakes and felt a sharp pain in his stomach as though he had been stabbed.

"Daddy! What's wrong?" Tracy wailed. She followed her father's eyes and began to cry when she recognized her mother's car. "Mommy! Mommy!" she screamed.

David turned toward Tracy. "It's all right, Pumpkin. I'm going to go check it out. You stay here and don't worry about a thing. Everything is going to be fine."

"Oh, God," he prayed, "please let her be okay." He threw open the car door and ran toward the wreck.

Chapter 41

Detective Bronson leaned back in his plain, metal chair, the bottom of his pen drumming a steady rhythm against his thigh. Across from him was a rectangular wooden table. On the other side, in another metal chair, Albert Henderson–alias Big Al–sat glaring at Bronson.

Bronson had hoped to wrap this up fast. He felt that once he had presented Big Al with all the staggering evidence he had against him, Big Al would realize it would be to his advantage to confess. Using his smoothest, fatherly type voice, Bronson said, "Now tell me again why you broke into Lisa's duplex."

"Man, you must be hard of hearing or something." Big Al crossed his arms. "I'll tell you again what I said. I don't know any dame named Lisa."

"Then why does she know you?"

"How the hell should I know? Maybe this dame is got something against me, you know? Maybe she saw me at a mall and got the hots for me. Maybe she's a lying bitch." He sniffed.

"Is that how you choose your victims? You spot them at a mall?"

Big Al frowned. "Man, you're way off line. I'm going to sue your fucking face."

Bronson stood up and went around the table. He sat on it, facing Al. "You're goin' to need a lawyer, all right, but not for a law suit. This time, Big Al, you went way over your head."

He leaned closer. "This time we can prove that you were hired to rape Lisa."

For a second, Big Al's eyes widened before clouding again with that non-committal look he'd been wearing since Bronson began talking to him. But that fearful look lasted long enough to tell Bronson that his suspicions were right.

"Look, Mr. Hot Shot Detective, you better start showing me this proof you've got, 'cuz I don't believe you have anything. Besides, I already told you, I have a room full of witnesses who are willing to testify that on the day I supposedly attacked this chick, I was with them."

"How long has it been since you've talked to these witnesses? Because if you haven't talked to them within the last two hours, you're in for a big shock." Inwardly, Bronson scolded himself. He should have said one hour. He needed to learn to bluff a little bit better. He was, after all, Mr. Hot Shot Detective.

Big Al's eyebrows furrowed, but otherwise he showed no emotion.

Bronson continued, "If you had taken the time to talk to them, you'd find out that they've changed their minds about lying for you. In short, Mr. Henderson, you've been set up. And you and I know you're the little man in this case. But you're goin' to fall very fast. Very hard."

Big Al shifted uncomfortably in his chair and swallowed hard.

Bronson eyed him speculatively. "Are you ready to talk?"

"You're lying," Big Al hissed.

Bronson shrugged and stood up. "Suit yourself," he said and walked out.

"Wait!"

Bronson stopped.

"What happens now?"

"Now we lock you in the slammer and throw away the key."

"You're bull shitting me."

"If you say so." Bronson reached for the doorknob. Damn! The fool hadn't swallowed his bait. He opened the door. "Jim, take him," he said.

The two guards by the interrogation room looked at each other then at Bronson. He signaled them to remain where they were and not say anything.

Behind him, Bronson heard Big Al stir. Good, let him squirm, he thought. Then he added loud enough for Big Al to hear, "Yeah, I'm through. No deals. Throw the book at him."

"That son-of-a-bitch," Big Al said.

Bronson closed the door and returned to the chair he had previously occupied. "You say something?"

Big Al frowned, crossed his arms in front of him, and leaned back on his chair. "I didn't say nothing."

"I'm glad you didn't say anything because now you're going to be off the streets for a very long time." He closed his spiral notebook and clicked his pen closed. "Do you know what happens to rapists in prison?"

"Don't know. Don't care. I'm not going to no prison."

"That's where you're wrong. That guy who hired you—he set it up so you'd get all the blame. Do you really think a person of his caliber would want to get involved with something like this?" Bronson returned his notebook and pen to his shirt pocket. "See ya, sucker." He headed for the door.

"Wait."

Bronson stopped but did not turn around.

"Let's talk."

Bronson turned. "I'm meeting my wife for lunch. You've got less than five minutes."

"Let's say I was hired, and let's say that same guy was supposed to provide me with an alibi, but he was lying to me. What happens then?"

"Then you go to jail, and he got what he wanted."

"And if I don't want to go to jail?"

"Then you talk."

"Is that a guarantee?"

"No guarantees here, but I do promise the judge will

know you cooperated. He'll be more lenient. That's a guarantee."

"You'll talk to the judge personally?"

Bronson nodded.

Big Al seemed to consider this for a moment, then he said, "What do you want to know?"

"How were you contacted?" Bronson chose his words carefully. He wanted a name, and he knew Big Al would never give it to him straight out, but hopefully it would slip out during the interrogation.

"I usually get this call at the bar, or Joe–that's the bartender–gives me a message. I'm to wait there at such and such time on such and such day. Then the driver arrives and takes me to Mr. Johnson's limousine. That's where we do all our business."

Bingo! Bronson thought, and as casually as possible, he said, "Just for the record, that is James Johnson, right?"

"Is there another?"

"And you're willing to testify against him?"

"If it gets me out." He wiped his nose with his open hand.

"I'll do what I can." Bronson left the room, nodded at the two policemen waiting outside the interrogation room, and returned to his desk.

He looked up Johnson Enterprises in the phone book and dialed the number. He asked to be connected to Mr. Johnson's office. His secretary informed him that he wasn't in.

"I have some very important information which he told me to get to him as soon as possible. How do you suggest I contact him?"

"You can give me the information, and I'll give it to Mr. Johnson as soon as he comes in."

"No, that won't work. There are several technical items I have to explain, and I know he'll have lots of questions. I need to talk to him directly."

"Mr. Johnson's son is here. Maybe he could help."

"I rather deal with Mr. Johnson himself."

A small pause followed, and Bronson knew that the secretary felt uncomfortable. She sounded like the type of person who always did her job efficiently, and depended on Mr. Johnson's constant presence to keep things organized. But things had changed. Lately, Mr. Johnson hadn't been present.   How long had this been going on? Since Lisa arrived in Dallas, Bronson would bet on that.

"If you give me your name and phone number," the secretary finally said, "I'll have him return your call as soon as possible."

"And when will that be?"

"I'm. . . not sure. He left about twenty minutes ago. He didn't say where he was going or what time he'd be back."

"Isn't that rather unusual?"

"Yes, of course, it is. Mr. Johnson has quite a bit on his mind lately, and I'm sure he meant to tell me. He just forgot."

Bronson thanked her and hung up. He searched and found Johnson's home phone number. There was no answer there. Next, he tried Lisa's phone. It rang ten times before Bronson cradled the phone. He was batting zero.

He'd try again in half-an-hour. Johnson was bound to return to his office sooner or later. Why not? He had no idea he was a wanted man.

While Bronson waited, he took out his notepad and re-read all of the notes he had taken dealing with this case. He skimmed most of the pages, and he stopped when he found the note he had been looking for. The note read:

> Tracy L., James J. = same smile
> Coincidence?
> Features somewhat alike.

Bronson had no idea why he had written that, other than it seemed to be important at the time. Well, maybe it was important.

It was time to do some research.

Twenty minutes later, Bronson had all the information

he needed. He knew that James Johnson had lied. He had never had a granddaughter, but at one time he did have a daughter, who, if she had survived the drowning tragedy, would be Lisa's age.

Interesting.

He picked up the phone to call James when the phone rang. "Bronson," he said.

"It's me, David. How are you?"

"Tired," Bronson answered. He rubbed his temples. He hadn't realized how tired he felt. "And you?"

There was a pause.

"David, what's wrong?"

"It's Lisa. She's in the hospital."

Chapter 42

Bronson was still on his way to the hospital when James Johnson arrived at his office. His secretary handed him a stack of messages, letters, and memos. He mumbled a thank you and slammed the door behind him.

He glanced through the pile and separated those he thought needed immediate attention. He picked up the letter on the top and read it. He had almost finished it when he realized he had no idea what it said.

He peeled off his glasses and massaged the bridge of his nose, then put his glasses back on. He picked up the same letter and read it again–for the third time. It seemed that the branch in–where? James scanned the paragraphs. Oh yes, London. The London branch was proposing to–to. . .to what?

His intercom buzzed, and James slammed the papers down. He pushed down the button. "Yes?" He was surprised at the harshness in his voice.

"I'm sorry to disturb you, sir," Stacey said. Her tense voice sounded strained. "But there's a man here who wishes to see you. He says it's very important."

"Who is it?"

"He says his name is Dwayne Wright."

"Never heard of him."

"He's been working for our security department for the past eighteen years."

James frowned. "Tell him I'm a very busy man, but that I can spare him five minutes at the most."

A few minutes later, James's office door opened and a

tall, slim, elderly man nervously stood by the door, as if afraid to move.

James pointed to the plush leather seat by his desk. "Sit down, Dwayne, and tell me what's on your mind."

"First I want to thank you for seeing me." Dwayne smacked his lips.

James plastered on a fake smile.

"I. . .I want you to know, uh, that my wife—her name is Susie—she's very sick. I. . .I got lots of hospital bills. Big ones." He smacked his lips again and shifted uncomfortably in the chair.

"Are you trying to ask for a raise? Is that what all of this is about?" James stood up. "I'm sorry. I'm the wrong man to see, but I will direct you to—"

"No! This has nothing to do with asking for a raise. It's about. . .about your son, Thomas."

James sat back down. "Go on."

"Please don't ask me how I know this. I. . .I just know." Dwayne smacked his lips again. "It seems that Thomas, uh, Mr. Johnson—Junior, that is—hired a man I work with. Please believe me. I. . .I don't want to get him in trouble or anything, but, uh, it seems like Tony Sheri—uh, this man was hired to...to kill your, uh, mistress."

James leaned over. "What?"

"Yeah. Uh, Lisa—I think that's her name." He smacked his lips, cleared his throat, and looked away. "If. . .if this information is, uh, good for you, I was wondering, maybe I, uh—maybe like a reward. M-my wife—she's awfully sick."

"Dwayne, I'm very sorry to hear about your wife. But what you've just said doesn't make any sense. Believe me, I don't even know anyone named Lisa. But you have been with us for eighteen years. Right?"

Dwayne's eyes glistened, and he nodded.

"You've given our company a lot of your precious years. It's time we pay you back. I will have the company pick up the amount of your wife's care which is not covered by insurance."

Dwayne sat unmoving, as though in a stupor. He

cleared his throat and said, "Mr. Johnson, thank you. If there's ever anything I can do for you or the company—"

"As a matter of fact there is. There are two things you can do." James raised a finger. "One, I don't know—or care—where you got this information, but I don't want it to go further than this room. Even though it is one-hundred per cent false, it could hurt the company, and that, I will not tolerate under any circumstances." James momentarily paused to let his words carry their full impact. He raised another finger. "Two, I want to hear the rest of the story."

"There's not much more, sir. Just that this security guy and your son botched—uh, excuse the word, sir—the attempted murder. He supposedly tried to drive her off a hill or something like that. From what I hear, your lady's in the hospital."

"If she really were my lady, do you think I'd be sitting here?"

"No, of course not, sir. I should have known better. You—and your son—have always been good people."

James leaned back, smiled an acknowledgment, buzzed Stacey, and told her to come in. As soon as she had done so, he said, "I told Mr. Wright that the company will cut him a check for his wife's illness after proper documentation of his out of pocket expanses has been submitted. You make sure all the paper work is properly done and that this man gets reimbursed."

"Yes, sir." Stacy turned and left.

James directed his attention to Dwayne with a look that said, That is all. You are dismissed.

Dwayne took the hint. He bolted out of his chair like a soldier at attention. "Thank you, Mr. Johnson. You have no idea what this means to me."

They shook hands and Dwayne left.

* * *

"We have a traitor among us." James intertwined his fingers behind his head and rested its weight against his hands. This, he hoped, made him look as if the subject bore no importance, but it was something, nevertheless, that needed immediate attention. James looked straight at the two men who sat ramrod straight, facing his desk. Their hands neatly rested on their laps. "Do you know who I'm talking about?"

Both of the men exchanged quick looks without moving their heads. "No, sir, we don't," said George, the smaller of the two men who nevertheless stood six feet one inch and topped the scales at two hundred forty-one pounds. His partner, Eric, was three inches taller and sixteen pounds heavier than George.

"His name is Tony Sheridan, and he works for our security department," James said.

Eric reached for his pocket spiral notebook and his pen.

"Don't!" James snapped and Eric froze. "I don't want any of this recorded in any manner, shape, or form. Is that understood?"

"Yes, sir." They answered in unison.

"I want him followed. I want to know whom he meets with and what they say. I want to know everything. If he blows his nose at a minute past two in the morning, I want that reported too. Questions?"

"When and where do we make our reports?" George asked.

"Daily. Carry the cellular. I will call." James opened the drawer, tossed George a phone, and stood up, signifying the meeting was over. Both George and Eric also stood up. "One more thing," James said as he led them out of his office. "There's no need to say what will happen if any word of this leaks out."

For the second time George and Eric exchanged looks. "No need to worry about that, sir," George said.

Chapter 43

As soon as George and Eric closed the door behind them, James let his relaxed expression disappear. He felt tense and his rock-like stomach churned. His breathing came at irregular intervals.

He loosened his shirt and tie and tried to let his mind relax. It didn't work. His mind was a jumble of incomplete thoughts and emotions.

Thomas knew about Bobbye. Did Thomas also know about his secret life? If so, would he keep quiet or expose him? Had Thomas become a threat to his security? Worry ate away at James' gut.

James was a top executive, capable of making crucial decisions at the snap of a finger. Why then was he hesitating? He knew the answer, of course. There were too many factors involved. What he needed to do was treat this like any other business deal. Break it down into its components. Deal with each factor separately.

The first factor, of course, was Bobbye. He had toyed with her long enough. He had inflicted physical and mental pain. He had raised her hopes and let them crash. She had suffered just as he had planned.

Revenge tasted sweet, but time had become a precious commodity. He could no longer afford the luxury of tasting her pain. Bobbye had to die.

He reached for the intercom button and told Stacey to come in. "I'm leaving for a couple of days," he told her once she stood in front of him.

"Where are you going?"

James shrugged. "Out someplace. I'm not even sure myself. I'm taking my airplane and whatever hits my fancy at the time, I'll do. It may be a beach, or a mountain somewhere. It could even be Mexico or Canada or Rome. I just want to get away for a few days."

"How can I reach you?"

"You can't, but I can reach you. I'll call in periodically."

Stacey frowned. It was obvious she wasn't pleased with this idea. She cleared her throat and said, "But what if–"

James cut her off. "I don't want to hear it. I've devoted my life to this company. I deserve a well-earned vacation. If any emergencies arise while I'm gone, let Thomas handle them."

"When will you leave, sir?" Her voice sounded strained.

"Right now. Just as soon as I make some calls and clear the most pressing of items off the top of my desk."

She stared at him with judging eyes.

"That is all," he said. Stacey turned to leave. "Oh, one more thing," James said. She stopped and turned around. "Hold all incoming calls. As of now, I'm not available."

"Yes, sir." She stormed off.

James waited until she had closed the door behind her. Then he reached for the Rolodex, found the number he was looking for, and dialed it.

Chapter 44

David headed for the hospital's waiting room located on the first floor. He immediately spotted Tracy. She sat quietly on the couch, her head hanging down, her hands folded across her lap. Several children played all around her, but she ignored them.

As David headed toward her, she bolted out of her sitting position, concern written all over her face.

"She's fine, Pumpkin."

Tracy let out a long sigh and hugged her father. "Can I see her?" she asked.

He scooped her up in his arms. "No, sweetheart, they don't allow little children in. I already explained that."

"But you said she was fine. Why isn't she here instead of up there?"

"The doctors want to keep her overnight–just to make sure. She's banged and bruised, but she was very lucky. She'll be sore for a couple of days, and she has a minor concussion."

"A what?" She bit her lip.

"Nothing to worry about, Pumpkin. She banged her head–that's what a concussion is. The doctor will check her tomorrow, and he'll probably let her come home."

Tracy rested her head on David's shoulder. "I was so scared, Daddy."

"So was I." He held her tightly, then set her down. "Hey, are you hungry?"

She shook her head. "Maybe later."

"Sounds good to me. Why don't we work up an appetite

and go play some baseball?"

"Baseball? Girls don't play baseball."

"They most certainly do, and it's time you started."

"But I don't have a bat and ball."

"We'll stop by the store first."

Tracy gave a small jump. "I think baseball will be fun."

David smiled, grabbed her hand, and stepped outside. Just as they did, Bronson arrived. "Uncle Harry!" Tracy ran to greet him.

Bronson hugged her and shook David's hand. "How is she?" he asked as they walked back inside.

David pointed to the waiting room. "Tracy, why don't you go in there while I talk to Uncle Harry?"

Tracy nodded and bounced toward the waiting area. This time she didn't sit on the couch but joined the other children on the floor.

David turned his attention to Bronson. "She's fine, thank God. She's bruised, but that's about the worst of it. She's upstairs, resting. They got her hooked up to an I.V.–to give her strength. I think that's what the doctor said. You know how it is when something like this happens. The doctor gives you a whole bunch of information all at one time and you're too scared or relieved—or whatever–to pay close attention. Well, that's me. All I got was that she was fine. I'll talk to him again tonight, after I take care of Tracy."

"She can stay with us, if you want."

"Thanks, but I think that'll scare her. She'll think there's something really wrong with Lisa."

"What happened, David?"

"She went to meet her mother–"

"Her mother?"

"Yeah, didn't she tell you? She's received three letters from her mother. The last one requested that they meet at Crestmont Hill Park, except that Lisa somehow lost control of the car. She hit a tree head on."

"Was this on the way to the meeting or on the way back?"

"It had to have been on the way back."

"Did she say so?"

"No, but I can assume that from the position of the car. Why? What is it you're not telling me?"

"What did she say about her mother?"

David felt his muscles tighten. Sometimes Bronson was so exasperating. "Lisa's drifting in and out of consciousness. We haven't talked about the meeting." He paused, making sure Bronson didn't ignore his questions this time. "Why? What's going on?"

"Lisa's biological mother is dead."

A blade of ice entered David's heart. "Whaaat?"

"Lisa's biological mother died when Lisa was only three years old."

"Then who sent Lisa those letters?"

"My question precisely." Bronson glanced through the notes he had scribbled in his spiral notebook. "What I want to know is why do you suppose Lisa thought this woman was her mother?"

"Her mother—or supposedly her mother—sent Lisa a picture of her as a baby. The picture is identical to Tracy's baby pictures. Same features. Even the same expression. There was no doubt in our minds. That picture is of Lisa as a baby. But if her mother didn't sent it, then who did?"

"If you give me the picture and the letters, we might get lucky and get a print. If not, we can have the letter and picture analyzed."

"Funny thing. Lisa misplaced the picture and the letters. Strange, huh?" David paused, contemplating the coincidence. "How did you find out that Lisa's biological mother died?"

"Because I've located her father."

David held his breath in anticipation. "Oh?"

"It's James Johnson."

"Dammit! I knew it! I told her not to trust him. What kind of game is he playing with her?"

"I'm not sure, but I'm sure as hell going to find out. As soon as I visit Lisa, I'm picking him up."

"Do me a favor."

"Name it."

"Don't tell Lisa anything right now. Please wait until tomorrow when she's feeling stronger."

"I understand. When is she going to be released?"

"Tomorrow, I hope."

"Tomorrow when she gets home, I'll come over and tell her. It'll be good if you're there to help."

"You can count on me," David answered.

"Good, I knew I could," Bronson said. "In the meantime, I have already ordered police protection. No one other than you, doctors, and nurses will be allowed to enter her room."

A wave of despair smothered David. He groaned aloud and grabbed his forehead. "Do you think she's in danger?"

Bronson threw his arms up in the air. "As the saying goes, better safe then sorry."

* * *

Bronson's visit with Lisa lasted more than an hour. He, along with his wife, Carol, made small talk. Bronson forced himself not to press for any details. Tomorrow would be soon enough. All the time as they talked about the weather, hospital food, or Tracy, Bronson's mind wandered back to James Johnson.

Feeling like a caged animal, Bronson could no longer stand the chitchat. He hit his forehead with his opened hand and said, "Gosh, look at the time. I really wanted to question a suspect. I gotta go. You understand."

Lisa nodded. "Thanks for coming."

Bronson turned to his wife. "I'm leaving, Baby. What about you?"

"I think I'll stay for a little bit longer."

"Good," Bronson said. "I hate to leave Lisa here all by herself." He kissed Carol, squeezed Lisa's hand, and walked out.

Outside the door, he stopped to talk to the guard. "Remember, only me or my wife, David, her husband, doctors, and nurses can come in. Is that clear?"

The young policeman nodded. "I got it."

"You bet you got it, because if you don't, you'll get it." Bronson hated to leave Lisa, but she did have police protection even if the force had sent possibly the greenest recruit. Besides, Bronson would be picking up James. Yeah, Lisa should be all right.

With that, Bronson stormed off and drove as fast as possible toward Johnson Enterprises. It was almost closing time, and he didn't want to take the chance on missing James.

Ten minutes later, Bronson was inside James' office. His secretary was a pleasant looking woman in her mid-fifties who looked like she was set in her ways.

"May I help you?" she asked.

"I'm here to see Mr. Johnson."

"He left town for a couple of days. Perhaps I can direct you to—"

"Where did he go?"

Stacey glared at him and Bronson flashed his badge. Curiosity sparkled in her eyes. Her orderly world had been disturbed.

"Now will you tell me where he went?"

Still she hesitated.

"You can make this easy on yourself or hard. You can tell me, or I can drag you to the police headquarters."

The newly acquired creases around her mouth deepened. "He wouldn't tell me. He said a beach somewhere or a mountain or Mexico or Rome. He's flying his own plane. He said he'd call."

"How long ago did he take off?"

She looked down at her watch. "Two, maybe three hours ago."

"If you hear from him, you will let me know immediately, won't you?" He set down his business card. "Also, I'd appreciate it if you didn't mention this to anyone, including Mr. Johnson."

He walked out, not bothering to wait for an answer.

As he drove toward the airport, Bronson reasoned that

if James Johnson had flown his own plane, his flight plan would show when he left and in which direction he headed. Bronson estimated that it would take him twenty minutes to reach the airport. Using his cellular, he called the airport and told them to detain James Johnson without arousing his suspicion.

"I'm sorry, Detective, but Mr. Johnson is already airborne," the lady at the airport informed him.

Chapter 45

A gnawing sensation ate at James' gut. It'd been ages since he'd been to the cabin, and he knew why. There were too many memories. That young woman–what had been her name?–rotting under the pool, and that phone call–that terrifying call informing him that his wife, his precious Kathy...

Her last words to him–"Why do you hate your daughter so much?"–still haunted him and echoed in his mind.

Why had he chosen to come to this place? It was filled with nothing but yesterday's ghosts. He should have gone someplace where he could rest for a couple of hours before returning to Dallas to finish Bobbye off. Instead, he had come to the cabin. This had been a horrible mistake.

It was best if he left now. He'd fly back, not to Dallas, but to one of the small communities around there, rent a car, and drive into Dallas. But before leaving, he'd run down to the store and charge something–anything. That would establish his alibi. At the time of Bobbye's death, he could prove he was nowhere near Dallas.

Being very thorough and careful had kept him out of prison all of these years. He wasn't about to get sloppy.

* * *

James chose to spend the night in the rented car. That meant no motel bills and one less way to trace him. He showed a fake driver's license and a credit card with the same name, which matched the bogus driver's license.

He drove until past one in the morning, stopping only when he spotted the perfect gasoline station. Its bathroom faced away from the main street, and that's what he wanted. Chances were that no one would see him enter the bathroom.

The only one to worry about possibly identifying him would be the cashier. James glanced his way, but the elderly man had his face buried in a magazine, and he was constantly nodding off. James felt safe. He knew no one would notice him as he slipped into the men's room.

Fifteen minutes later he was dressed in doctor's scrubs and sported a bushy mustache and glasses. His normally gray-peppered hair was solid black, thanks to the magic of the perfect wig. He studied himself in the mirror. Not bad. He looked at least ten years younger. To add to his perfect disguise, he walked with a limp.

Glancing around, seeing the area still deserted, he got in the car and drove off. Four blocks away from the hospital, he realized that with all of the preparations and gathering of information, he'd neglected to attend to the smallest of details. He knew which hospital Lisa was staying in, but he didn't know the room number.

He found a convenience store and hurried to the pay phone. He found the number to the hospital and carefully dialed. "Hello," he said to the receptionist. "I've just arrived in town and was told that Lisa Littau is one of your patients. Could you please give me her room number?"

"Just a minute. I'll check," said the voice over the phone. From the sweetness in her voice, James assumed that it had to belong to a grandmother. "Ah, here it is. She's in room two-o-six."

"Thank you," James said. "How's she doing?"

"Are you immediate family?"

The question stumped him. "I'm her father." The sentence, once spoken, made him realize that he *was* her father. He was someone who was supposed to protect her. Just like he had promised Kathy.

"I'll connect you to the second floor," said the grandmotherly voice.

Before James could answer, the phone on the second floor began to ring.

James hung up.

Chapter 46

The hospital loomed like a giant monster before James. He knew that when he set foot on the hospital floor, his life would be changed forever. He'd be leaving a peaceful life behind only to be replaced by the screaming silence of anxiety. For a second, he hesitated, then swallowed hard and headed for the building.

As he hurried down the corridor, James reached into his pocket and felt the syringe he had carefully filled with potassium chloride. He would enter Bobbye's room, inject the lethal solution into her I.V. tube, and leave. The whole matter would take only a few seconds. Bobbye would be in cardiac arrest by the time he got back to his car.

He looked around. The halls were deserted. He could breathe easier. He threw his shoulders back, raised his head, and stormed down the hall, daring anyone to stop and question him. Not that anyone would. He was, after all, dressed like a doctor.

While he waited for the elevator door to open, a nurse walked past him. She looked him straight in the eye and said, "Hello, Doctor."

James nodded a hello and stepped inside. To his relief, the elevator was empty and the second floor was as quiet as death. When he noticed the policeman in front of Bobbye's door, he faltered, then quickly realized his mistake. He nodded at the policeman and went into the room across from Bobbye.

He found an elderly man sleeping. James waited what

he considered to be three minutes before stepping out. Then he strolled towards Bobbye's room.

"Rather late to be making rounds," the policeman said.

"Not for me. This is my normal time. I hate working the graveyard shift."

"Tell me about it," the rookie said and continued to work on the crossword puzzle.

James let out a silent sigh of relief, opened the door, stepped in, and closed the door behind him. The room wasn't as dark as he wished. The Venetian blinds remained open and the moon's light filtered in, casting strange shadows in the room.

Maybe one of these shadows is Kathy, he thought. She's here to beg me not to hurt her daughter, *my* daughter.

"You promised," a voice inside his head said. "You said she'd be safe with you." He took a step toward Bobbye's bed, and Kathy's voice surrounded him like an icy ointment smearing itself all over his skin. James felt sweat burst out of every pore in his body.

He had loved Kathy so much, still did. He'd do anything for her.

Including sparing Bobbye's life?

His hand tightened around the syringe. Time and space lost meaning. He felt disoriented.

He studied the figure on the bed. It was Kathy, his precious Kathy. He turned away from the bed and took several deep breaths.

Kathy was dead. This was Bobbye. He looked down at his right hand, the one that clutched the deadly syringe. Using his left hand, he reached for the tube.

Bobbye's eyes fluttered just as Kathy's had done right before she died. Suddenly James felt himself being transported to another time. *Oh, Kathy, please don't die. Don't leave me. I'll change. I'll promise I'll change. I'll do anything, just please, don't leave me.*

Don't leave me.

Not again. I can't go through that again.

Again?

What was he thinking?

Bobbye's eyes popped open. They stared into each other's souls for one long minute.

"Da–daddy?" Bobbye whispered.

Then, as if Kathy were standing right there, he heard the words: "Why do you hate your daughter so much?"

Kathy's eyes glistened with tears.

James dropped the syringe.

He turned, walked away, and tried not to run down the hospital's corridors. He knew that would attract unwanted attention, but it was so hard to walk at a normal pace, to pretend everything was all right.

The thought of losing Kathy was tearing him apart. He wanted to hold her, tell her how he would never–could never–love another.

As she held on to that last string of life, she would tell him that she too adored him. Nothing–not even death–would ever separate them. She'd close her eyes and think of his love. That love would grasp the strings and weave them into a strong cord of life.

Kathy, then, would never leave him.

James reached the elevator door and pressed the button. Its doors opened and James stepped in. He was leaving now. Nothing he could do would bring his Kathy back.

In the end he hadn't been able to save Kathy. Instead of focusing on their love, she'd been thinking about how he hated Bobbye. Kathy's last thoughts weren't with him as they should have been. Instead, she was concentrating on...on...their daughter. That's why Kathy had died.

His hatred for Bobbye had killed her.

He had killed her.

James reached the car, opened the door, and got in. He put the key in the ignition hole but didn't start the engine.

Hate had killed Kathy.

His hate.

James closed his eyes, and the image of his sister

flaunting her golden hair flashed before him. He had killed her once. How many more times did he have to kill her? Why couldn't she stay dead? Why did she have to come back as Bobbye?

He had known that was what had happened the first minute he saw Bobbye. There it was, the same blond hair. Michelle's curse and now Bobbye's curse as well as his own curse. He had to do something about it. He knew he had to kill Bobbye before the curse spread, but he also knew Kathy would never allow that. So he killed other blond-headed women, hoping each time it would relieve his anger. His hatred.

The hatred that had killed his Kathy.

James folded his arms over the steering wheel, laid his head over them, and for the first time since Kathy's death, James Johnson cried.

He knew he could never kill Bobbye.

That much he owed Kathy.

Chapter 47

Lisa sat rigidly in bed, trembling as she remembered the dream. It had seemed so real. She had stared at a stranger and in his eyes, she had found her father.

But where there should have been love, there was only hate. Where there should have been kindness, there was only evil. A chill covered her body.

She looked up at the clock beside the television set. It was a few minutes past nine. David was late. He said he'd be here by nine.

Five minutes later he walked in, a big smile on his face. "Good morning," he said. He bent down and gave her a kiss on the lips. "Sorry I'm late, but I've been downstairs checking you out. We're all set. We can bust out of here."

Like magic, the dream vanished when she saw David. "Great!" She stood up and gasped. Every muscle in her body ached. "I'm really anxious to leave this place and twice as anxious to see Tracy."

"Well, she's anxious to see you too. She's downstairs waiting. And speaking of waiting, I can't wait until I get you home. I missed you." He leaned over and kissed her again. "By the way, did I tell you that Tracy has a new hobby?"

"What kind of hobby?'

"Baseball. In fact, the bat and ball are still in the car."

"What are you trying to do? Turn our little girl into a tomboy?"

"She already is."

Lisa smiled, then got serious. "I've been thinking, Dave."

"Oh, oh." David sat on the edge of the bed. "I don't

think I'm going to like this, but go ahead anyway."

"The accident–going down that hill–all I could think of was you and Tracy. I need to know. When this is over, what's going to happen to us?"

"Jeez, Lisa, you want to talk about that now? Here in the hospital?"

Lisa nodded. "I need to know."

"All right. Fair enough." He stood up. "Let's lay all the cards out on the table. Let's assume you find your biological father, and let's say that he's filthy rich. And let's say that he wants to make up for lost time. What will you do?"

She eyed him speculatively. His question didn't make much sense. "What do you expect me to do?"

"Will you accept his money?"

"Well, yeah, I guess. It depends." Lisa folded her arms, then remembered reading somewhere that people who did that were being defensive. She quickly unfolded them. "Let me just make something perfectly clear. I didn't come to get their money. I came to find my roots."

"But your mother told you that your biological father is filthy rich. Assuming that she was right, wouldn't that bother you any?"

"No, it wouldn't, and it shouldn't bother you either. David, what is it with you and this money hang up you have?'

"I don't have a hang up. I'm afraid that if you have access to a lot of money, you won't be satisfied with just a car salesman."

"You don't have much faith in me, do you?'

David frowned. "Lisa, don't twist around what I say. You always do that."

The spidery webs of anger gathered in the corners of Lisa's mind. Why did he always have to accuse her of things? "I'm not twisting anything."

"Oh yes you are. Why can't you admit it?" David's harsh tone vibrated through the room.

"Me? Admit it? This isn't about me. It isn't even about me twisting things around. It's about money."

"It's always about money." David raked his hair with his fingers.

"Not just money, but what you think money will do."

"It has always divided us." He looked up at Lisa, and she saw sorrow walk across his face and stomp out the lights in his eyes.

She reached for his arm, but he yanked it away from her and moved away. "Let me finish. Your biological family has lots of money. You're going to be rich, and I will still be just a car salesman."

"We could change that."

A distant, sleep-like look came to his face. He sighed, shook himself, and came back to focus. "I don't want to change that. I'm happy as a salesman, but you will always be just a bit ashamed that I am not something better."

"Maybe at one time I did dream of money. But that was before I went searching for my birth parents. I tried to explain to you that it was all part of memories. It's not so much that I wanted money, it's that I remember having money."

"And when all that money comes your way, then what?"

"I. . .don't. . .know. There might not be any money. My memories may be all wrong."

David's glance rested on Lisa. "You'll have your money. I have no right to take that away from you. Nor from Tracy. Both of you will live a life surrounded by wealth. But, Lisa, I can't be part of that life. That's just not me. We've had this discussion many, many times and it ended in divorce. Let's leave it that way before we hurt each other again."

Each word David spoke was an ice knife that ripped out her insides. She'd been thrown into a bottomless pit with no hope of escape. This time it was over. She'd never have David again. The black emptiness swallowed her.

There was nothing she could do but waddle out of the room. She wished she had the strength to storm out, but waddle was the best she could do.

David said, "Lisa."

She stopped and turned. "You're right. This ended in

the courtroom, and I was a fool for thinking we had a second chance." She turned to leave but an orderly pushing a wheelchair blocked the doorway.

"This is for you," he told Lisa.

"No, thank you. I'm perfectly fine."

"Sorry, hospital rules." The orderly shrugged.

Lisa nodded and sat down in the wheelchair.

* * *

On their way home, Tracy suggested going to McDonald's to celebrate Mommy's safe return. Immediately, David answered, "Maybe you and I will go later. Right now we're going home."

Perhaps sensing that something was wrong, Tracy sank all the way back into her seat and remained quiet for the rest of the ride.

Up front, Lisa felt a bolt of pain travel through her body. She shifted positions and hit her ankle on something. She reached down and felt the baseball bat. She opened her mouth to ask about the game, but David's face was firmly set, his jaw slightly protruded. Lisa closed her mouth and stared out the window.

David turned onto the street where the duplex was and Lisa noticed Bronson's white, broken-down '70 Ford parked in front of her driveway.

Chapter 48

"Now, Lisa, ma'am," Bronson said as he sat on the sofa and balanced his hot cup of coffee on his lap. "What I have to tell you is only a theory, and I don't like talkin' about theories. But I'm going to make an exception here because I think you could help me out, okay?"

"I understand," Lisa said as she played with the pleats in her skirt. She had the feeling she wasn't going to like what she was about to hear. "Go on."

"We picked up Albert Henderson–alias Big Al."

Lisa glanced out the living room window, toward the backyard. David and Tracy were playing catch. She wished she could run outside and bring David in.

Lisa sighed and turned her attention to Bronson. "Did he confess?"

"That's why I'm here." Bronson took a large sip of coffee. "May I?" he asked as he reached for the television tray and set it next to the couch. He set his cup down. "I have some rather unpleasant news for you."

Outside, Tracy squealed and David began to chase her.

"I'd like David to hear this too," Bronson said.

"I don't know if Donna told you or not, but David and I are divorced. He's here only because of Tracy." She listened to her voice. It sounded stiff and formal.

"Then you must excuse me for sayin' this, ma'am, but you're blind. It's very obvious that he's here for you too." He reached for his coffee and drank some more. "And excuse me for stickin' my nose where it don't belong."

"Don't worry about it." Again, Lisa sneaked a look outside. Her eyes briefly settled on David, and her heart filled with pain. "What bad news do you have?"

"Did I say it was bad news?" Bronson massaged his forehead as though attempting to figure out how to word what he had to say.

Lisa thought, no, you ding-a-ling, you said unpleasant. She bit her tongue to keep from sounding rude. She didn't want to take out her anger and frustrations on Bronson.

The ringing of the phone disrupted Lisa's thoughts. She frowned. She should let it ring, but what if it was her biological mother? She glanced at Bronson, then at the phone.

"I won't go away," Bronson said. "Go ahead, answer it."

Lisa nodded, excused herself, and stood up. Her muscles protested the sudden movement.

"Is this Lisa Littau?" asked the female voice over the phone.

"Yes." Behind her, Bronson stood up, went to the kitchen, and poured himself another cup of coffee.

"Lisa, this is Lucy at the Whitanger Real Estate Agency."

"Hi! I've been planning to call you. Have you had any luck finding the house?"

"I think so. I've located a white house with the fountain outside. I hope it's the right one."

Lisa felt a rush of adrenaline flow through her body. "That's wonderful news. When can I see this house?" Lisa watched Bronson return to the living room, stirring his coffee.

"Today would be fine with me. Could you possibly bring your boss and his wife over, and I'll drive the three of you to see the house?"

"I don't think that'll be a very good idea." Lisa turned around, giving Bronson her back. She lowered her voice and spoke directly into the phone. "His wife is very temperamental, and if it's not the right one, she'll fire you and find someone else to handle it. I suggest that you give me the address, and I'll check it out."

There was a small hesitation before Lucy gave Lisa the

address. Lisa wrote down the number, stuffed the paper in her skirt pocket, thanked Lucy for a job well done, and cradled the phone. She turned to Bronson. "Sales people–they never leave you alone."

Bronson smiled. "No, I suppose not."

Lisa returned to the recliner and slowly lowered herself into it. Her sore muscles screamed out and she winced. "You were about to tell me the unpleasant news," she said once she got comfortable—or at least as comfortable as possible.

"Yeah, I was, wasn't I?" He reached for his coffee cup and took a sip. "I believe I might have found out who your biological father is."

"What!" The word burst out of her like a bomb in a cavernous room. This wasn't what she expected to hear. This wasn't unpleasant news at all. . .unless. . . "Is he in jail or something?"

"No, quite the contrary. In fact, he's one of our most respected citizens. Not just here in Dallas, but in the entire United States. And you've met him."

Lisa shrunk back into the recliner, as though Bronson had punched her in the face. With stunned shock, she remembered her dream.

The eyes!

The face was wrong, but the eyes belonged to someone else. Someone she knew.

"James Johnson," Lisa whispered.

"Yep, that's who I think it is," Bronson said.

Startled, Lisa hadn't realized that she had spoken the name aloud. "What makes you think he's my father?"

Bronson reached into his shirt pocket and pulled out his small, spiral notebook, flipped a few pages, and cleared his throat. "Ah, here it is." Bronson pointed to the notes. "Lisa, you said that when you first met Mr. Johnson, he looked very familiar."

"But that's because he's famous." Even though she stared at the floor, she felt Bronson's eyes scrutinizing her.

"Really, Lisa? Do you really think that's why you

recognized him?"

Slowly, Lisa shook her head and sighed. "Deep down, I guess I have always carried my father's image. I recognized him, not because he's famous, but because he is my father."

"Then why didn't you say somethin'?"

Lisa looked past Bronson's head toward Tracy's picture resting on top of the television set. She crossed her arms and rubbed them as though she were cold. "I guess that I intentionally blocked out that information. I hadn't even realized I had done that until now."

"Why would you block it?"

Because of the eyes. This, she kept to herself. When she spoke, her voice was barely above a whisper. "He hated me. Even though I was a little girl, I could tell he hated me." Tears stung her eyes. "I was always so careful when I was around him. I tried not to make any noise or do anything which would draw attention to me." The memories came rushing back, accompanied with the fury of suppressed anger and–

Fear.

Lisa began to shake. "Sometimes he would look at me in that eerie way and...and it frightened me."

"What do you mean, eerie way?"

Lisa shook her head, stood up, and began to pace. "It was like–like if he wanted to hurt me or something."

"Lisa, did he ever–"

"No! Never." She stopped her pacing and massaged her forehead. "But still I was so afraid of him. It was like living with the boogie man." She hung her head low. "He was my father, and he hated me. I was so afraid of him, and all I wanted was for him to love me. That's all I ever asked of him–his love. Why did he come back to see me and pretend not to know me?"

"I was hopin' you'd be able to tell me that."

Lisa searched her mind, trying to come up with a logical conclusion. She found none. She shook herself and sat down. "Why is that so important?"

Bronson reached for his cup and drank the last of the

coffee. "Excellent coffee. I don't suppose you have any more?" Bronson stood up. "Why don't we finish this conversation in the kitchen where we can be next to the coffee pot?"

As they moved from the living room to the kitchen, Lisa asked, "Are you trying to avoid my question?"

"You are most perceptive." Bronson touched his forehead as though saluting Lisa. "But, Ms. Lisa, ma'am, I'm not avoidin' it, merely postponin' it. Are you one-hundred-percent sure that James Johnson is your father?"

She thought for a moment before answering. "Yes." She poured some coffee into Bronson's cup. "Now let me ask you: what makes you think he's my father?"

"It's all circumstantial evidence." Once again Bronson retrieved his notebook. "First, current data: James Johnson is now married to Elizabeth Bridges Johnson who is currently away in Europe. They have one son, Thomas Lee Johnson who is the sole heir to Johnson Enterprises."

"And?" Lisa handed him his cup.

"And," Bronson continued as he reached for the sugar bowl and poured two spoonfuls of sugar into his cup. "This is not his first marriage."

Lisa was about to open the refrigerator door, but her hand stopped in mid-air. "Then this Elizabeth you mentioned, she's not–she's not my–my–"

"Mother?" Bronson finished for her.

Lisa nodded.

"Probably not. Assuming James Johnson is your father, then we can assume that your mother was a woman named Kathy Bierce Johnson."

Lisa glanced toward the desk in the living room. Its top drawer had once contained the letters she thought her birth mother had written. If she was dead, she obviously hadn't written them. Then who did? And where were those letters now? She felt a tremble deep inside her. "Was?"

"She was killed in a car accident, and a couple of weeks later, James and Kathy's four-year-old daughter, Bobbye, drowned in a swimming pool accident."

Lisa covered her eyes with her hand. "I had a twin." Her words were a whisper in the wind.

"No, Lisa, I don't think you did."

"I don't understand." Lisa's mouth felt as dry as cotton.

"I believe that you are Bobbye," Bronson explained.

"Wait." She handed him the milk. "You just finished saying that Bobbye drowned."

"I did," Bronson said, pouring a bit of milk into his coffee. "But I have reason to believe that Bobbye never died as a result of that accident."

"Then who died? Who did they bury?"

Bronson pulled up a barstool and sat by the kitchen counter. He stirred his coffee. "I have a feeling that if we were to open Bobbye's grave. . ."

Lisa held her breath.

". . .it'd be empty." Bronson sipped his coffee, then continued, "Bobbye's and your birthday fall on the same day, and had Bobbye lived, she would be the exact age that you are now."

Lisa frowned. "Detective Bronson, there's—"

"Uncle Harry," Bronson corrected.

"Uncle Harry, it's possible for more than one person to be born on the same day."

"True, but not in this case. There's no matching birth records." A heavy silence hung in the room like a dense fog. Finally, Bronson said, "I'm sorry to lay this on you. But there's more."

Lisa looked up.

"James Johnson hired Big Al to rape you."

"Oh God." A vast feeling of emptiness hit the pit of Lisa's stomach. She longed for David to hold her, comfort her. She almost ran to him. Only sheer determination forced her to remain in the kitchen.

"I need your help, Lisa."

Startled, Lisa looked up at Bronson. "My help? How? Why?"

"I need you to help me solve this case. James Johnson tried to scare you off when he could have just as easily ignored you. Do you have any idea why he'd do this?"

Her father's eyes flashed before her. He gazed at her through direct, cold, and hard eyes. The narrow eyes smoldered, and the brows remained level. The look of open hostility clutched at Lisa's heart.

Lisa took a step backwards as she fought for control. She swallowed hard and shook her head. "I–I don't know." She let the air out through her mouth as she looked upwards. She needed time to think, to sort things out.

"Lisa. . ." Bronson began. After a brief pause, he added, "What is it?"

But Lisa didn't hear him. She had been catapulted back in time. Again, her father's eyes flashed before her. But this time, they were wide open and focused on her. Bobbye had no choice but to shuffle toward her father.

He reached down and buried his hands in her hair. It tickled and Bobbye giggled. James squatted so that he was now eye level with Bobbye.

But his eyes did not look at her face. They were focused on her hair. "It's beautiful. Blond. Soft." He smelled it and rubbed his face with her hair. "Oh, Michelle. Michelle."

"I'm Bobbye. My name is Bobbye."

"I know. I know." He continued to stroke her hair, but where once he was gentle, now his movements were rough and jerky.

"Father, you're pulling my hair. It hurts."

When he answered, his voice sounded rough and dry. "You need to be hurt. You need to be punished. Your blond hair is your curse and my curse. I must rid you of it."

The door opened and Mommy stepped in. "What's going on in here?"

Bobbye ran to the safety of her mother's arms. Even as she comforted her, Bobbye could hear her father's voice, "You must be punished."

Punished.

* * *

Lisa found herself plastered against the kitchen corner, her hands over her mouth. Her heart beat so fast, she was sure it was going to pop out.

"Lisa, what's wrong?"

She shook her head.

"Lisa, speak to me."

Her eyes drank in every detail in the kitchen. Her kitchen. She wasn't a little girl anymore. She had nothing to fear.

"Lisa, your mind was miles away. What were you thinkin'?" Bronson wore a concerned look.

"I. . .I'm not sure. I need to get away and think. Remember." Lisa walked out of the kitchen. "I'm sorry. I just can't help you now. I've got to go."

"Where?"

"Oh, don't worry. I'm just going in there." She pointed toward the hallway. "I need time alone."

Bronson followed her. "Lisa, I also need to know about your so-called mother and those letters she supposedly sent you."

"I'm sorry. Not now," she said. "I've got to get my head on straight. Give me fifteen, twenty minutes. Then I'll be back out, and we'll talk."

Bronson nodded. "I'll wait outside with David and Tracy." He pointed to the couch. "Sit down, relax. Do you want me to get you a cup of coffee?"

Lisa flashed him a weak smile. "Thanks, but no. When I have a major problem, I lie down, close my eyes, and think. Please make yourself at home. I know there's a lot we need to talk about, but I just can't right now. You understand, don't you?"

Bronson nodded and gave her the thumbs up signal.

She felt his eyes follow her as she went into the bedroom. She gently closed the door behind her. But instead of going to bed like she had said she was, she leaned her ear against the closed door.

She waited until she heard the back door open. Then she grabbed her purse, opened it, and fished for the car keys. Her body ached when she raised the window, but she ignored the pain. She wasn't going to let it interfere with what she had to do.

She climbed out the window.

Chapter 49

The intercom in Thomas Johnson's office buzzed. Immediately Thomas answered it. "Yes, Liz?"

"Your ten-thirty appointment is here."

"Send him in." Thomas stood up and walked around his desk. The door to his office opened and Tony stepped inside.

Thomas arched his eyebrows in surprise. As long as he'd known Tony, he had never known him to wear a suit. Yet, today he was sporting a three piece beige outfit which made him look more like an executive than a security guard. Even the dark brown attaché case he carried gave him the appearance of a V.I.P.

"You got it?"

Tony nodded. He set his briefcase on top of Thomas's desk, worked on the combination lock, and opened it. He reached underneath some blank papers, pulled out a handgun, and handed it to Thomas.

"Is it clean?" Thomas stroked the gun, deriving some satisfaction from its cool, metallic feel.

"No one will be able to trace it to you." Tony sat down in the leather chair that faced Thomas' desk. "It cost plenty though. It–"

"That doesn't matter." Thomas interrupted him. "What matters is that I have an untraceable gun in my possession."

Tony nodded and shifted position. He might look like an executive, Thomas thought, but he certainly doesn't act like one. Thomas returned the gun to the bottom of the briefcase and slammed it shut. "How much do I owe you?"

"My standard fee, plus the cost of the piece."

"Which is?"

"One thousand." Tony cleared his throat and again wiggled around in the chair. "May I ask what you plan to do with that?"

Thomas glared at him. "I don't see how that's any of your business."

"True, but if you just bear with me, sir, I'd like to have my say."

Maybe it was the suit. Maybe it was because Thomas needed Tony's silence. Maybe it was because he knew he would be hiring Tony again sometime down the road. Regardless of the reason, Thomas granted him permission to air his thoughts.

"If you plan to use that on Lisa, I would advise you to take care. There'll be a nasty investigation that will probably lead directly to you. I suggest that you make it look like a burglary that went bad. If you're not sure how to do it, let me handle it in my own way."

"When?"

"The first available opportunity, surely not more than two, three days from now."

"Give me your thoughts on the burglary."

"I'd wait until she's home alone. Then walk in on her, shoot her. Mess up the place a bit, take a few things. Make it look like an attempted burglary where the burglar got surprised and in panic, shot the owner. I could even leave some hints of drugs behind so that the police could go searching for a junkie." He looked up expectantly at Thomas.

Thomas rubbed his chin. Several seconds elapsed before he spoke. "Maybe that would work."

"Good! In that case, I need the gun back." Tony leaned forward, his eyes wide with anticipation.

At last, he resembled the Tony that Thomas knew.

"Get yourself one. I'm keeping this one just in case."

For a long second, Tony studied Thomas. "Just don't do anything stupid."

* * *

Thomas sat at his desk, staring at the requisitions and contracts he had to either approve or disapprove. His eyes drifted toward the briefcase. He shook himself and turned his attention back to the paperwork. He stared at the words, but his mind wouldn't register their meanings. He slammed the papers down and opened the briefcase. The gun was a toy that demanded its share of attention–a toy that wasn't quite complete.

Bullets–that's what made the gun come alive. Thomas pressed his intercom button. "Liz, what is today's agenda?"

"At eleven o'clock you have an appointment with Senator–"

"Never mind, Liz. Cancel all of my appointments."

"These are important meetings, sir. What do I tell them?"

"Tell them I had to leave on urgent business."

"When will you be back, sir?"

Thomas spoke as he put his sports jacket on. "Probably not until tomorrow."

"Where can I reach you?"

"I'm going to stop at a store, and after that I'll be home, but they don't need to know that."

As Thomas walked out of his office, Tony's words reverberated in his mind: "Just don't do anything stupid." He wasn't planning to, but he was ready to do whatever was necessary to protect his interests.

Chapter 50

James decided that life should return to normal. With that goal in mind, he flew his plane back to the Dallas airport, had Joe pick him up, and drive him to work.

Stacey was surprised to see him back so soon. She glanced anxiously at Detective Bronson's business card resting by the phone, then quickly back up at her employer. "Mr. Johnson, it's good to, uh, see you. I, uh, wasn't–"

"Vacation is going to have to wait. There's work that needs to be done. Bring me my mail." He stepped inside his office and saw a stack of letters waiting for his signature.

His intercom buzzed. "Yes," he said, pressing the button down.

"Eric and George are here to see you, sir. They don't have an appointment."

"Send them in and come pick up the letters." He finished signing them. The door opened and Stacey, followed by George and Eric, stepped in. James handed Stacey the letters. He waited until she walked out and closed the door behind her before he turned his attention to Eric and George. "Give me your report." He signaled for them to sit down.

Eric cleared his throat while George glanced down, refusing to meet James' eye. Eric nudged George. "All right," George grumbled at Eric, then turned his attention to James. "This thing has taken a strange twist, and I want to remind you, Mr. Johnson, sir, that you did hire us to report on all of Tony Sheridan's activities."

"I'm aware of that."

"Tony met with Hank Sanders."

Obviously, George expected James to know who Hank Sanders was. He didn't, but instead of asking the obvious question—so who the hell is he?—James waited for him to continue with his narrative.

Eric, the larger of the two mountainous men, realizing that James was not familiar with the name, explained, "Hank Sanders is a shady character, a jack of all trades, you could say." He leaned forward, and James thought that the only reason Eric was larger than George was to accommodate all that extra common sense he seemed to possess.

"Among other things," Eric continued, "Hank is infamous for dealing with guns."

"That's right," George picked up the conversation. "If anybody wants a gun—you know the kind, the one the police can't trace—you simply go to Hank Sanders." He seemed a lot less nervous and more animated, like a toy that had been wound too far. "Anyway, Tony goes to see this guy Hank Sanders, and he buys a gun from him."

"If Hank Sanders deals with all types of merchandise, what makes you think he was there for a gun?" James asked.

"Hank is not known for his loyalty," George answered. "For a hundred bucks he would sell his mother."

"And for another hundred he gave us the exact conversation between him and Tony."

"And that was?"

"Supposedly, Tony could not decide whether to buy a twenty-five-caliber automatic or a thirty-eight. He finally chose the twenty-five because it is a much faster gun—or something like that. The way Hank said it was like this: 'Tell your client that he can put five rounds in some dude's head while a guy with a .38 is just barely putting one in his gut.'"

"Afterwards," Eric broke in, "Tony went to see your son. When he went into his office, he was carrying a briefcase in which we're sure he was carrying the gun. When Tony walked out of the office, he no longer carried the briefcase."

James thanked them for their report and escorted them out. Afterwards, he stared at the telephone in his office as though any minute now it would grow fangs and attack him. "Oh hell," he said aloud and reached for the phone. His hand rested on the phone's handle and without picking it up, he spoke to it, "Lisa, there's a mad man out there who plans to kill you. Be careful, he just purchased an untraceable gun."

James shook his head, "Lisa, I've spent all my life hating you. And now isn't this ironic? I'm calling to warn–" He let his voice trail off.

He cleared his throat. "Lisa, this is your father. My son wants you dead."

James stared at his hand resting on the phone. It recoiled. "What the hell am I doing?" Again, he reached for his console, but this time he pressed his intercom button. "Stacey, get me my son."

There was a slight pause. "Your son? Oh, you mean Thomas Johnson. Yes, of course, sir. It's just that I never heard you call him *son*. It sounded rather stran– I'm sorry, sir. I'll get him right away."

James drummed his fingers on his desk while he waited for what seemed to be an eternity. Even though he expected his intercom to buzz, he jumped when it did. Immediately he answered it, "Thomas?"

"No, sir, it's me, Stacey. Mr. Johnson's secretary said that he's gone home."

James looked at his watch. "Now? At 11:00 o'clock? Was he feeling ill?"

"No, sir, he just said that he needed to tend to some unfinished business and that afterwards, he could probably be reached at home."

He's up to something, James thought and his nerves twisted in a knot. Out loud he said, "I see."

"Would you like for me to get him for you?"

"No, that won't be necessary. I'll be going home myself." A feeling of dread engulfed James as he gathered the papers on top of his desk and stuffed them into his briefcase.

Chapter 51

The all-glass, ultra-modern, multi-level building which housed Johnson Enterprises mesmerized Lisa as it loomed before her. She swallowed hard and stepped in. Its main floor consisted of a large reception area and a series of hallways that led to important looking doors.

Lisa headed for the receptionist, a curvaceous blond who couldn't possibly be more than twenty. The nameplate on her desk read Sandie McGuire.

"Hi Sandie," Lisa said in what she hoped was her sweetest, most business-like voice. "I need to see James Johnson."

Sandie flashed her a should-I-know-you smile and said, "I'm not sure if he's back. Let me contact Mr. Johnson's personal secretary." She picked up the phone and spoke briefly into it. When she hung up, she looked up at Lisa and said, "I was right. He's not back yet, and she doesn't know what time he'll return."

The world sank under Lisa.

"Gee, I'm sorry." Sandie said. "It must have been awfully important."

"It is." Noticing that Sandie had a sympathetic heart, Lisa quickly added, "My boss will be awfully mad at me now. He said to deliver this message today, and like a fool, I waited until the last minute."

"Oh gosh. That is bad." Sandie's face brightened. "Hey! I can deliver it for you tomorrow, and you can tell your boss it was delivered today."

Lisa shook her head. "That won't work. It has to be

personally delivered because it needs an immediate answer."

Sandie frowned.   "You sure it couldn't wait until tomorrow?"

"I'm sure." Lisa glanced at the floor and sighed deeply. "It has to be done today. I just hope I don't lose my job."

Sandie looked around the room and lowered her voice to a near whisper, "Look, don't say I told you this, but just a few minutes ago, Mr. Johnson came down and waited for his limousine to pick him up. I overheard him tell the chauffeur to take him straight home."

"Thanks!" Lisa brightened up. "You wouldn't happen to have his address."

"Honey, I don't even have his phone number."

Lisa reached into her pocket and found the paper where she had scribbled down the address the real estate agent had given her. Maybe. . .

"Do you have a street map?" she asked.

Chapter 52

James sat in the back seat, his mind quickly formulating–and just as quickly rejecting–words and phrases he would use when confronting his son. He leaned forward so that his chauffeur could hear him. "Joe."

Joe, still concentrating on his driving, leaned back, "Yes, sir?"

"I'm not quite ready to get home. I want you to drive around for ten to fifteen minutes, then we'll see."

"Yes, sir." He waited for a few seconds before asking, "Are you having problems?"

James was expecting the question. Anytime he had problems he'd ask Joe to drive around, then they'd discuss them. The only thing different about this problem was that it wasn't work related. He sighed. "I suppose you could say that."

"Anything I can help with?"

There was a long pause. "I'm not sure, Joe. This is a family matter."

"Oh." There was a small pause, then, "That's unusual. If you pardon me, sir, as long as I've been working for you, it's always been business problems. In a way, sir, I'm glad to see you're thinking about the family for a change."

James looked out the window. As long as Joe had been working for him, James had never known anything about his personal life. All he knew was that Joe was a good listener. His eyes drifted toward Joe. "Are you a family man?"

"Yes, sir. I've got one son and one on the way."

"Congratulations, Joe. When is your wife due?"

"In a month, sir. And it's going to be a little girl!" His voice beamed with pride.

A little girl. Would she be blond? James folded his hands on top of his lap and stared at them. "Suppose, Joe, that when you were very young you had fathered a little girl. And suppose she was all grown up and was looking for you. What would you do?"

"My own flesh-and-blood? I'd welcome her with open arms."

"Even if she opened up old wounds?"

"She's still family."

"What about your son? How would you tell him so that his financial security doesn't feel threatened?"

"If I were very rich, sir, like you, I would show him a will where he would get everything he wants, but I would still leave something for my daughter. You know, to kinda make up for lost time. I would sit down with my son and specifically ask him what he wants, and what he suggests his sister should get."

James nodded. "I suppose that if I had a daughter and she showed up, I would do the same." Surely, he could reason with Thomas and make him understand. He had to do this for Bobbye and for all those other blonds he had killed.

He reached up and massaged his forehead. "Drop me off at home, then go back to my office and tell my secretary to give you the J file. Bring it to me immediately."

"Yes, sir." Joe made a turn and began to head toward the Johnson mansion.

James leaned back and pressed the button that would raise the partition between them. He stared out the window. Once he had the file, he and Thomas would reach some agreements. He'd–

The limousine's buzzer interrupted him and his thoughts flew away. "Yes, Joe."

"I'm sorry to disturb you, sir, but I believe that there's a car following us."

James turned around to see if he could recognize anyone. Unable to do so, he asked. "Which one?"

"That small, tan Dodge Colt, sir."

"Slow down," James ordered. The chauffeur did and soon James had a clear view of the driver. He could now make out a shape. It was a woman. Lisa–Bobbye!

Worry, mixed with curiosity, gnawed at his insides. Why was she following him?

"Excuse me, sir," Joe said. "Do you want me to keep on going or do you want me to pull into the driveway?" He slowed down so much that the car was barely rolling.

"Pull in and let me out." His voice sounded old and tired, even to his own ears. "Then go and bring me that file." He stepped out and turned to face Bobbye who by now had pulled in behind him, parked her car, got out, and stood close to his car. Behind Bobbye, James caught a glimpse of Thomas, watching them from the living room window, pulling back when he realized he'd been seen.

Chapter 53

David sat on the edge of the couch, his back arched, his head bowed, his hands tightly clasping each other. He repeatedly shook his head. "I don't know, Detective Bronson–"

"Harry," Detective Bronson corrected him.

"Harry. Well, as I was saying, Lisa is a highly intelligent woman, but sometimes she lets her emotions–instead of her brain–rule her. She'll probably want to go see James Johnson, and it scares the hell out of me. What do you think we–what do you plan to do?"

"Let's talk to her. It's been about fifteen minutes. Can you go get her?"

David nodded and went inside.

He knocked on the bedroom door. He waited, but she didn't answer. He knocked louder. "Lisa?" He looked at Bronson, shrugged, and opened the door. A minute later he was back, his eyes wide-open. "She's gone. The window's open."

Bronson dashed to the front window and saw the car was gone. He hit his forehead with his open palm. "Stupid! The oldest trick in the world, and I fell for it. Stupid, stupid, stupid!" He hit his forehead again and headed out the door, his car keys in his hand.

"What should I do?" David asked.

"Stay here, in case Lisa comes back. If she does, don't let her out of your sight. I'm going to go look for her. I'll call you and keep you informed." He climbed inside his car, gunned the engine and drove off.

Twenty minutes later–record time, even for Bronson–he

was facing James Johnson's secretary. She looked up at him, eyebrows arched, eyes popped open. "You sure got here in a hurry," Stacey said.

"What do you mean?"

"I just called your office no more than five minutes ago."

"Mr. Johnson is here," Bronson said.

"No, he's left again, but he was here for just a few minutes. He was going home, he said."

Bronson ran out of the office.

As he walked briskly toward his car, he noticed an elderly lady clutching her purse. She was on the opposite side of the street, moving away from Bronson. He should warn her not to hold the purse so tightly. It was a sure advertisement that she had just cashed her social security check or had withdrawn some money from her savings account.

As though wanting to contradict Bronson's thoughts, she tucked the purse in tighter against her flower-patterned dress and wrapped both of her thin arms around the brown purse. She looked suspiciously around her, bent her head, and continued at a pace which was probably quite fast for her, but in essence was really rather slow.

Oh hell, Bronson thought, I don't have time for this. Then instinct told him to look down the block, and Bronson spotted him.

Probably a druggie. Wild, unharvested brown hair. A glazed, crazy look in his eyes. Lips slowly moving, anticipating the moment he'd be able to taste his next fix. And suddenly he was running toward the elderly lady.

Bronson dashed across the street, and all he heard was the shrill screech of slamming brakes. Panic arose as he eyed the driver, who by now had lowered his window and was verbally throwing Bronson some obscenities. Bronson chose to ignore him and instead continued pushing his way toward the punk.

Chapter 54

The water fountain was still there, but somehow it didn't seem as huge and impressive as it had been when Lisa was a little girl. And the six-foot juniper hedge separating the mansion from their neighbor's house—had that been there when she was growing up?

Lisa's attention turned to the limousine when its back door opened. James Johnson stepped out and the limousine drove away. Hesitantly, Lisa stepped out of the car, dropped her keys in her purse, and slammed the car door closed. She stared at the man who was possibly her father.

For the first time, Lisa noticed that James Johnson carried himself in such a way that it made him look taller than he actually was. And this is how she remembered him: tall and proud.

Lisa felt her father's eyes scrutinizing her. Under his steady glare, she became a little girl again. She wanted to run to him and throw her arms around him. Her mind repeated the words she used to say to herself countless of times: "Oh, Daddy. Please love me. Please love me. Please. . ."

The more her mind cried out in anguish, the more she wanted the comfort of his arms, his love.

No! Be realistic, Lisa ordered herself. This is the same man who—even if he is my father hired Albert Henderson to rape me.

To rape me. . .

To rape. . .

Rape. . .

And once again Lisa wanted to run to him—but this time

not for warmth or comfort–but to pound her fists on his chest and shout at him, you're a bastard! Why did you do it? Why? *Why?*

But she didn't move.

Nor did James Johnson.

They stood staring at each other for what seemed to be an eternity. Slowly, like layers being peeled off, James's strength seemed to evaporate, leaving behind an old, weak man. He sighed. "Lisa," he whispered.

Lisa almost ran to him–almost told him she'd forgive him if only he would provide her with some halfway decent explanation. But instead, she willed herself not to move. Her face–she hoped–wore a mask of contempt.

"We need to talk," he said.

Lisa nodded.

"Won't you come in?"

"Then I am–" Lisa couldn't bring herself to finish the sentence. Somehow the words "your daughter" seemed to dry up like silvery dust in her throat. "Who am I?"

James' eyes remained glued on Lisa. After a brief silence he said, "You are Lisa Littau, but at one time you were Bobbye. Bobbye Johnson."

Lisa looked away. So now she knew, but instead of making her feel good, the knowledge made her feel miserable.

"Come inside," he said. "I have to know how much you've remembered." As he moved to head toward the mansion, he spoke, his voice barely above a whisper. "Somehow I've always known this day would come. In a way I'm kind of glad. I have lived my entire life in fear, and I'm tired. I want to let go." He glanced toward Lisa. "Do you know what I'm talking about?"

Lisa remained perfectly still. Her father's voice echoed in her ears, "Your blond hair is your curse, and you need to be punished." How many other blonds had he punished?

Her young father's eyes haunted her.

Lisa gasped and put her hands to her throat, like the heroine of a silent movie.

"Yeah, you know," James said and resumed with the walk. "And Thomas knows the other half. He's been at my desk, I know." He shook his head and a sad, far-away look enveloped him, but it didn't dwell there long. He stood up straight, threw his shoulders back and said, "I just hope that when you learn it all, you can forgive me. I owe you an apology, Bobbye Johnson." Abruptly, he stopped. Something–someone?–behind her captured his interest.

Lisa followed her father's eyes and noticed that a young man perhaps a few years younger than she stood blocking the way. Then he began to walk briskly toward them, his right hand shoved deep into his sport jacket's pocket.

"Thomas–son."

Lisa recognized the controlled note of panic in her father's voice.

Thomas's face appeared startled when he heard his father call him "son." For a second he hesitated, then resumed his pace.

Lisa's eyes met James'. She could literally see her father's confidence seep out of him like water draining through a sieve.

"I have a lot of explaining to do," he said.

Thomas glared at his father for a second, then switched his attention to Lisa. She made a weak attempt to smile, but it dissolved even before it could blossom on her lips.

"Let's talk," James said.

Even though Thomas directed his statement to his father, he continued to stare at Lisa. "It's too late for that, Father." He stressed the word "father," making it sound obscene.

"No, Thomas, it's never too late." He moved methodically and carefully, as though powered by a tense inner spring. As the spring became taut, James seemed to derive some source of inner strength. "Look at me, damn it!"

Thomas's gaze drifted back to his father, but only for a second. Filled with a look of defiance, he purposely looked away from his father and glared at Lisa.

"I know about Tony Sheridan," James said.

"Then you know about this too." Thomas slid his hand out of his pocket, his fist tightly wrapped around the gun. He pointed it at Lisa. "Like I said, it's too late now."

"Put the gun down, son." James used the tone of a father who was scolding his misbehaving child.

Thomas' face tightened and a glassy look veiled over his eyes. "I have never been your son," he said and cocked the gun.

"Thomas, wait!" James thrust his arms out and waived them. He stepped to his left, using his body to shield Lisa.

Fear gripped Lisa, and she stood unmoving.

James, using a powerful voice, continued, "Thomas, I've hurt you. I'm sorry. Give me a chance to make it up." He took a small step toward Thomas.

For several seconds, Thomas seemed to break. James took full advantage and inched forward some more.

"Stay back!" Thomas ordered. He squinted and his lips formed a fine line of determination.

James stopped but did not retreat.

"You can't save her," he said as he took two steps to his left.

"Ah, but you're wrong." He too moved to his left, once again shielding Lisa.

"No!" James screamed and pulled the trigger. The bullet slammed into James' head.

Lisa gasped and went down on her knees. "F...father?"

His eyes flickered. "Bob-bye, I'm. . .so s-sorry. Y-your m-mom loved. . .you s-so much. . . She. . . died. . .w-with y-your name. . .on her lips. Th. . .Thomas f-forgive me, s-son." A veil covered his eyes and he took one last breath.

Lisa's gaze met Thomas'. His eyes were opened as wide as saucers and he hyperventilated. He had lowered the gun, but he still held on to it.

"I didn't think he'd move." His hands shook violently. "I-I didn't see him move. He. . .he wasn't supposed to. . .to move. He wasn't. . .supposed to die."

Slowly, Lisa stood up and inched backwards.

"Don't!" Thomas said trying to recover from the shock of what he'd just done. "I—I've got to think." With his free hand, he tugged at his chin. "Don't you dare move," he snorted. "Don't you even dare breathe." His body went slack as he looked down at the inert body. "Father?"

While Thomas focused on his father, Lisa slid her purse down her arm and psyched herself to muster all the strength she possessed. She threw the purse at Thomas with the determination of an Olympic athlete who had her heart set on winning. Lisa's body, still sore from the accident, screamed in pain. She winced, and heard the voice of victory cheering her. The purse hit Thomas's midriff. Amazingly, he dropped the gun.

"Bitch!" he roared.

Lisa bolted for the safety of her car. She opened the door and hesitated. The car wouldn't protect her from a bullet. She thought about running, then remembered the baseball bat. It was underneath the front seat. It could serve as a weapon, then again, it would also slow her down. Uncertain as to what to do, Lisa glanced at Thomas.

He was staring at his father, not paying attention to her.

Lisa picked up the bat, turned, and ran.

Chapter 55

The gun landed next to James's body as though, even in death, he was protecting the same daughter he had wanted to kill.

But it's not going to work, Thomas thought. I'll kill that bitch, drag her over here, tell the police she killed dear ol' dad, then turned the gun on me. I wrestled her for control of the gun and it went off.

Using the edge of his foot, Thomas kicked the gun away from his father's body. He picked it up and glanced up in time to see Lisa running down the long driveway. He aimed and fired.

* * *

A neighbor.

Surely there was someone out there who could help her. As Lisa ran down the driveway, she realized just how huge each lot really was. It seemed an impossibility that she would reach the neighbor's yard and still be alive. Maybe if she weren't so sore, she could run faster. No matter, she had to try.

She pushed on harder, her breath coming in long, audible gasps. She had almost reached the end of the driveway when she heard the gun go off. She had no idea where the bullet went, but it had been close enough to send adrenaline pumping through her.

The shock of the blast caused her to drop the bat. It fell in front of her. She stumbled and fell. Deadly fear pierced her chest. She tried to get up as quickly as possible, but her right leg throbbed with pain. Somehow, when she fell, she had hurt her leg. Drops of blood oozed out of the badly scratched leg.

Fearing the worst, she stole a quick glance behind her. Thomas was more than half the way down the driveway.

Ignoring her pain, she stood up, using the bat for support, and forced her mind to concentrate on reaching the end of the driveway.

Thomas' voice shrilled behind her, mocking her terror. "That's not going to do you any good," he hissed.

Lisa ignored him.   Somehow she had to find the strength to survive this. She dashed behind the wall of shrubs which separated the two yards.

"There's no one to help you," he said. "My mother went with our neighbors to Europe. That means you'll have to make it clear to the other neighbor's house. That's the Alberts—and they are hardly ever home." She heard him laugh like a man on the verge of madness.

She'd never be able to outrun him. Her strength was failing her, and her muscles felt like warm Jell-O. Her head throbbed, and her vision blurred.

The best she could do was hide and pray he wouldn't find her.

Chapter 56

Lisa stood as perfectly still as possible. She didn't even dare to breathe. From between the branches of the shrub in which she was hiding, she could clearly see Thomas moving directly toward her, as though he knew where she'd hid.

"Oh, yoo-hoo. Where are you?" he teased in a high-pitched voice. He held the gun in a ready-to-use position.

Lisa's stomach tightened into a hard knot. She hadn't left herself any alternatives. If he knew where she was hiding, her chances of survival were next to none. All she could do was pray and remain motionless, listening intently.

He stood so close to her now, that if she reached out, she could touch him. She closed her eyes, willing him to go away.

Above them a jet zoomed by. Somewhere close to them, a car sped away. These sounds were replaced by something else. It was the smallest whisper of a laugh. "I know where you are," it seemed to say.

Lisa wished she could scream as her heart pounded wildly in her chest.

A bug crawled up her leg. Instinctively she shook it off. Too late she realized her mistake. Thomas must have heard her move as he smiled, raised the gun, and cocked it.

Desperately, Lisa looked around. There was no way to go but down. Keeping her eyes on Thomas, she bent down as quietly as possible.

Just as Lisa did so, Thomas fired into the hedge. A lump, the size of a lemon, caught in Lisa's throat. Then, thankfully, Thomas scoped the bushes by slowly moving the gun in a horizontal direction.

Lisa released the air she hadn't realized she'd been holding in her lungs. She watched the barrel sweep past her range. She waited until it was aimed at the furthest point from where she crouched. She knew this was her one and only chance.

She raised the bat and jumped out of her hiding place. Holding the bat with both hands, she swung it like a baseball player aiming for a homerun.

It smashed into Thomas's chest with a loud, hollow thud. His eyes popped to the size of saucers, and he fell backward. The gun went off, but the bullet missed its mark.

Before he had a chance to get up, Lisa kicked him in the groin. Thomas moaned in pain.

With her foot, she pushed the gun away from him and toward her. She knew she should pick it up and shoot him. But even as this thought formed in her mind, she knew she wasn't capable of shooting anyone.

By now, Thomas had gotten up, but was bending forward with pain. His hand clasped his crotch.

"Bitch!" he screamed and lunged toward her.

Lisa swung the bat once more, this time aiming for his head. The loud, crushing sound the bat made when it slammed against Thomas's head caused Lisa to throw the bat as far away as possible. She picked up the gun and bolted down the driveway back toward the Johnson Mansion.

She had almost reached her car when she stared at her hands–her empty hands. What had she done with the gun? She must have dropped it while she was running.

If Thomas was still conscious. . .

She spotted her purse and retrieved it. Jittery fingers opened it. She dumped the purse's contents. Her car keys were nowhere. She scattered the items. There. Under her wallet, she could see the keys.

From behind her, she heard movement.

She forced herself to ignore it, to look for the keys or maybe a weapon. She frantically searched through all of the contents. Nothing, not even a small pocket knife. A pen, then? Was it sharp enough to inflict pain? If she aimed for the eyeball. . .

She felt fingers wrap themselves around her arm.

She screamed.

"Calm down, Lisa, it's only me."

Lisa turned around and relief flowed through her veins. It was Bronson. "Over there," she said, pointing to the other side of the hedge. "James Johnson's son. He accidentally killed his father, and then he tried to kill me. He's got a gun."

Bronson quickly pushed Lisa away, pulled his gun from his shoulder holster, plastered his body against the hedge and slowly stuck his head out far enough to assess the situation. He went around the hedge and for a few seconds, he was out of Lisa's sight.

She held her breath and released it when she saw Bronson coming her way.

He carried two guns, his and Thomas'. He put his away. "You didn't tell me he was knocked out. You do that?"

Lisa nodded.

"We could use someone like you in the police department," Bronson said. "Ever think of joining the force?"

Lisa began to shake and big tears formed in her eyes.

"I guess not," Bronson said.

Chapter 57

At the foot of the elaborate tombstone were two dozen fresh, red roses. The inscription was simple:

Kathy Bierce Johnson
Beloved Wife and Mother

The word *mother* stuck in Lisa's throat.

Lisa looked down at her own bouquet of half-a-dozen carnations and compared them to the roses James had probably brought. She set her flowers down beside the roses. "Hi. . .Mom. My name is Lisa Littau, but you know me as Bobbye Johnson. But I guess you knew that, huh?"

Lisa's eyes swam with tears. "I'm sorry, Mom, I don't remember what you looked like, but when we meet again, I'll recognize you." She paused to compose herself.

"Do you know my mom and dad? You would have liked them. They're wonderful people. They were good to me, and I wanted you to know that. I miss them very much—just like I miss you, Mom. I'm so sorry we didn't have more time together."

Lisa wiped her tears and signaled for Tracy to join her. She and David sat in the car and waited for Lisa while she visited her biological mother's grave.

Lisa bent down and wrapped her arm around Tracy. "This is your other grandma," she said, then turned to the tombstone. "Isn't your grandchild absolutely beautiful?"

"Can she really hear you?" Tracy asked.

"I think so, honey." She smiled. "No, I know so."

"Are my two grandmas up there together?"

"I'd like to think that they are."

"Me, too. Maybe they go to the Park in Heaven together or to the movies. Do they have movies in heaven?"

Lisa smiled and stood up. "I'm sure they have everything you want in heaven." She noticed that David got out of the car. She signaled him to join them.

"James—my father—told me that my mother died with my name on her lips," she told David.

He flashed her a sympathetic smile, and the three of them stood staring at the grave.

* * *

"Would it be all right to ask how much longer you plan to stay here in Dallas? I'd like to know because of Tracy," David told Lisa. He was stuffing the last of his items into his suitcase.

Lisa sat at the edge of the bed and shrugged. "I don't know. It depends. The police want me to hang around for a while–just to answer questions."

"Bronson told me that if you wanted to, you could put in a claim for part of the Johnson Enterprises' millions." He checked the drawer, saw it was empty, and gently closed it. "I think you should go for it. You always wanted to be rich. This is your chance. You made it into the big time. I'm happy for you." He slammed his suitcase shut. "I really am." He carried it out of the bedroom.

"David."

He stopped but did not turn around.

"I'll probably need help–you know, with Tracy. I'll be going to the police station. That's not a good place for her to be. Besides, she'd be bored. Couldn't you possibly stay just a bit longer, for Tracy's sake?"

He turned, set the suitcase down, and seemed to consider the question. His features hardened, as though they had been carved out of a single piece of rock.

"No, Lisa," he said. "I'm not needed here anymore. I have a job back home that I need to get back to. That job is important to me. Tracy will be fine with you, or I can take her back with me, if you prefer."

Lisa hung her head. "You're going back to being a salesman."

"That's what I like doing." He picked up his suitcase and turned around. "Good-bye, Lisa." He walked out.

Lisa glanced at the alarm clock. David's plane wasn't due to take off for another two-and-a-half hours. Surely he could stay at least one more hour. One more minute. But instead she whispered, "Good-bye, David."

She heard him go into Tracy's room. She could hear the low murmuring of voices, but she couldn't make out any words. A few minutes later the door to Tracy's room opened and David stepped out, holding onto her hand.

Tracy walked her father to the door and kissed him good-bye. Softly she sobbed, as she watched her daddy through the window for several minutes. When she finally closed the living room curtains, she walked over to Lisa who was still sitting on the edge of the bed, her hands folded together in her lap.

"Mom?"

Mom, not *Mommy*. Lisa looked up and noticed that Tracy had been crying.

"Why did you let Daddy go?" Tracy's narrow eyes accused her.

* * *

David sat at the DFW Airport Coffee Shop. He really didn't want the coffee, but it gave him something to do while he waited for his plane to start boarding.

He had hoped he and Lisa—

He sighed. Well, it didn't matter now. Lisa had always wanted the better things in life. Now she could have them. As he had told her, he was happy for her.

And angry with her too. God, was he angry! They could have so easily—

David forced himself to take a sip of coffee. It tasted like a cardboard box. He retrieved two dollars from his wallet, set them next to the coffee cup, and walked out. He'd buy a newspaper and read it while he—

David stopped. At the end of the corridor he spotted Tracy and Lisa. As soon as Tracy spotted her father, she ran toward him. He bent down and scooped her in his arms. Holding Tracy, he waited until Lisa came to him.

They stood facing each other, neither uttering a word.

Lisa was the first to give in. "David, before you go, there's something I want you to know."

"I'm listening."

"I understand Mrs. Johnson has been notified. She's flying in tomorrow."

"And?"

"And I feel I need to talk to her. That's the only way I'll be able to understand what happened. Thomas isn't talking."

David's features softened with concern. "Are you going to be all right?"

"I think so, at least for the time being. I don't know how long it will be before Thomas' trial comes up."

"You plan on being here that long?"

"No, I'll go home, but when the trial begins, I'll need to be here. Bronson already told me that. He also said that he expects that once the trial comes, there will be some very dirty laundry aired."

"He's probably right. I tried to warn you about that guy."

Lisa nodded. "As usual, you were right. But still he was my birth father, and he died trying to save me. That's the image of him I'll always carry." She cleared her throat. "But that's not what I came to tell you. Lately, I've been doing a lot of soul searching. I've found that money can't bring happiness. In fact, it can tear families apart–families like ours. Everything I've always needed I had in Dad, Mom, Tracy, and you. It's not money. It's families that bring happiness. I've searched a long time to find where secrets lie, and all the time happiness was right under my nose. I now realize that."

She looked at David and tears glistened in her eyes. "David, I don't want anything to do with Johnson Enterprises. If I am entitled to some part of it, I'll sell my shares. But I don't plan to fight for any of their wealth. If I do get any money, I thought I—we—could set up a trust fund for Tracy, and David, I feel you're the best salesman in the entire world and I'm...proud of you."

Lisa stopped and cleared her throat. "I. . . I came here to find my biological parents, and I did that. I'm satisfied, and now I want to go home. . .and I want to start over. That's if you're willing to take that one last chance with me."

David set Tracy down and sought Lisa's eyes. "I'm afraid I haven't been quite honest with you."

Lisa gasped. "What do you mean?"

"You know my parents are divorced."

Lisa nodded.

"I've never told you—or anyone else—why. My parents were happy once. They loved each other. Then my mother inherited this vast amount of money and everything changed. They fought constantly over how to invest it, how to spend it. It was just one fight after another. Finally, one day my mother walked out. I was seven then, and I've never seen her since."

"Oh, Dave, I'm so sorry. You should have told me. After all these years, why didn't you tell me that's why she left?"

"I don't know, I guess I was ashamed."

"Ashamed?"

"Ashamed, that my mother loved money more than her own son."

Lisa reached out and wrapped her hands around his.

"I've grown to hate money, but I have no right to deny you your inheritance. Go for it. It's yours."

"You apparently weren't listening. It's not the money I want. It's you."

David's eyes sparkled like bright stars on a dark night. "Are you very sure that's what you want?"

"I've never been more sure of anything in my entire life."

David wrapped his arm around Lisa and kissed her forehead. "I never stopped loving you," he said. "Have I told you that before?"

Lisa nodded. "But thanks for repeating it. I need to hear that as often as possible."

"I love you." He wrapped his arms tightly around her. "And I always will."

Tracy bounced with excitement.

Both of her parents looked at her, then at each other, and smiled.

David glanced at his watch. It was time to board the plane. He gave Lisa one last kiss. "We've got some talking to do, so hurry home. I'll be waiting for you."

Lisa looked up at him and smiled.

Other Novels by L.C. Hayden
Who's Susan?
When Colette Died

Also from Top Publications
by William Manchee
Undaunted
Brash Endeavor
Death Pact
Second Chair

by Lynnette Baughman
A Spy Within
Thin Disguise

by Carl Brookins
Inner Passages

by Tricia Allen
Texas Weather

by Aaron Master
Queen of Aces

by H. J. Ralles
Keeper of the Kingdom

by Melody Bussey
Crazy Cats

By Tony Fennally
Don't Blame the Snake

Visit the Top Publications' website.
http://toppub.com